To: Fl

With love,

Sauyn Bennett

SHAKEN, NOT STIRRED

Shaken, not STIRRED

New York Times and USA Today Bestselling Author

Sawyer Bennett

ISBN: 978-1-940883-27-4

Find Sawyer on the web!
www.sawyerbennett.com
www.twitter.com/bennettbooks
www.facebook.com/bennettbooks

Table of Contents

PROLOGUE

Casey

"JESUS, CASEY. THAT was amazing."

Yeah, it kind of was, I think as I look down at Richard. At thirty-seven, he's a little older than the men I normally date, but I have found that to be a benefit in the bedroom. I'm sorry... but older men just really know how to please a woman.

It also helps that Richard fits my other qualifications. He's rich, so he can treat me to nice things, moderately cool to hang with, and best of all... he understands the concept of no strings. He's a minor owner in a NASCAR franchise and lives in Charlotte, but I met him several weeks ago when he was vacationing here in the Outer Banks. Since then, he's flown back every weekend on his private plane—which he flies himself, so that's kind of hot—to see me. He's wined and dined—and yeah, sixty-nined—me very, very well. Then he leaves, goes back home, and I'm contented.

"Yeah, sugar," I tell him with a little kiss to his

jaw. "That was awesome."

And it was. He got me off once with his tongue, and I got me off once while I was riding him.

Easing myself off Richard, who is still half-hard within me, I roll right off the bed so I can start gathering up my clothes. I hear Richard take the condom off and throw it in the garbage.

"Don't go," he says softly behind me and then his arms are wrapping around my stomach. He pulls me back into his chest, which is beautifully tanned and muscular, and leans his chin on my shoulder. "Stay the night with me, Casey."

I give a light chuckle, push his hands off me, and with a chastising look over my shoulder, I say, "You know I don't do overnights."

"Christ," Richard explodes as he drags a frustrated hand through his hair. "You're driving me nuts."

I quickly slip on my panties, keeping my eyes on him the entire time. "Come on, Richard. Don't be like that. You know my boundaries."

"Yeah, yeah," he says with exasperation, throwing his hands out to the side. "No getting close. You don't do relationships. Blah, blah, blah."

"Blah, blah, blah?" I mimic with a cocked eyebrow while deftly putting my bra on. Over the years, I've learned to dress fast for a quick escape.

Richard's eyes get sidetracked a moment by my breasts as I adjust the straps, but then come back to me. Very quietly and with serious eyes, he says, "I'm falling in love with you, Casey."

Ice fills my veins even as I feel a tinge of remorse within my chest. I step toward him and in a voice that I mean to be firm yet gentle, I say, "No, Richard. You aren't."

"Don't tell me how I feel," he snaps at me.

"You don't love me," I repeat with steely confidence. "You're in lust with me… fine, I accept that. But it's not love."

"It's love I'm—"

"It's not love," I say again… calmly, patiently, but with a little more punctuation. "You don't know enough about me to love me. We don't share secrets or intimacies. We share meals and we fuck. That's it, Richard."

"It's more. It may not be love, but I have feelings for you," he says again, trying to insist, but even I hear the heat has died down out of his voice.

I know his type. He loves having sex with me, and who wouldn't? I'm pretty much awesome in the sack, but I'm also a realist. I know that the only reason men look at me is for my beauty, and the only reason they stay with me is because of what I can do to them in between the sheets. I learned a long time ago exactly how men like him feel about women like me.

Sometimes, they're cool with the boundaries I place. Sometimes, they proclaim to love me, which is horseshit. Not one of the men I've been with even knows my middle name or where I live. They don't know about my brother being a convicted murderer, the name of my best friend—which is Gabby, for the record—or where I flunked out of college. They know I have gorgeous tits, an ass tight enough to bounce a quarter off of, and I'm great at giving head.

That's all they care about if they're being honest with themselves.

Honest to me.

So when along comes the man that starts talking about love and commitment, I know exactly what it is. It isn't that they love me or that they want more from me on a personal level. It's that they want me by their side more. They're not satisfied with the weekends I'm willing to give them. They want me in their bed seven days a week... nothing more.

Certainly nothing less.

With a sigh, I step away from Richard and finish putting on my cocktail dress. It's made of a shimmery, mint-green satin, tight around the bust but still tasteful enough to wear out to the five-star restaurant we dined in tonight. With efficient motion, I put on the strappy, crystal-studded sandals that bring my five-foot-nine up to where I can almost look six-foot-tall Richard directly in the eye.

Grabbing my handbag off the nightstand, I turn to face him. He's standing there gloriously naked, completely unabashed, looking like I just kicked his favorite puppy. It's a shame, really, because while I may not let my feelings get involved, I do enjoy a nice, monogamous, but light mutual endeavor. I've gone weeks happily content with one man, as long as he doesn't cross the line I've drawn in the sand.

The line that Richard just crossed, which, unfortunately for him, that bell can't be unrung.

"I'm sorry," I say as I walk up to him. I lean in… kiss him on the cheek. "I hope you understand. But I've never led you on. I've told you my boundaries. I told you it could never be anything more."

He sighs heavily but holds my gaze. "I know you did. I don't know what I was thinking. You won't hear it from me again."

Shaking my head sadly, I bring a palm up and touch it to his cheek. "I know I won't."

He hears the tone of my voice. He understands what I mean. "You're not going to see me again, are you?" he asks hesitantly.

"No," I tell him as I continue to look in his eyes. "The line's been crossed, and it can't be undone for me."

I wait for it.

I know it's coming.

I've been here before.

Richard's eyes turn frosty, the cut of rejection bringing out all of his defense mechanisms. The need to reclaim his manhood and the upper hand rises forth. "Fine. Whatever. You're not the first or last piece of ass I'll have."

Ahh. There it is. Exactly what I knew was lurking

under the surface.

What is *always* under the surface.

I give him a polite smile before turning toward the door. "Goodbye, Richard. I hope you find what you're looking for."

Curses follow me out. A few degrading remarks. It all bounces off me because I refuse to let it sink in. I've heard it before, and he's no different. In fact, I'll even accept I might deserve a little of it since I willingly engaged in some really fantastic sex with him that I could see definitely making him think it could lead to other things.

But it's the God's honest truth. I never led him on.

I don't lead any of them on.

I tell them how it is right up front and just as is typical to any man, they have no problems accepting my conditions because hey… the sex is phenomenal.

Because, after all, men really are looking for one thing only.

I hastily exit the hotel, my high heels clacking on the pavement. The warm summer breeze floats over my exposed skin, and I breathe in deeply of the sea salt that permeates the air.

Damn, I love my home here in the Outer Banks.

I love my family. I love my friends.

Contrary to what most men would believe about me, I have tremendous capacity to love. It's just something I would prefer to avoid outside of my friends and family.

I get in my Jeep, a present I bought myself last year after I made a killing off just one sale. Unfortunately for me, the real estate market is tight, and there aren't many houses available on the island nowadays. In hindsight, it was probably a stupid idea to become a realtor, but shit… I didn't know what else to do with my life. It didn't help that my first sale was of a mega mansion to famed author, Gavin Cooke, because I just sort of assumed everything else would be that easy.

Wrong!

It's freakin' hard to make a living in real estate. And to make matters worse, Gavin ended up stealing my roommate, which has really put a ding in my budget.

Okay, well… he didn't steal her. Just knocked her up and moved her in with him. And fine… they're in love (gag) and they have a beautiful daughter now (nothing to gag about there—she's adorable), but what about me? I'm floundering here and don't know what to do. So poor right now that the only good meals I get are on the weekends when I might have a date.

It's definitely time to step up and figure out what the hell to do with my life, because I can't keep living this way. I wonder to myself if when I say that, I only mean as far as expenses go, but I think I might mean something else. That scene back there in the hotel with Richard is getting really old, and as much as I like to pretend that I always hold the upper hand in these situations, I know that, deep down, it still makes me feel like shit about myself.

CHAPTER 1

Casey

I LOVE THIS bar.

Just like the song that gets played on the juke-box quite often. My older brother, Hunter, bought this property going on almost two years ago, refurbished the interior, and renamed it The Last Call. Since then, it's become one of the hottest places on the Outer Banks to hang during the summer months.

It's casual and laid back, just like the beach bum my brother is and always has been. The Markham family has salt water in our veins, having lived here forever. Me and my other brother, Brody—who is Hunter's identical twin—are what I'd call frolickers. We like to sit on the beach and play in the ocean, but that's the extent of our communion with the sun and surf. My dad, however, is a fisherman and Hunter was on a surfboard from the time he could practically walk, so both have a much more personal connection to the ocean. That doesn't mean I love it less but just in a different, gentler way. So very different from

Hunter, who respects the ocean and knows he can never control it, can only ride what it gives him. Dedication and natural talent led Hunter to a very successful professional surfing career, from which he retired to buy this bar.

Or rather... he actually retired from surfing to stay here on the islands so he could be with his one true love, Gabby Ward.

Who also happens to be my best friend since we were little bitty things.

It took a while to get used to the idea of Hunter and Gabby being together. At first, it just plain gave me the wiggins to see them showing open and sensual affection with each other. I mean... for God's sake... we all grew up together.

But the concept of those two being a couple has grown on me. Hunter and Gabby are engaged, and she will one day be my real sister in addition to being my best friend.

"Can I get another beer, Casey?"

My head swivels to look at ol' Roy Becham, sitting at the opposite end of the bar. He's a fixture in here. I give him a quick smile and head down his way, grabbing a fresh and newly chilled pint glass from the cooler. "Sure thing."

And this is where my life currently stands.

Tending bar at The Last Call because I can't afford to continue living on my own with what I make as a real estate agent.

About three weeks ago, I plucked up the courage, swallowed my pride, and begged Hunter for a job. Now, don't get me wrong… there is nothing shameful about working in a bar. Not only does Hunter cover frequent shifts here, but Brody also worked here for a while when he first got out of prison.

No, the part that has me swallowing my pride is in having to beg a family member for help.

Turns out… no begging was needed. Hunter gladly gave me the work, offered to loan me money if I needed it, and then proceeded to grill me on the state of my finances to see how much trouble I was really in. After an hour of assuring him that I wasn't starving to death, but just needed a little extra to make up for losing Savannah as a roommate, he finally left it alone.

My mom, on the other hand, is not happy I'm working here. While both my parents love my brothers and me unconditionally, I know that I am the "disappointment" in the family. And that's saying a lot, seeing as how Brody spent five years in prison. In fairness, however, his transgressions are forgiven by all of us because he didn't actually do the crime.

I, on the other hand, have not measured up in any way. My senior year in high school was very difficult for me, and I sucked at college. I barely lasted a year there, partying my ass off and having the time of my life. I don't think I really caught on to the concept of needing to buckle down and study. How could I when it was just so much damn fun to be free and young with no one to make me do anything?

"Casey, baby," my mom had said with obvious affection but a little bit of annoyance one night at a family dinner. "It's time to figure out what you want to be when you grow up."

I'm almost twenty-six years old, and my mom doesn't think I've grown up yet.

She may be right.

I pour the beer from the tap, keeping the glass tilted at an angle to keep the foam head minimal. When it's full, I set it down before Roy and reach out to grab the appropriate amount of money he has laying in front of him on the bar.

"Keep a couple dollars for yourself, honey," he says in a gruff voice.

I take two extra dollars and stick them in my tip jar. "You're a sweetie, Roy."

"So you gonna marry me then?" he asks with a toothless grin. Roy has to be in his eighties. He's a retired shrimper and used to hang out at this bar before Hunter bought it. He was displaced for a bit during the remodeling but once it was re-opened for business, Roy's butt has pretty much been parked on that same stool at the corner of the bar.

"I'm not marrying any man," I tell him with a wink. "No way am I going to be pinned down."

Roy cackles and holds his beer up to me in salute.

"You remind me of my sweet Georgia Mae. Did I ever tell you about the time she left me at the altar and I had to hunt her down and drag her back kicking and screaming? She was a pistol that woman, but after the honeymoon, she was smiling big."

I shake my head and smile at Roy, and even though I've heard this story twice, I put my elbows on the bar and lean toward him. "I haven't heard that one."

Roy drones on and on. Sweet old man really, which is why I listen to his repetitive stories. This is his life... just as it's mine... sitting in a bar and whiling the time away.

Continuing from one story to the next, Roy tells me about his wife, Georgia. She died long before I was born so I didn't know her, but she sounded like a hoot. A few more customers start to straggle in, mostly fisherman at this time of the early afternoon, telling me the shrimp aren't running anymore.

I call out greetings and serve up beers as well as some harder liquor for the more salty men. Periodically, I shoot the shit with Roy or some of the other locals.

I've found the key to enjoying this job is to stay busy, so I like it when people start coming in. It makes the time fly by. While the afternoon shifts that I work are generally slow, I still can get in a good hour or so of busy traffic, which means better tips.

Right at six PM, Kent comes in to relieve me. He

started working at The Last Call about a year ago and is one of Hunter's more seasoned workers. He's also really hot with sandy blond hair that he wears long and shaggy, with a beard of about four days' growth. It never gets any longer or shorter, so I know he must be in to grooming. On top of that, he's a generally nice guy. I mean, really nice.

I've often thought about going out with him. He's asked me a few times, and I always turn him down with a bit of levity. He's a little younger than I would like—I think twenty-three—but ultimately, I can't do it.

He's a bartender. Blue collar, working class. Definitely not rich.

Which means definitely not my type.

Some would think that makes me shallow, and I would have to agree with them *if* I went out with these men for their money. But that's not why I go out with them. I couldn't care less about their fancy cars and expensive gifts. It amuses me to get them because I know just how little that stuff really means to these men. It's a way to impress and seduce. It's classic and dull, but I accept it.

It also means they are the shallow ones, and shallow people are easy to keep at arm's length.

The reason I don't go out with people like Kent is because he's too nice. Too stable. Too dependable. Wouldn't want to hurt a woman intentionally. Knows the meaning of honest work. He has character.

Those are the men I stay away from. Those are the type of men that would threaten to unravel me.

"Hey Kent," I greet him with a smile as he walks back behind the bar.

"Hey Casey," he says with a pearly white grin. "Looking gorgeous today."

"Why, thank you, kind sir," I say with a little curtsy and then give him an appraising once over. "You're not looking bad yourself."

He chuckles and opens the register to start zeroing out the tallies for my shift while I finish washing up some empty glasses and giving a good wipe down of the bar. When I'm done, I fish out my tips but leave a dollar behind. It's some sort of karmic tradition all the bartenders here do, and I'm not about to mess with the tip money juju.

A quick count and I see I've netted a grand total of thirty-two dollars. Actually not bad for a slow afternoon shift of six hours.

"Casey Markham… girl, do I have a bone to pick with you," I hear yelled from behind me. It's a voice I've known most of my life.

With a grin, I turn to face Gabby with her chocolate-colored hair and Cherokee heritage cheekbones that make her so exotic looking. "What have I done now?" I ask with smirk as I walk out from behind the bar.

"Can we get two beers when you get a minute?" Gabby asks Kent as she points me out toward the back deck, indicating she wants to sit out there.

"Sure thing, Gabs," Kent replies, and immediately starts pouring two pints of Harp's, which is a new beer Hunter started carrying on tap that Gabby and I began drinking recently. We're going through an Irish phase or something.

Kent slides the beers across the bar to us and Gabby fishes in her purse, pulling out a ten-dollar bill to hand to him. Immediately holding his hands up defensively, Kent backs away and shakes his head. "No way, Gabby. I can't take your money. The boss will fire me this time if I do it."

"What?" she asks, her voice bordering between pissed and flummoxed. I'm enjoying this show, so I just grab my beer and take a sip.

"Hunter said you can't pay for anything here anymore. He said he'll fire me if I take your money," Kent says solemnly. "And I'm sorry, Gabby. I like you and all, but not enough to lose my job."

Gabby starts muttering curses, and I hear Hunter's name in every other word. *Love is very strange*, I think to myself.

Throwing the money on the bar, Gabby grabs her beer. "Then consider that your tip, Kent. And I'll be talking to Hunter about this later."

She spins away and stalks through the bar, past the pool tables and to the door that leads to the outdoor deck. I actually like to think of it as *her* outdoor deck, since Gabby is the one that built it from scratch. Yup… my girl is such a dude when it comes to building things. She's a general contractor, and there isn't anything she can't create from wood.

The multi-tiered deck is stunning with quarter walls dropping from the ceiling that hold various surfboards of Hunter's that he won as trophies in some of his competitions. The covered portion of the deck contains a framework that has plastic drop walls so you can even sit out here in the winter and look at the ocean. Adding this deck is one of the things that helped propel The Last Call into bar-stardom status here on the island. Hunter hires live bands to play out here in the summer, and it's just the coolest place to hang with your friends.

Gabby sits down at an empty table closest to the beach, which is nicely shaded by an umbrella that's slightly tilted to block the late afternoon rays coming from the west. I sit down next to her and prop my feet up on the chair beside me.

"So what's the bone you have to pick with me?" I ask her nonchalantly as I gaze out at the ocean. The water is a dark green this late in the afternoon and the waves are small, barely making a rumble as they roll in.

"You lied to us," Gabby says, and that gets my attention. My gaze jerks over to her and my eyebrows raise in question, but I know damn well what she's talking about. I don't lie to my friends—much—but I have told one recently and it's apparently biting me in the ass.

Still, in the off chance I'm wrong, I decide to play it close to the vest. "How do you think I lied?"

Gabby rolls her eyes at me. "This past weekend… you said you couldn't go out with us because you had a date with that NASCAR dude… what's his name? Richard?"

"That's right," I say neutrally, not copping to anything other than what I had told her a few days ago.

"You weren't on a date with him," she snaps at me.

Well, shit. I'm busted… I think. There's still a chance she's bluffing me.

"What makes you say that?" I ask with a forced measure of indifference.

"Oh, cut the crap, Casey, and just fess up. Hunter and I saw him at the Soundside with another woman on his arm," she says in exasperation.

"Oh my gosh," I say with bubbly excitement as I lean toward her. "Y'all ate at the Soundside? Was it fabulous? I bet it was fabulous."

Gabby's eyes flutter closed, she inhales deeply and then lets it out slowly through slightly parted lips. When she opens her eyes, I see patience with a good deal of annoyance just underneath. "Dinner was wonderful, and as I said… Richard was there dining with another woman. So I want to know why you said you were with him Saturday night and you couldn't hang out with your friends?"

I give her a wink. "Who says I wasn't with him after that dinner? Maybe I was with him later."

"You're full of shit," Gabby sneers at me. "You may shun any type of relationship that has feelings involved but when you do see a man, you are completely monogamous."

"Fine," I say as I hold my hands up before me. "Busted. Gonna spank me?"

"Gonna slap you," she says with a huff. "Why, Casey? Why didn't you want to come out with us, and more importantly, why lie about it?"

I take a large sip of my beer before answering her. When I set it down, I put on my most apologetic face. "I didn't feel like going out that night. That's all. But I knew all of you would keep at me until I agreed. Hell, you probably would have brought the party to my little house. So I told you I had other plans. Little lie. Big deal you're making of it."

"What happened with Richard? Aren't you seeing him anymore?" she asks, her eyes going soft at the thought of me breaking up with someone.

Again.

I snort at her and lean back in my chair. "Get that look off your face. I ended it with him. He was getting too warm and fuzzy with me." And to prove my point that this was not an incident deserving of her sympathy, I give a mock shudder of disgust.

Gabby looks at me... studies me. She taps her

finger on her chin. "You know… I do believe I know what your problem is."

"Oh, yeah?" I ask sarcastically. "Lay it on me, Yoda."

"You need a Joe," she says simply.

"Had one of those," I say with an impatient wave. "A rich playboy spending Daddy's shipping money. Wasn't packing a huge amount between the legs, but he more than made up for it with his stamina."

Gabby reaches out and punches me on the shoulder, causing me to yelp. "No, you moron. You need an average Joe. Someone who's down to earth. Who appreciates you."

Still rubbing my shoulder, I cock an eyebrow at her. "You seriously think that's what I need?"

And damn… she's probably not far off the mark. I know if I didn't have "issues," a good ol' boy is probably the type that would bring me to my knees. That's why I needed to stay far, far away from them.

"I *know* that's what you need," she says with a smug look. And then her eyes go soft again, and she reaches out to lay her hand on my forearm. "Oh, Casey… I want you to fall in love. I want you to see how wonderful it is when a man worships you and treats you like a princess. You deserve that more than any of us, and yet you're the only one without it."

"And don't want it," I add on firmly, knocking the gentleness out of her eyes.

She huffs in frustration and picks up her beer to

take a slug. "You're going to be one of those old cat ladies."

"No way," I disagree. "I'm going to be a prowling cougar when I get older. When I'm forty, I'll only date twenty year olds, when I'm fifty, thirty year olds, and when I'm sixty, I'm going back to the twenty year olds. Now that right there is the good life."

Gabby rolls her eyes at me again. Seems she does that a lot but thankfully, she changes the subject and we start discussing what to do about Andrea's birthday, which is coming up.

Andrea Somerville is the newest addition to our crew. She just opened up a law practice here in Nags Head and managed to get engaged to a dear and longtime friend, Wyatt Banks. Wyatt and Hunter have been best friends since they could walk, much like Gabby and me. I know a lot of people thought he and I would get together at some point, seeing as how we were the last two remaining single peeps in the crew, but eww… gross… he's like my brother.

Don't get me wrong… he's like my hot-as-hell-older-step-brother, but no way was I ever interested in that. Because as Gabby pointed out, regular Joes were just a little too dangerous for me. Wyatt is a cop thus that puts him in the regular category of men.

"Isn't Andrea's brother, Kyle, coming in to visit soon?" I ask as I start thinking about how we could throw Andrea a surprise party.

"This week sometime. Supposedly riding cross

country from Wyoming on his motorcycle with a buddy."

"Ooooh… maybe Andrea's brother is some hot biker dude," I say as I settle back deeper into the deck chair with my legs propped up in front of me.

"Hate to tell you this," Gabby says drolly, "but bikers are ordinary Joes."

"I can look and appreciate," I respond with a dismissive wave of my hand.

Because that's about all I would ever allow myself to do. Anything more would be far too tempting.

Far too dangerous.

CHAPTER 2

Jenn

W E PULL INTO the apartment complex called Crane's Landing, and it looks nice enough, I suppose. It's well landscaped, and there is a large pool and recreational area within the center of the buildings. I'll have a better idea of whether or not this place is good enough for Zoey once I can see the inside. I slowly drive around the perimeter with my buddy, Kyle Somerville, right behind me, looking for the building number Brianna texted me a few days ago before we left Wyoming. The rumbling growl of our Harleys causes some of the residents milling around to look at us in interest.

It took Kyle and me just about four days to make it here to Raleigh, North Carolina on our bikes. My Heritage Softail has been kind to my ass but then again, we didn't push it, instead deciding to take our time and enjoy the cross-country summer drive. Besides, neither one of us are on a rigid time clock, so there was no sense in rushing.

I finally spy the building that Brianna and Zoey live in and carefully back my bike into a parking spot, with Kyle easing his in beside me. We both cut our engines simultaneously and remove our helmets. I place mine on the small seat behind me, and Kyle hooks his to a handlebar.

With my feet firmly planted on the ground, I twist slightly so I can reach my saddlebags and pull out a bottle of water I have in there. I remove the cap and take several long drinks, then look over at Kyle and hold the bottle out to offer him some.

He shakes his head full of long, shaggy blond hair, which is tamed only by the Harley Davidson bandana he wears over it. "I'm good."

Finishing the bottle off, I put the empty back in my saddlebag before getting off my bike. I look around the area with a discerning eye and note good security lighting and open-access parking.

"Nice place," Kyle says as he swings his leg over the bike and stands up with a long stretch.

"Seems like," I tell him as I look around with interest. "You want to hang for a bit and see Zoey?"

"Yeah," he grunts as he reaches up and re-tightens the tie on his bandana. "I'll give my ass a break for a bit before I move on. Besides, I have to take a monster piss."

I nod in understanding. We may not have a lot of words pass between us, but men seem to be much simpler in our dialogue. Besides, it's not like I didn't know Kyle's plans at this point. We rode together from Wyoming to Raleigh so I could see my daughter, Zoey. She moved here with her mom and my ex-wife, Brianna, about two months ago, and this has been the first opportunity I had to visit.

No doubt, a plane trip would have been easier and taken less time, but right now, I have the luxury of time on my side. I quit my job last week after much thought and deliberation over Zoey and her new home in North Carolina. I can't fucking stand to be away from her and while Brianna and I share joint physical custody for Zoey back in Wyoming, since Brianna has primary legal custody, she gets to dictate where they live. Bolstered by a very healthy savings account I have diligently added to from every paycheck, as well as the sale of my house in Wyoming, which netted me a pretty penny, I can afford to take some time off and evaluate this area for a potential move to be near my daughter.

Pisses me off because it's not like Brianna wants to live here. She merely took the first opportunity she could find to leave Wyoming as a means to punish me by taking my daughter away. The thing that sucks is she fully expects me to follow them here. She figures that I won't stand to be parted from Zoey, and she'd be right about that. But the crazy bitch that she is, she sees this as me following "her" and not following my daughter. Still harboring hope that I'll get back with her, but that ain't ever going to happen.

That's definitely something I'm going to set her straight on during this visit.

When Kyle found out I was heading east, he offered to go with me as he has a sister that lives on the coast of North Carolina in the Outer Banks. He took two weeks off from work, a move that did not go over well with his boss, since that also happened to be the same job that I just quit.

I met Kyle five years ago when I needed to get a new paint job done on my Heritage, which I had bought for a song and a dance on Craig's List and rebuilt the engine myself. That landed me at Teton Choppers, a custom motorcycle shop offering full engine and bodywork services. Kyle was the manager and the senior man when it came to bodywork. He took one look at my bike and was extremely impressed with the rebuild I had done on the engine. One thing led to another and before you knew it, I was talking to the owner about my experience as a mechanic. Granted, everything I knew about engines came from my work in the motor pool while I was in the Marine Corps, but I found an engine is an engine is an engine. It just sort of makes sense to me and I have a knack for it, but most of all… I just like figuring out how to make things work right.

And because I absolutely hated working on my father's cattle ranch in Wyoming, I was more than ready to make a move. Much to my dad's dismay, I started working at Teton Choppers as a mechanic and gave up my legacy as a cattle rancher.

Well, I gave it up temporarily. Whether I can walk away permanently remains to be seen, but that's another story for another day.

Kyle and I head up to the second floor of Brianna's building. My nerves hum with anticipation, a mixture of frenzied excitement to see Zoey and anxiety over having to deal with Bri's shit that I'm sure I'll be handed in spades.

When we reach the second-floor landing, I immediately see the door to her apartment with a note attached to the front. Warning bells go off inside my head, because nothing is ever easy when it comes to dealing with Brianna.

I stalk up to the door and snatch the paper, which is held in place by a piece of transparent tape.

Tenn,

Change of plans. Kip got discounted tickets to Disney World, and we're taking Zoey there. We'll be back next week and you can pick her up then.

Bri

My hand squeezes the paper, curling it into a tight ball within my grasp.

Motherfucking son of a bitch.

"What is it, dude?" Kyle asks from behind me.

I ignore him and pull my phone out of my pocket, stabbing at the screen with my finger until I pull up Brianna's contact information to dial her. As expected, she doesn't answer but lets the call go straight to voice mail.

After I listen to her short message, I grit out my own. "This is fucking unacceptable, Brianna. You knew I'd be here today for Zoey, and you had no right to take her. Call me back ASAP."

I disconnect, knowing she won't call. She'll ignore me, playing her stupid and sick little mind games that I suffered under for the nine years we were married. And continue to suffer under as a way to punish me for having the audacity to divorce her ass.

Pushing my fingers through my hair, I blast out a frustrated huff of air. "Zoey's not here. Bri took her to Disney."

"What the fuck, dude?" Kyle growls. "The bitch knew we were driving cross country and would be here today."

"Yeah, she knew," I say tiredly as I make my way back to the staircase that leads out to the parking lot. With heavy feet, my steel-toed boots clomp loudly down the cement steps as Kyle follows along behind me. "Said she won't be back until next week."

"What are you going to do?"

"Guess I'll just get a hotel. Check out the area since I'm considering a move here."

Fucking bitch.

"Look man," Kyle says as we reach the bikes and

he grabs his helmet from the handle bar. "Ride with me to the Outer Banks. Hang out on the beach for a week and relax. No sense in staying here by yourself."

I glance back up to Bri's apartment, anger still gurgling like acid in my gut. I should have known it wouldn't be easy. She's so full of herself. I know she thinks I traveled all this way for her... like some dog sniffing after a bone. It would never even occur to her that I'm here for Zoey and nothing else.

I slide my gaze back over to Kyle. "Yeah... okay, sure. Got nothing better to do right now."

"Fucking aye," he says with a grin. "We'll cruise the coastal highway, drink beers, and watch babes on the beach in bikinis. It will be epic."

Chuckling, I grab my helmet and put it on my head, fastening the strap under my chin. "Babes in bikinis, huh?"

"Can you think of a better way to spend a week?" he asks rhetorically just before starting his bike.

I follow suit and our engines roar to life, causing me to yell to be heard. "Let's ride, man."

◆

IT'S ONLY ABOUT a three-hour ride straight east from Raleigh over to the Outer Banks of North Carolina. Kyle's sister, Andrea, just opened up a law practice there a few months ago, and I'm actually curious to meet her. She was apparently an FBI agent working criminal cases in Pittsburgh but decided to give it up and use her law degree instead. I find it interesting that Kyle and his sister were, for a time, on opposite ends of the spectrum when it came to the law, and yet, they seem to be pretty tight.

My love of motorcycles and the freedom of the ride pretty much goes no further than the fact I own a Harley and I work on custom-built choppers. Kyle's goes a little further in that long before I met him, he patched into a motorcycle club called Mayhem's Mission that's based out of Jackson, Wyoming. The owner of Teton Choppers, a grizzled, old military veteran that earned the nickname ZZ because of his long ZZ Top-like beard, employs quite a few members from the club. ZZ isn't part of Mayhem's Mission, but he also doesn't seem to have a problem with them either, seeing as how they provide a lot of his recurring business.

I'm not exactly sure if there are any criminal workings inside of the club. I've never asked Kyle and he's never volunteered, but I have to think there's something going on there because Kyle carries a gun on him at all times as well as a burner cell phone in addition to his regular one. Doesn't take an advanced degree to know something shady goes down, but it's none of my business. He doesn't bring that shit around our workplace and otherwise seems to be a solid dude.

Kyle rides ahead of me and by my calculations

and the fact that I can smell salt on the air, I figure we're getting close to the ocean. He's a classic biker. Arms raised in the air as he holds onto his ape-hanger bars, long, blond hair flying behind him. The skull on the back of his leather vest leers at me... a creepy, hollow-eyed skeletal head with pointed teeth dripping blood and flames leaping from the eye sockets. I think it's a patch that's designed to inspire fear in the average viewer, but it doesn't affect me in that way. I've come to know quite of few of the guys that ride with Mayhem and while some could be considered a little certifiable, they're mostly dudes that share a love of Harleys and the lifestyle that comes with riding them.

Kyle only talked to me once about joining the club. I listened patiently while I was repairing a cracked cylinder head on a 1988 Sportster and tuning in to only about half of what he said. I heard things such as camaraderie, riding free, wild parties, and all the free pussy you could ever want. While my ears perked up slightly over the abundance of pussy within the club, it just wasn't something I was interested in. I was only interested in doing my job and riding in my spare time, providing a good life for Zoey, and trying to figure out what the fuck I wanted to do with my life.

Yeah... had no clue what I wanted to do, but I certainly knew what I didn't want to do, and that was to be a cattle rancher. While I loved certain aspects of the job, it just wasn't what I wanted to devote my life to. It was expected of me to following in my dad's footsteps. However, a part of me was holding out hope that my younger brother would step up to the plate, take an interest in the family business, and alleviate me of the responsibility.

Up ahead in the distance, I see a long bridge spanning over a wide body of water, which I know from the map I had looked at earlier was the Roanoke Sound. I knew just on the other side of that bridge we'd officially be on the barrier islands known as the Outer Banks and for the first time since we left Raleigh after lunch, I was starting to get a small feeling of excitement. It would be nice to take a break and fuck… I can't remember the last time I took a vacation just for myself. Ever since Zoey was born fourteen years ago, I'm not sure I've done anything just for myself.

Which is fine by me.

Zoey is and always will be my number-one priority. She comes first in all things.

I follow along behind Kyle as we rumble down the highway and cross over onto the island. We head north toward Nags Head and the ocean opens up on my right, the midday summer sun sparkling on the blue-green waters.

I'm no stranger to the Atlantic. I was stationed for a brief time in North Carolina, just a few hours south of here aboard Camp Lejeune Marine Corps base, which abuts right up to the ocean. It was my first duty station after I got out of boot camp, and it's also where Bri got her first taste of the East Coast as I brought her and Zoey out here to live with me when Zoey was just six months old. We stayed here for almost two years until I was sent to Camp Leatherneck in the Helmand Province of Afghanistan and Bri and Zoey moved back to Wyoming to live with her parents during that eighteen-month deployment. I spent the rest of my enlistment in San Diego, where... before I knew it... my time in the military had come to a close, and I was once again faced with the prospect of joining the family cattle business or finding something else that would keep me out from under my father's thumb.

Now, it had never been my original intent to marry Brianna. It was not something I remotely wanted to do. I had dated her for a few months after I graduated high school, but it only took those few months for me to realize she was bat-shit crazy. And apparently, it only took the same amount of time for her to end up pregnant so when she showed up on my doorstep claiming I would be a father in less than eight months, I panicked. I wasn't ready for fatherhood. I sure as shit didn't want a wife. I was enlisting in the military to get far away from my current life, and now I was saddled with responsibilities I didn't want.

Some would say that with a young wife I detested

but a beautiful daughter who I adored, it would have been stupid for me to turn down my father's offer of joining on at the ranch again. I'd have free housing and a good paying job. It was the smart decision to make.

Instead, I took the job as a mechanic at Teton Choppers and have been somewhat satisfied with my life. It doesn't pay what ranching pays but it paid enough, and I was able to support my family just fine.

That worked out for me for almost nine years, during which time I ascended among the ranks to become ZZ's top mechanic and I shared management duties over the shop with Kyle. During that time period too, I finally wised my ass up and realized I didn't have to be married to a woman I didn't love only for the sake of sharing a child. I finally wised up enough to realize that I wasn't teaching Zoey what a healthy relationship would look like, and I was doing her no favors by continually putting up with her mother's shit just to keep the peace in the house.

But... after nine years, I am not feeling that full measure of satisfaction any more. I've been itching for something different, and this is made more so by the fact that my dad has been pressuring me to come back into the fold. My brother has decided he doesn't want to grow up apparently, and my father wants someone to pass the business on to.

I have a decision to make.

Go back to ranching or figure a way to do something with my life that will have enough meaning to sustain me personally and professionally.

I'm hoping my buddy, Nix Caldwell, can help me reason this shit out. He's in New Jersey so I'll make a quick trip up there so we can discuss an idea I've had brewing, which has really been consuming my thoughts since I'm considering a move to North Carolina.

Kyle's brake light comes on, pulling me out of my thoughts, and he starts to slow down as I see a teal-blue Jeep on the side of the road up a ways. As we get closer, what becomes even more interesting than the Jeep is the woman that's standing behind the vehicle with her emergency flashers on.

Leave it to Kyle to want to pull over and help a damsel in distress, but fuck… how can I blame him? The woman is beyond magnificent.

We cruise slowly past her to pull over in front of her Jeep. She tilts her head to the left to watch us cautiously and in that brief glimpse, I catch golden-blonde hair that comes down to her mid-back. It's all windblown and messy with whiter streaks of high-lights filtering throughout. She's got on a pair of the tiniest cutoff shorts I've ever seen, cut so high in the back I can see the crease of where her ass cheeks meet the backs of her legs, a spot on a woman I find to be so fucking sexy.

Long, long, long tanned legs spill downward out of those shorts, and a quick glance back up her body reveals a gorgeous C cup set of tits mounded nicely under a tight white tank top.

But what really catches my interest is her face as we idle on by her.

It's stunning. I mean fucking runway model-like.

High cheekbones, straight nose, sweetly puffed lips slicked with gloss, and crystal-blue eyes. Her skin is golden everywhere, and there is a slight dusting of freckles over her nose and cheeks. She looks like the all-American cheerleader blessed with the body of a Victoria's Secret model.

No wonder why Kyle was pulling over to offer assistance, but there's no doubt I would have pulled over myself had I not been with Kyle. This woman was too fucking gorgeous not to stop and render assistance to.

CHAPTER 3

Casey

MY FIRST INDICATION that I had a flat tire was the *fwapping* sound that made me first think a helicopter was flying overhead. It took only a few seconds and a brief glance upward since I had the top off my Jeep to know it wasn't.

I pulled over and having no clue what to do with a flat tire, immediately called Hunter before I even got out to look at the damage. When I reached his voice mail, I left a brief message. "Baby sister here. I'm stuck on 158 with a flat tire. As soon as I can get some stud to stop and help me change it, I'll be in to work. Or, you could get your butt out here and change it for me. I'm just about a quarter mile south of Wilby's. Later, gator."

When I hung up, I called Brody. It paid to have two helpful older brothers.

Unfortunately, I got Brody's voice mail as well, but I didn't even break out into a sweat that I couldn't reach him because I had other options.

Which meant I called Wyatt and while I did reach him, he told me I was shit out of luck because he was still on duty and as much as he was a cop and lived to serve and protect, his captain would not appreciate him leaving to help a friend change a flat tire. The only other bit of help he offered was the number to the local garage, which I declined. That would take too long and being as it was the start of the summer season, I knew it wouldn't take long for someone to stop and help me. Especially not when I was wearing a hot pair of Daisy Dukes.

Just so no one would misinterpret my need for help, I switched on my flashers and got out of the Jeep, walking to the back where I vaguely remembered I had a spare tire attached to the rear swinging tailgate. It's not that I really noticed it before, and I'm sure the salesman must have mentioned it to me when I bought the vehicle, but really… why would I need to know that? Even if I knew where the spare tire was, I wouldn't know what to do with it.

I see a car in the distance coming up from the south, so I immediately start rummaging through my very empty rear trunk area. I'm not looking for anything in particular but I figured it would at least look good to be bent over slightly so that any person of the male species that might be in a rush and not inclined to stop would think twice about that.

The car approaches and flies by, honking with two guys sticking their heads out the windows and yelling, "Damn baby… you're hot."

Assholes.

If I'm so damn hot, why don't you stop and help me change my flat tire?

Two more cars pass, neither eliciting a honk or catcalls, leading me to believe they were filled with girls heading out for a day on the sunny beach.

With an impatient glance at my watch, I consider calling the garage when I hear the deep and unmistakable rumble of motorcycles approaching. Holding my hand up to my forehead to shield the sun, I see two approaching from the south and a small thrill runs through me. There's just something about a man on a motorcycle that gets my own metaphorical engine rumbling.

Quickly turning toward the rear of my jeep, I again strike a distressed damsel pose and pretend to rummage around, bent over, ass sticking out nice and perkily. The bark of the engines gets louder, and I can tell they are slowing down. I lift my head, turn it to the left, and see two potentially gorgeous and maybe even badass bikers slowly gliding by. The first one looks a little scary with long, blond hair and a full beard. As he starts to pull off the road in front of my Jeep, I notice the black leather vest he's wearing has a freaky-looking skull with bloody, dripping teeth on the back and the word "Mayhem's" written over the top and "Mission" across the bottom.

Before I can even think to be a little leery, my eyes

cut to the next bike slowly crawling by and Oh. My. Freakin'. God.

Now, this is the type of biker that would star in my fantasies. He's not wearing a leather vest but just sporting a simple black Harley Davidson t-shirt that fits tightly across a broad chest. Both of his arms are covered in tattoos, and I even see a peek of ink running up the right side of his neck. Faded jeans with a small hole in the right thigh that only draws my notice because of the way they form to a long and solid leg, accompanied with some kick-ass black boots. My eyes lift quickly to his face and although I can't see his eyes because of the dark frames he's wearing, I can see plenty of shaggy, black hair that curls and flips out from under the small helmet that covers just the top part of his skull. His head turns to face me as he rides by and although I can't see what color his eyes are, I can feel them running all over my body. By the small quirk to his lips, I know they are finding appreciation in what he sees. I, in turn, appreciate the thin, dark goatee that surrounds those lips and a perfectly square and dimpled chin just below.

Both bikes pull over and stop about twenty feet in front of my Jeep. The silence is almost deafening when the engines are cut, but then the squawk of seagulls in the distance and waves crashing on the beach takes up residence in my ears.

I shut the back tailgate and walk down the driver's

side of my Jeep toward them, careful to make sure no other traffic is getting ready to drive by. Both men have their long legs on the ground, balancing those massive machines between their thighs. They remove their helmets almost in synchronicity and while the blond tightens a bandana he has around his long hair, the other guy runs his fingers through his choppy, dark layers. While I'm not into guys with extremely long hair like the blond, the dark one's looks just long and soft enough that a woman's fingers would get lost in there and never want to let go.

When I reach the front of my Jeep, I rest my hip against the fender and cross my arms under my breasts, which yeah... I know will make them the center of attention.

My eyes focus on the dark-haired guy as he stands up from his bike and lifts a well-muscled leg over. He's tall and that's something I appreciate since I'm unnaturally tall for a girl. His backside is as nice as his front in those faded jeans and the black tee pulled just as tight across his shoulder blades. His arms are corded with muscle and one bicep flexes beautifully as he reaches up to take his sunglasses off as he turns in my direction. Even from twenty feet away, I can see his eyes are the lightest of blue, which pop from underneath thick, dark lashes and slashed eyebrows that give him a dangerous sort of air.

Both men walk toward me. I glance quickly at the blond and as he removes his sunglasses, his eyes immediately lower down to my breasts. The other guy though casually tucks an arm of his glasses into the neckline of his t-shirt and holds my gaze as they walk closer.

"Flat tire?" the blond asks and when I look back at him, his face holds a friendly smile.

"Flat as they come," I quip and flash him my pearly whites.

"Good thing we stopped to rescue you then," the blond replies, flashing me his own grill.

Pushing away from the fender, I turn to walk to the back of the Jeep, knowing both men have their gazes pinned to my ass as they walk behind me. "It's the back right tire."

I abruptly stop at the back corner of my Jeep where I point down at the flat, only to have a solid male body connect with mine. Large hands come to my hips and I hear a deep, rich rumble. "Whoa, Goldie... give a man some warning before you stop your trajectory."

I know, without looking, that this is the dark-haired biker, because his voice rolls deeper than the blond's does. The sound of his sexy voice coats over my skin like a velvet blanket and his hands are warm as they grip me surely just below my waist. With a slight pushing motion, he moves me to the side and steps past me, releasing his hold so he can squat down beside my tire.

Reaching a hand out, he touches a finger in between the treads and gives a slight tap. "You picked up a nail."

I squat down beside him to take a look, not because I really care, but because I want to get a little closer to him. My knee bumps his as I tilt my head to the side to look. "What does that mean?"

Both of our gazes lift up and connect... his light blue eyes latching on to my cornflower ones. God, this man is pretty with his hard jawline and just about the most perfect set of lips I've ever seen on the male species. The goatee is what sets that face apart though, giving him a sexy, rough look.

"What that means," he says with a smile as he stands up and holds a hand out to me. I place mine in his and he helps me rise from my squat position, "Is that we need to put your spare tire on. You can then get the nail pulled and the hole plugged as an easy fix."

The blond-haired guy opens the back of my Jeep, pops open a little compartment on the side wall that I hadn't noticed before, and pulls out a lug wrench and a jack. I watch him as he closes the tailgate and proceeds to work on getting my flat tire off.

When I turn my attention back to the man who is still holding my hand in his, I give him my prettiest smile and briefly pull my bottom lip in between my teeth while I look at him coyly. When I let it pop free, a move that I know makes men think certain things about my lips and mouth, I say, "Well... it's my lucky day to have had two hot men stop to help me."

The blond gives a bark of a laugh as he pulls the tire free, and the dark-haired guy's hand tightens on mine. "I think we're the lucky ones," he says with a wink, and then takes a step in closer to my body.

Because he's so much taller than I am, I have to crane my neck to look up at him. He stares right back down at me with a hint of challenge in his eyes. Then he surprises the shit out of me when his free hand comes back to my hip where he smoothes it along the denim down to the frayed edges. With just his fingertips fingering the fluff around the cut hem, he murmurs, "I mean... what's a guy to do... seeing a sexy woman like you standing here on the side of the road just waiting to give a man a heart attack in these little shorts."

His words are low and seductive, yet still loud enough that his friend heard him because he snorts loudly as he starts to work the jack underneath the Jeep. My eyes slide down to look at the blond as he squats, and I see a knowing grin on his lips.

"Eyes back here, Goldie," the dark-haired man says and just to make sure he has my attention, he tugs on the hem of my shorts just enough to pull me in a bit closer to him.

My eyes slowly lift up... taking in his muscled and tattooed arm... the strong hand holding onto mine just at his stomach. Right up that massive wall of a chest, over the swirling tattoo design coming up out of the collar of his t-shirt and right back to that beautiful face.

I sigh inwardly because this man here... standing intimately close to me and exuding all kinds of male dominance and alpha tendencies, is exactly the type of man that is dangerous to me. He's the type of man that I couldn't control, which makes him immensely appealing to my inner psyche... that most secret part of me that is tired of being the one calling the shots all the time. Of course, the reason I have to call the shots is so I don't get hurt, but that's something that would take a few psychologists to get untwisted in my brain.

Oh, this hot biker man.

The things we could do to each other. I can feel it... the vibe of attraction between the two of us pulsing almost tangibly in the air. I wonder what it would feel like to be with someone like him. A common man that exudes raw sexuality from his entire being. I bet he's the type that has to possess a woman... make her a slave to his whims, and just the thought of doing as he commands causes a naughty shiver to snake up my spine.

"What are you doing tonight?" he asks in that sexy, rough voice.

Tonight? What am I doing?

I blink hard and my mind races to figure out the immediate future. But then it all comes crashing down on me. It doesn't matter what I'm doing... whatever it is, it can't be with him.

Definitely not with someone like him... all tall, dark, and so completely far out of my comfort zone that I would be crazy to entertain even the notion of hooking up with this guy. He doesn't look like someone that could be so easily discardable.

Stepping away from the man, I tug my hand loose and push my hair behind my ear just so I have something to do to justify my withdrawal. "I have plans tonight."

"So cancel them," he murmurs and steps toward me again, his eyes intensely serious.

Yes, cancel them. Go out with this man and just experience one super and stunning night of hot, out-of-control passion.

I give myself a mental slap.

Shaking my head, I give him an apologetic smile. "Can't. I have a date tonight with my boyfriend."

Lie, lie, lie.

Those light blue eyes stare at me for a moment, considering whether he should argue with me, but then they quickly fill with disappointed resignation. He gives me a slight nod of his head and an ironic smile. "Lucky man."

Unlucky me, I think to myself, and I'm on the verge of telling him that I had a momentary lapse of idiocy and that I would love to do something... anything... with him, when my phone rings. Giving him a short smile, I pull my phone out and see it's Hunter calling me back.

Turning my back on the two men, I walk a few paces away from the Jeep as I answer his call. "Hey... did you get my message?"

"Yeah," he says, and I can hear music in the background so I know he's at the bar. "Do you need me to come get you?"

"No," I assure him. "I had two good Samaritans stop to help me out. They're putting my spare on, and I should be there soon. But I apparently have a nail in the tire and need to get that fixed."

"I'll take the tire for you this afternoon, get it plugged, and then change it out for you. It will be all good by the time you get off your shift this evening," he says, and then his voice becomes muffled as I assume he covers the mouthpiece on the phone to yell at someone in the background, "Hey... get off the damn table before you break your neck."

I snicker and shoot a glance back over my shoulder. The blond guy has the spare on and is releasing the jack from under the Jeep. The dark-haired guy is leaning back against my tailgate, hands casually tucked in his pockets, watching me.

Damn, he is so amazingly gorgeous that I'm struck a bit stupid for a moment.

"Sorry about that," Hunter says. "Stupid college frat kids in here getting drunk all day. You're going to have your hands full when you get here."

"Crap," I grumble as I turn back away from the gorgeously hot biker watching me. "College kids don't tip worth a shit."

Hunter chuckles. "Well, at least it's a Friday and you'll have more customers so that means more tips."

"Aren't you just a ball of sunshine," I quip at him. "I'll be there soon."

I disconnect, shove the phone in my back pocket, and turn to walk back to my Jeep. Both men watch me approach with appreciative eyes and while I never mind a man checking me out, I have to say I very much like it coming from the dark-haired biker. I saunter past them both toward my driver's door where I reach in and grab my purse.

"Here... let me give you guys some money for helping me out," I say over my shoulder, not really having the money to spare but feeling obligated to offer it all the same.

"No need," that deep voice says from right behind me, but then sounds further away when I hear, "Glad to help."

I push back from the interior and look over my left shoulder, watching both men walking back toward their bikes. The dark-haired one doesn't give me a second glance but the blond looks over his shoulder before turning around to face me, then walking backward right alongside the other guy. His eyes rake up and down me, and he gives me a wolfish grin. "It was our pleasure for sure, Goldie."

I smirk at him, shake my head, and get in my Jeep. By the time I have my seatbelt on and the engine cranked, they're just swinging their legs back over their bikes. I check the traffic in my rearview mirror, see it's clear, and pull out onto the road.

With a few short punches of my fist to the steering wheel, I beep my horn in acknowledgement and take off down the road, leaving that dark, sexy biker behind in reality... but I guarantee he'll make an appearance in my future fantasies.

CHAPTER 4

Tenn

A S I STRAP my helmet back onto my head, I watch the blue Jeep pull away with my fantasy woman inside and try to tamp down my annoyance. Of course she'd have a boyfriend. What woman that looked like that, walked like that, talked like that… wouldn't have a boyfriend?

"Fucking eleven-plus," Kyle says from beside me.

My head swivels his way as I pop my kickstand back with the heel of my boot. "Eleven plus?"

"Goldie there," he says as he nods his head down the highway where I can barely see her vehicle as it drives away in the distance. "Eleven plus on the scale."

H*igher*, I think to myself, because fuck… a woman like her was created to define the word beautiful. But what I really liked about our brief interchange is the confidence in which she bears that beauty. Not in a cocky or self-absorbed way, but more in an assured, intelligent way. Like she works what was given to her in calculated measure, and I've always respected a woman that has the independence to want to look out for her own best interests. Don't get me wrong. There's nothing wrong with taking care of a woman... protecting her. But I like the confidence of one that knows she can do it herself, and that without a doubt, is the type of woman Goldie represents.

Golden from fucking head to toe... except for those dark blue eyes that held secrets within them. Secrets I wouldn't mind torturing out of her with my mouth between her legs.

"I'd sell my left nut to know what you're thinking right now," Kyle says, and I blink my eyes to dispel the fantasies I had started conjuring before I ended up with an embarrassing hard-on.

I grin at Kyle. "Just thinking she's more than an eleven."

"Which makes your strike out all the more painful," he observes, and that is completely true. "So I say let's go grab a beer. Andrea doesn't get off work for another hour, and she texted me the name and address of a bar she said she'd meet us at. I don't think it's too much farther up the road."

"Sounds good to me," I say just before firing up my bike.

We pull back onto the highway and motor on, and just three miles north, Kyle slows his bike to make a right-hand turn into a gravel parking lot. A long building with gray, salt wood siding backs up to the ocean dunes with a sign across the front door that says "The Last Call."

Clever.

We park to the left side of the building, which gives me a glimpse of a huge outdoor deck coming off the back that is packed with people slugging back beers in their bathing suits. I'm thinking I'm a little overdressed in my jeans, t-shirt, and shit kickers out here on the beach, and I know I'll need to make a store run for some appropriate clothes this week. I didn't pack but a few changes of clothes in my saddlebags, figuring I could do my laundry at Bri's apartment, but nothing I brought was with the idea in mind I'd be spending a week at the beach.

As I start to unstrap my helmet again, Kyle reaches out and gives me a slight punch to my shoulder. When I look at him, his head nods at something just over his right shoulder. My eyes slide past him and focus on the teal-blue Jeep parked on the other side of the lot.

My eyebrows raise and my gaze slowly moves back to Kyle. His grin is almost evil, and I answer with a sly smile of my own.

"Well, what do you know," I muse. "Looks like Goldie didn't get very far down the road."

Kyle steps off his bike and hooks his helmet to the handlebar. "Maybe you can get her drunk and take advantage of her."

I snort and level a hard stare at him. "Not my

style. Besides, she has a boyfriend."

"At least we'll have something nice to stare at while we wait for Andrea."

"Truth," I agree as I swing my leg over my bike and run my hand through my hair.

We walk into the bar, and I give my eyes a moment to adjust to the interior darkness. There is a long bar to the right with a few patrons nursing drinks. A pretty, dark-skinned girl with long, silky black hair smiles at us from behind the bar. "Welcome to The Last Call."

I nod at her and a brief glance around yields no Goldie. I hear a racket of voices from the left, seeing a hallway that disappears to what I'm thinking is another room. I follow it down, Kyle just a few paces behind.

As we emerge into a larger area filled with another bar, pool tables, dartboards, and a ton of partying people, my eyes do another quick scan. When they reach the bar, they immediately focus in on that long, golden hair that seemed to have sparkled in the sunshine but now just seems to glow in the ambient lighting behind her.

Her back is to me as she pours a beer from a draft tap.

Huh… I wouldn't have pegged Goldie as a bartender. Even though she was casually yet sexily dressed, I figured her more of an office-type worker for some reason.

Kyle brushes past me and walks up to the middle of the bar, taking a seat at a stool right in front of the beer taps. Goldie's eyes lift up in welcome to the new customer and when they focus on Kyle, she holds his gaze for only a nanosecond before her eyes immediately scan around the room. When they lock onto me, her gaze fills with recognition and fuck me… pleasure to see me standing there.

A sly grin comes to her face, and her gaze focuses back onto the beer she's pouring. "You guys following me?" she asks, and I'm not sure if she's talking to Kyle or me.

"Nah," Kyle assures her. "Just meeting someone here in a bit."

I walk up and take a seat to Kyle's left, resting my forearms on the bar. Those blue eyes lift back up to mine as she pulls the glass away from the tap. "Give me a second and I'll be back to get your orders."

"Can't wait," I murmur and fucking dig the sexy incline of her lips I see just before she turns away. As she walks down to the far end of the bar, Kyle actually stands up on his stool a tad, leans over the bar, and eyeballs her retreating ass for a moment.

When he sits back down, he looks at me and shakes his head in amazement. "Damn dude… fucking fifteen I'm thinking."

A million, I think to myself.

It only takes a minute for her to deliver her beer to an old man at the end of the bar, give him a soft smile, and take a few dollar bills from the small pile of money resting in front of him. She puts one dollar in the tip jar, the rest in the cash register, and walks back up to Kyle and me.

"What are you two drinking?" she asks with a smile. "And it's on me because of all your kind help."

We both order bottled Budweiser, as we aren't into fancy microbrews or drafts. I watch her with sharp eyes as she efficiently gets our beers, takes some money out of her tip jar, and puts it in the register before delivering our orders to us.

"Enjoy," she says as she sets a bottle in front of each of us.

I take the beer and hold it up to her in salute. "Thanks, Goldie."

She winks at me and sets her forearms on the bar, leaning slightly in toward us. It makes the edge of her tank top dip a little, and I can't help my eyes when they drop for a moment to admire the swell of her breasts and dark shadow of cleavage.

My gaze slides back up to hers, and her eyes are sparkling with mischief. She knows exactly what she's doing... working her assets and all that.

Sticking her hand across the bar at me, she says, "It's not Goldie. It's Casey Markham. I take it you two are new to the island?"

I've already held that delicate hand in mine, but I'm not going to pass up another opportunity. I reach my digits across and take ahold of her again. "I'm

Tenn and this is Kyle," I say, jerking my head to the right.

She gives me a soft squeeze, angles her head, and gives a smile to Kyle. When she looks back at me, she pulls her hand back and asks, "Ten? That's an unusual name. Your parents mathematicians or something?"

I chuckle and shake my head. "No. It's spelled T-E-N-N."

"As in the abbreviation for the state?" she asks as her ear dips toward her shoulder in curiosity.

"No, as in the poet."

"There's a poet by the name of Tenn?"

"Not that I know of," I tell her conspiratorially. "But I'm not a real big fan of poetry, so I'm not really sure."

She looks at me inquisitively and waits for me to enlighten her, instinctively knowing there's more to the story of my name.

"Lord Alfred Tennyson," I supply.

"Ah… now that's a name I do recognize. I think we had to read him in college, but I hate shit like that."

"Me too," I commiserate.

"Going to take a piss," Kyle butts in and stands up from his stool.

Neither Casey nor I look his way but continue to stare at each other.

Her lips curve upward in amusement, and I focus

in on how full and soft they look. She leans a little more across the bar, and I struggle not to let my eyes drop to her breasts again. "Your parents are romantics then," she hypothesizes. "Lovers of poetry?"

I smile at her and shake my head. "Literature in general. And more my mom than my dad, God rest her soul."

She gives me a sympathetic look over the reference of my mother's passing but doesn't dwell on it, which I appreciate. "Interesting. Any siblings?"

"Smart girl," I compliment her. "Younger brother. Woolf."

"As in Virginia?"

"As in," I say with a smile as I hold my bottle of beer up to her again in salute.

Casey takes a hand and traces an unrecognizable pattern on the wood of the bar with a fingertip. She watches her progress for a moment, and then raises her eyes back to mine. It's a subtle yet flirty gesture. "Your name should be Woolf. It's a better biker name."

Chuckling, I shrug my shoulders. "I'm not a biker."

"Yet you ride a bike," she points out. "You wear the Harley t-shirt, have your shit kickers on, tats all over the place, and a dangerous look about you. Very *Sons of Anarchy.*"

I snort and slap my hand on the bar. "You watch too much TV, Goldie."

Casey slides her hand closer to mine and with the end of her finger, strokes it lightly across the side of my wrist. My skin fucking tingles from the contact, and her subtle flirting goes full on in my face. I find it fascinating that the woman who proclaims to have a boyfriend is so free with her touches, and all of a sudden... I'm not feeling so gentlemanly about her being involved with someone already.

"A shame," she whispers, her eyes moving from our hands to my face. "Something just really hot about bikers."

My hand snakes out and wraps around her wrist, my thumb coming to rest right over her pulse, which I can feel fluttering madly against me. "I'm a biker then," I assure her with a growl. "Whatever you want if you'll cancel your date with your boyfriend tonight."

Casey's head turns left and then right, looking down both ends of the bar and assuring herself that she's not needed by any customers at the moment. When she looks back at me, her eyes spark with playfulness. "Just out of curiosity, what would you do with me tonight if I didn't have a boyfriend?"

Many women have flirted with me. I understand it is often a playful, back-and-forth banter that ultimately seeks an outcome of two people coming together. Sometimes, I enjoy that shit, other times, not.

Now is one of the times I'm not into it, because

Casey is too direct and forward to engage in that crap. So I just decide to throw the truth out to her. "If I had you tonight?"

She nods at me, her gaze locked to mine.

I lean across the bar and in a tone so low I can barely hear myself, I tell her, "I'd make you come over and over and over again. And when you insist you couldn't give me any more, I'd make you come again just to prove you wrong."

Casey inhales through her nose sharply and her pupils actually dilate. Her soft, pink lips part and a tiny huff of spearmint breath blows out. "You don't mince words," she observes with a murmur.

"Not when I see something I want," I tell her, my thumb now stroking the silky skin of her wrist. And then I command her, "Dump the boyfriend, Goldie. Come spend the night with me."

And there it is… in her eyes, I see it—the first signs of acquiescence. I want to stand on the bar and beat my fists against my chest in victory.

But I don't dare let go of her wrist until I get the words I want from her.

She opens her mouth but before she can speak, a hand claps me on my shoulder and I hear Kyle say, "Look who I found, dude."

I don't turn to look at him. I don't let go of Casey' wrist. I continue to stare at her and wait for her to give me the words I want. To tell me that I can have her… at least for tonight.

But the heat and promise dies from her gaze just a tad, and she slowly turns her head to the right to look at Kyle as she pulls away from my grasp. Her eyes light right back up again in more than just nominal recognition of Kyle, and a smile forms on that beautiful mouth.

"Hey Andrea," Casey says brightly, and I realize all at once that Casey must know Kyle's sister. Not so unusual, this being a tiny community and Andrea recommending we meet up at this bar.

I turn to give my attention to Kyle and his sister, and I'm momentarily stunned when I see how beautiful she is. Like Casey, she has blond hair but hers is a bit darker and more yellow in tone. She's tall but still comes a few inches shorter than Casey does and without being obvious, I notice that her body is built to almost perfect proportions. I say "almost perfect" because Casey has true perfection down to a science, and there's no touching that.

"You must be Andrea," I say with a genial smile as I reach a hand past Kyle. "I'm Tenn Jennings."

"Pleased to meet you," she says as she pumps my hand, and then her gaze flicks back and forth in question between Casey and me. "I see you already met my friend, Casey."

"Kyle and Tenn helped me change a flat tire a little while ago," Casey supplies an explanation.

"Hmmmm," Andrea muses. "That was nice."

"Yeah, we're regular fucking Boy Scouts," Kyle says as he loops an arm around Andrea's shoulders and pulls her in close. Leaning over, he gives her a kiss on top of her head. "Missed you, little sis."

"Missed you too," she says with a smile and slides her arm around his waist as she looks at me pointedly. "Why don't you guys grab your beers and let's go sit out on the back deck. You can tell me all about the trip out here."

I don't mistake the tone of her voice. It screams right at me, *I don't trust you. Stay away from Casey.*

But I won't be scared off so easily.

I give her a charming smile. "What are you drinking, Andrea? I'll grab it for you and meet you and Kyle out there."

Her eyes narrow at me, but her tone is polite. "Anything on draft is fine."

I nod and turn away, effectively dismissing her and giving my attention back to Casey. "How about a draft, Goldie?"

Casey's eyes slide over my shoulder and I watch as they move across the room, presumably following Andrea and Kyle out to the back deck. She doesn't look back at me but turns and bends into a cooler to pull out a frosted pint glass and sticks it under the tap labeled "Stella". When it's full, she sets it in front of me and says, "That will be $2.75."

Her voice is distant, and I know the spell that we were both under just a few minutes ago has been completely broken. But I'm just cocky enough to know I can get it back with a little effort. There's a connection there. Sexual, of course, but a connection all the same.

Reaching into my wallet, I pull out a five and hand it to her. "Keep the change."

She smiles and nods her head in thanks. As she starts to turn away, my hand jets out again, latching onto her wrist. The minute my skin connects to hers, the spell is back in full force again. I can feel it pulsing through me, and I know she sure as shit can.

Casey sucks in oxygen and drags her gaze from our hands back up to mine. Her eyes are immediately warm and expressive. Her chest rises and falls deeply.

"Dump the boyfriend," I tell her again, daring her to defy me. "Let me have you."

Her eyes roam back and forth between my own, and she nibbles on her lower lip in contemplation. The majority of me... the part that is a reasonable and logical man... doesn't really expect her to give in. I'm a perfect stranger and she seems like a nice enough girl. While she may be a big flirt, she doesn't seem the type to just jump into the sack with anyone. She could have her pick of any man on this island, as a matter of fact.

So I'm utterly shocked when she leans across the bar and whispers to me, "Okay."

My head jerks back slightly. "Okay?"

She nods and pulls her wrist out of my grasp. "You can have me. I get off at six."

Holy fucking shit.

She's mine.

CHAPTER 5

Casey

I MUST BE crazy.

That's the only explanation to account for the fact that I'm giving myself to a man that I know nothing about and had maybe ten total minutes of conversation with.

At least that's the conclusion Andrea had come up with when she hissed at me about an hour ago while we were in the bathroom together. "Are you fucking crazy?"

"Pretty sure I am," I told her as I washed my hands.

"You don't know anything about him," she pressed in an urgent whisper as she leaned against the vanity. "He could be a murderer or a rapist."

"He's your brother's friend," I pointed out. "And besides… it's not like I haven't done one-night stands before, Andrea. You know this about me, and you've never been all judgy about it before."

"I'm not judging," she said with an apologetic

smile. "I love your freedom and sass to live your life your way. It's just... have you seen him? He looks dangerous."

Yes, he does look dangerous. It's why he's appealing to me so much. He's like forbidden fruit. He's like fire. He's all the things I shouldn't touch but the temptation is too strong to ignore.

I dried my hands and threw the paper towels in the trash can. Turning to Andrea, I took her by the shoulders and leaned in to her. With an assured voice, I told her, "I'll be fine. Now go out, have dinner with your brother, and reconnect."

Andrea nodded in defeat and I ushered her out the door. While they had been out on the back deck, she had invited both Kyle and Tenn to dinner with her and Wyatt as he was getting off duty, and they were going to meet him on the north end of the island.

Apparently, Tenn had declined, instead telling her that he had a dinner date with me. That, of course, sent her scurrying into the bar where she demanded I go to the bathroom with her and she proceeded to tell me how crazy I was because she was sure the only dinner that Tenn had on his mind was feasting on me.

Yup... pretty sure I'm crazy to be doing this, and yet I can't think of one logical reason other than the fact I may be insane to call it off. Tenn had left at the same time Andrea and Kyle did, telling me that he had to go find a hotel he could check in to and that he'd be back to pick me up when I got off work.

Which is right now.

Kent relieves me on time, and I quickly count out my tips and wipe the bar down. I glance around the bar, which is really starting to fill up with more tourists out looking for a good time. I don't see Tenn and for a moment, I consider that maybe he got cold feet. Or maybe even Andrea scared him off, which, if that's the case, I'm going to be pissed.

By the time I grab my purse and yell out good-byes, I still don't see Tenn and disappointment starts to well up inside of me. I made a command decision to give in to him, something that I've never done in my life for a man. I've always been the one to decide my course, and I've yielded to no one.

This was huge for me. I mean, a massive departure from my normal way of thinking when it comes to the opposite sex. And maybe I can blame it on the feelings of unrest I've been having, or maybe it's the fact that I've been unfulfilled for so long, just stepping one foot in front of the other as I walk my way through endless days. But, for whatever reason I capitulated, I recognized in myself a major break-through and I wasn't about to back down from it.

But apparently, Tenn was going to, as I don't see him as I weave in and out of customers on the way out to the front door. I give one last look over my shoulder, desperately looking for his tall frame and dark hair, and my stomach bottoms out when I come up empty.

With a sigh, I turn and push the door open, stepping out into the humid summer air.

"Hey Goldie," I hear, and my eyes immediately lift and lock with Tenn's as he sits sideways on his bike, his muscular legs stretched out in front of him, one booted foot crossed over the other at the ankles. His arms are crossed over his massive chest, and he gives me a lazy smile. "Want a ride?"

Hitching my purse up over my shoulder, I saunter over to him, my eyes locked to his. I put a little extra sway in my hips and then tuck my thumbs into the belt loops of my shorts, just at my waist. The move pushes the denim down a bit, revealing the skin on my lower abdomen. Normally, that move is enough to draw a man's eyes down but Tenn's gaze remains focused on my face, his lips arced up in a sexy smirk as if he knows all my tricks.

"Turns out," he continues on as he stands up from his perch on the motorcycle and bends over to one of his saddlebags where he pulls out a small helmet, "you have a nice bike shop just down the road and figured I'd pick you up a helmet so you can ride with me."

My eyes flick down and then back up again. "You want me to ride with you?"

He nods and steps up to me, placing the helmet on my head. As he fastens the strap under my chin, he confides, "I want that gorgeous body pressed up against me sooner rather than later."

His fingers move from the straps to my cheeks, and he holds me firmly in his grasp. Leaning down until his nose is almost against mine, he whispers, "Still going to let me have you, Goldie?"

My eyes nearly flutter closed over the husky promise in his voice and my bones go liquid on me. I'm in very near danger of rolling over and baring my proverbial throat in complete surrender to this sexy predator.

In an effort to get some control back, I raise a hand and lay it on his hard chest. Raising up on tiptoes and angling my face to the left, I bare my teeth and nip his jawline, which causes him to groan. "For tonight," I clarify, because I need the safety of my boundaries. "You can have me just for tonight."

"Hmmmm," he murmurs as his hands drop to my waist and he pulls me into the warmth of his body. "A one-night stand kind of girl."

"Queen of," I provide, throwing light on exactly the type of woman that I am.

Tenn dips his face and brushes his lips over my neck. My head tilts to the side to give him better access as my fingers dig into the soft cotton of his tee.

"Gotta go back to the boyfriend tomorrow?" he asks in a teasing tone before scraping his teeth along the path his lips just took.

I can't help the shudder that ripples through me,

and I give a slight shake of my head. If I'm being all honest about my boundaries, I need to make sure he understands me fully. "There's no boyfriend."

He hums approval as a hand moves behind my head and grips into my hair. He tugs, and my back arches slightly as he raises his face to look down at me. His eyes are shadowed as the outdoor lighting of the bar is at his back, but because they are so pale, still shine brightly at me. "Even better."

"It's still just one night," I insist, knowing that the minute I promise myself that, I won't go back on it. I'm too disciplined in the way I parcel out my intimacy.

"We'll see," he murmurs. Stepping away from me, he grabs my hand in his and pulls me toward his bike.

◆

"I CAN'T ANYMORE," I gasp as the last tremors of my orgasm fade away and my muscles start to unclench.

What is that? Three so far?

Tenn isn't dissuaded. He merely pushes his face harder into me, his tongue driving in deep. My back arches and my fingers curl tight into his hair—which is softer than it even looked—and I try to wrench his head away from my sensitive flesh.

He lifts his lips from me just enough to growl, "Gotta give you one more… just to prove you wrong. Remember?"

I weakly lift my head and look down my naked body at him as he lies in between my legs. He's still fully clothed while I'm completely bare to him, but then again… he didn't give me any choice the minute he closed the door behind us when we entered his hotel room. His hands came to frame my face, and he proceeded to kiss the breath out of me. His mouth was hard, demanding, and completely controlling. His tongue erotically captivated my own as his hands roved all over me, pulling at my clothes and stroking over my skin.

When he had me completely naked, he took a step back and looked at me with lust blazing out of his eyes. "Over and over again, Goldie," he promised as his eyes traveled down the length of my body. My nipples got hard, and I felt twitchy all over.

His eyes came to rest on that part of my body that felt the twitchiest of all, and he licked his lips. "Want my mouth on that pussy," he murmured, and my knees almost buckled.

None of the rich and dapper men I go out with ever talk to me like that. They always murmur words of endearment while they reverently look upon me with wonder and awe. None of them have such a raw look of need and desire etched upon their faces, and none of them ever look at me like they want to devour me whole.

In my experience, the men I've been with tend to be selfish in nature. I've bemoaned to my girls time and again over the serious lack of oral attention I usually get, instead settling on a man that just wants to get his dick wet so he can pound out his own orgasm. I've never had anyone look at me the way Tenn did in that moment, telling me he wanted his mouth on me as if I was the only sustenance he could ever crave.

And his mouth was on me... and over me... and inside of me. He licked and sucked and ate at me, over and over again. My first orgasm came on brutally strong and amazingly fast, knocking the breath out of me and causing me to go dizzy. Tenn merely muttered against my wet flush, "Fuck yes, baby. So sexy," before he started licking and sucking at me again.

His fingers got added. One, two, and then three... stretching and plunging into me. My hips bucked and circled, trying to drive him deeper into my body. Orgasm number two wasn't far behind number one, and my toes curled from the immense pleasure he gave me.

But he didn't stop.

He didn't attack me harder though either, instead slowing his pace and leisurely lapping against my pleasure-numbed skin. His hands stroked the insides of my thighs, and he whispered how sweet I tasted. The fire stoked slowly inside of me because he ate me out slowly, taking his time with me.

When number three hit, I called out his name and

arched my back off the bed, faintly recognizing a chuckle of triumph out of him. And finally, yes, finally, I figured he'd fuck me.

Instead, he was demanding I give him one more, and I didn't think I had it in me.

"Just fuck me, Tenn," I moan as he slips a finger inside of me, curling it just right.

"One more, Goldie," he says, tilting his head to the side to suck on the skin of my inner thigh. With a prick of his teeth against me that elicits a startled yelp, he surges upward and pulls me from the bed.

I'm so limp. I'm like a rag doll in his arms as he spins me around and has me face the dresser at the foot of the bed, which comes complete with large mirror attached to it. I watch with glazed eyes as he brings his huge body behind me and wraps his tattooed arm across my breasts to hold me up. His eyes bore into mine through the reflective glass and his other hand trails down my stomach.

His fingers splay out and cover my mound, pushing me back against him until I can feel his erection burning into my lower back. He watches his own hand as he slides lower over my flesh and then sinks his middle finger into me.

"Watch me," he commands with a nod of his head downward. "Watch me finger fuck you to another orgasm, Goldie."

My head falls back on his shoulder as I close my eyes to gain composure. He's going to kill me. Death by orgasm.

"Watch, baby," he murmurs as he starts pumping his finger in and out of me. "Look how beautiful you are in my arms. Face flushed, nipples hard as rocks, my finger sliding in and out of you. So warm and tight. Can't wait to have my cock in there."

My eyes take in every detail as he describes it for me, and I feel wanton as I watch how sexy we look in the mirror together. I watch his hand moving against me, let his dirty words seep into my pores, feeling the pressure miraculously start building inside of me again. My gaze slides up to his and I find his eyes no longer watching his own actions, but locked onto my face. His cheek lowers, and he rests it against the top of my head.

"Feel good?" he asks me quietly.

I don't answer right away and he pulls his finger out, circling it slowly around my clit. My hips arch away from his body, seeking a harder touch from his fingers.

"Feel good, Goldie?" he asks again, and I nod my head vigorously as his fingers move faster against me.

"Going to come for me again, aren't you?" he asks, but it's not really a question. It's a command.

"Gotta let you prove me wrong," I gasp, and he chuckles as his eyes drop down to his hand.

"I believe fucking you with my words is just as hot as fucking you with my fingers," he murmurs. "You like my dirty talk?"

"God yes," I moan as I can feel my orgasm starting to fire up.

"Want more than just my fingers?"

"Yes," I gasp out again as I circle my hips against him desperately.

"Then you gotta come for me, Goldie. One more."

And that's all it takes.

My entire body stiffens as wave after wave of pleasure takes me hostage, rolling through me as I cry out my release. With hazy eyes, I see Tenn's eyes light up with victory and his lips curve up in appreciation as he watches me in the mirror for a moment more, his fingers plucking at me gently.

"I think that may be the hottest thing I've ever seen," Tenn mutters as he takes my shoulders and pushes me forward over the dresser. My hands come out to rest on the edge for balance, and I lower my face a moment as I try to catch my breath.

The jangle and swish of Tenn's belt being undone causes me to raise my face again, and I watched mesmerized as his movements have a sense of choppy urgency about him. He reaches into his pocket, pulls his wallet out, and takes out a condom, which he puts in his mouth to hold between his teeth.

With his hands free, he undoes his jeans and pushes them down over his hips. Although my body is blocking much of my view, I can see his erection sticking out past my left hip.

And oh, my word… it's beautiful. It's huge… monstrously big, and my blood starts pulsing again with desire for him at the thought of him putting that inside of me.

Tenn pulls at the condom wrapper still held tightly in his teeth and rips it open. While he seemed in such control just moments ago while he was guiding me to another orgasm, he seems to be overwhelmed with urgency right now.

Spellbound and captivated by the anticipation of what's to come—over how frantic he seems to be to get inside of me—I watch as he rolls the condom on and steps up behind my body. One hand dips down and he drags his fingers through my folds, causing me to huff out a pent-up breath of impatience.

Tenn moves his hands from my flesh to his own cock, takes it in hand, and lines it up to me with his eyes lowered to watch his progress. He rubs the enormous tip through my wetness, letting it sink in just a fraction of an inch, and my body starts to tighten with excitement.

His eyes lift up, and I let mine rise right along until we are staring at each other in the mirror. He doesn't move… holds absolutely still while his gaze melds with mine.

Then his hands grab onto my waist and he pulls back on my body as his own hips flex forward, causing his shaft to slide slowly into me. I stretch to capacity, feeling every nerve and fiber leaping in pleasure. When his pelvis presses tight against my ass,

Tenn hisses through his teeth and his eyes squeeze shut.

"Christ, Casey," he grits out, his voice raw with controlled lust. When he opens his eyes, he gives me a sheepish grin and a slight shake to his head. "That fucking feels good."

I nod at him, my own ability to produce speech seemingly on hiatus.

"I'm going to fuck you now," he promises, and it sounds so sexily threatening that I almost combust right there. "You're going to come for me again too."

I shake my head, because *that* is not going to happen. I have absolutely nothing left in the tank to give him. I didn't even know that many orgasms so close together were physically possible.

"You are," he tells me with smug cockiness, still holding himself absolutely still within me, although I can feel his dick jerking in anticipation.

"I can't," I finally manage to say.

Tenn slowly pulls out of me, causing the most beautiful feeling of friction I've ever had before.

"Gonna prove you wrong, Goldie," he says as he sinks back into me slowly, and even though I can feel all of my internal muscles quivering with expectancy, I still shake my head in denial.

Bending over me, he whispers assuredly once more. "Gonna prove you wrong."

And fuck everything I thought I knew about men and their capacity for giving pleasure, but he does indeed prove me wrong.

CHAPTER 6

Jenn

FOUR DAYS SINCE I've seen Casey.

Six fucking orgasms—five for Casey and a massive one for me that nearly stroked me out—and she walked right out of my room without a backward glance four days ago.

I'll admit it—only to myself—that I'm fucking pussy whipped after just that one encounter. Whipped for a woman I knew less than twenty-four hours before I fucked her, and yet I can't deny the way my entire being is itching to see her again.

Yeah… she was a fan-fucking-tastic lay. Without a doubt the sexiest, most smokin' hot woman I've ever been with in my entire existence. Fuck, I could have feasted on her for hours and never gotten my fill. So, no doubt… my cock wants another crack at her.

But the sex alone isn't what has me fully whipped.

It's the intrigue.

Casey Markham is the most puzzling person I think I've ever met. She's gorgeous beyond compare, but I didn't find her to have much of an ego. She's independent and self-assured, somewhat of a flirt but also an immensely private and controlled person. I've talked with her enough to get a peek at a razor-sharp mind and yet she tends bar for a living, making me wonder whether she has aspirations in the making or failed attempts to meet them.

She's positively fascinating and while I want to fuck her again, I more than anything want to find out why she's the self-proclaimed queen of one-night stands. That shit does not jive in my book because women are notoriously stuck on romance and love, connecting with their minds and hearts. Men are all about the fucking, thinking with our dicks most of the time.

It's true and I admit it.

But Casey isn't typical. She's aloof in her feelings, and I'll never forget what she said to me before she left. While I disposed of the condom, Casey used the bathroom. When she came out, I attempted to pull her onto the bed so she'd lay with me a bit until I could recharge, but she skittered away from me with a stern shake of her head.

"I have to get going," she said as she started getting dressed.

"No fucking way, Goldie," I told her firmly. "I'm not done with you yet."

"And yet, I'm done with you," she said with frost in her voice and determination in her eyes.

I blinked at her in surprise, because what fucking woman talks like that, but then narrowed my gaze on her suspiciously. "You promised me a night. Remember Queen of the One-*Night* Stand?"

"I said you could have me," she corrected with a chuckle. "I didn't promise an entire night. Besides, I don't do sleepovers."

What the fuck? That's something *I* would normally think... using my inside voice, of course.

I scrubbed my hand through my hair in frustration. Normally after a meaningless fuck, I was trying to figure a way to get the woman out the door without a fuss. Here I was trying to get her to stay, and I'm guessing it's because the fuck wasn't so meaningless to me.

By that time, Casey was zipping up her shorts but her posture remained stiff and resolute. Sensing that this was not a woman who could be swayed, I gave a sigh of resignation as I turned toward the door. "Come on. I'll give you a lift back to your car."

"No need," she chirped as she bent over to grab her purse off the floor. "I called a friend who lives close by. She's picking me up."

Well, fuck. There went my chance to spend just a little more time with her while I drove her back to her car, maybe using said time to try to figure out a way to see her again.

Casey then gave me a sweet smile as she stepped up to me. She rose up on her tiptoes and brushed her lips against my cheek. "Goodbye, Tenn."

When she stepped away, I searched her eyes for something... anything that would give me a clue as to what this woman was all about. I got nothing back but a vague and polite smile, effectively telling me the door had been closed tight against me.

Casey started to turn to the door, but I found myself muttering out loud as I reached my hand out to grab a fistful of her hair at the back of her head, "Fuck that, Goldie."

I reeled her in toward me, taking heart from the way her eyes flared and sparked with interest. Pulling her right back up on to her tiptoes, I leaned down just a bit, until her face was just inches from mine. "I don't buy it," I told her simply.

"What's that?" Her words came out in a whisper as her hands rested against my chest.

"This act you got going on," I murmured while my eyes roamed over her face for some glint of the real truth. I looked hard... I looked long, and for a moment, I thought she'd deny me.

And that's when I saw it.

I saw a small flash of sadness ripple through her blue irises, and it was so naked and in such contrast to the effervescent woman before me, that I dropped my hands away from her and took a step backward.

Casey quickly schooled her features and then leveled me with another cool look. Her shoulders squared and her chin rose up a notch. "No act, Tenn.

This is all there is to me."

Fat fucking lie, Goldie. Fat fucking lie.

But I didn't say that to her. I merely gave her a nod of my head and made a sweeping motion toward the door. "Then I guess you have a ride waiting for you."

She stared at me a moment before turning on her heel and walking out of my room.

Fascinating woman, that Casey Markham. She has some part of her locked away… something that she's protecting and thinks is untouchable. Whatever this is—this thing she's hiding—I'm like a kid in a candy store with grabby hands and I want to touch it.

The knock on my hotel door spurs me off the bed where I had been lying on my back while I mused about Casey. I cross the small room and open it up, expecting Kyle to be standing there.

"Ready to roll?" he asks.

I grunt my ascension as I step out the door and pull it closed behind me. "Where we headed?"

"Over to Manteo," he says as he follows me down the outside stairwell that leads to the parking lot. "That chick I was with the other night said there's a great bar over there that serves po' boys and cheap beer. She's going to be there."

I grunt an acknowledgment, remembering the woman Kyle was with the other night. We had gone to some dive bar we stumbled across when we had been out cruising around and ended up getting so trashed, I had to cab it back to my hotel. I had found Kyle fucking said chick in the men's bathroom, right up against the wall. I turned my body around quickly to avert my eyes and said, "I'm heading out, man."

Kyle just grunted at me while the sounds of slapping skin came at me faster. The woman started moaning, and Kyle managed to huff out, "Later, dude," while he plowed her against the water-stained wall. I hastily exited the bathroom and pulled the door closed behind me, but not before I wanted to pour acid in my ears when the woman cried out, "Give it to me you, you big stud."

"Her name's Jenny," Kyle says conversationally as we make it to our bikes and mount up. "She sucks dick like a damn Hoover."

I snicker as I put my helmet on. "You're a poet, man."

"Well, it's true," he says as he nudges his kickstand up. "And this is the point that you reciprocate."

Turning my head to look at him, I cock an eyebrow and say, "Not sucking your dick, dude."

"Douche," Kyle grumbles and then leans back in his seat, planting both feet firmly on the ground to hold the bike steady. "I mean, this is where you share with me a little bit about Casey. You hooked up with her, right? Four damn days, man. You've been silent and it's killing me."

Ordinarily, I'm all about swapping stories about great pussy. It's a man thing... bragging about the details and comparing the lengths of our dicks, which seem to get longer with every story. But for some reason, I'm not in the sharing mood when it comes to Goldie.

"She's a nice girl," I say and then reach out to my ignition.

Kyle reaches over and knocks my hand away. "Oh, fuck no, you don't. You do not get to lay 'she's a nice girl' on my doorstep and expect me to be satisfied with that. She's a fucking fifteen, dude."

A million. Not a fifteen. A million on that ten-point scale.

"You want details?" I ask him with a grin.

"Fucking aye."

I lean in toward him conspiratorially and murmur nice and low. "She was fantastic, man. In to all kinds of kink. Let me tie her up and whip her with a rubber hose, then she let me fuck her in every way imaginable. It was epic, man."

"Are you serious?" he asks in jealous wonder.

"No, I'm not fucking serious," I say in exasperation as I straighten back up and reach for my ignition again.

"If you give me one true detail, I promise to tell you everything I learned about her from Andrea. And trust me, dude, I learned quite a bit."

My head swivels slowly to Kyle, who smirks at me with fonts of untapped information just waiting to be poured out. I appraise him, trying to figure out if what he knows is worth giving him something in return.

Fuck yeah, it is.

"You'll spill it all for just one tiny detail?" I ask to confirm the rules.

"All of it," he says as he leans closer to me, his eyes wide with anticipation.

I shake my head as I look down at the pavement, a wry grin forming on my face. When I raise my eyes to look back at Kyle, I reach my hand back to my ignition. Just before I start my bike, I tell him, "Man… she tasted sweeter than anything I've ever had on my tongue before."

Kyle's eyes go round and a Cheshire smile forms. "And just where did you have your tongue?"

"That's all you get, dude," I tell him with a hard look. "And when we get to Manteo, I want all the details about her."

I start my bike and rev the engine a bit just to drown out any more questions from Kyle.

♦

BY THE TIME Kyle got done telling me all about Casey Markham while we munched on po' boys, I had come to a clear and absolute resolution in my mind that I would be wasting my time trying to figure her out and reach that untouchable part of herself she's been holding back. And Kyle had discovered quite a bit while he and Andrea pounded beers the other night at her house while Wyatt was on duty.

Apparently, Casey Markham is indeed a one-of-a-kind woman as I suspected. From what Kyle could gather, she's like the male version of... well, pretty much any single man that's prowling around these days. She truly is the Queen of One-Night Stands, which fine... that rubs me a tiny bit wrong even though I know that's hypocritical, but after having her once... I don't like the thought of her "one nighting" it with anyone else.

The real kicker, though, was when Kyle told me that Andrea was completely shocked that Casey showed any interest in me, because I'm apparently not the type of man she normally hunts. Yes, he said the word "hunts" like Casey is in it for the sport, but I don't know if that was his word or Andrea's.

The way Kyle told the story—with a bit of relish, I might add—Casey is only interested in super wealthy men who can give her pretty baubles in exchange for some amazing fucking. While Kyle didn't come right out and say it, I was getting a clearer picture of a woman who uses rich men.

She must have gone slumming when she decided to give this biker a try, I think wryly.

Do I feel used?

Fuck no. I had an amazing time with Casey and don't regret fucking her one bit.

Am I looking at Casey in a new light and questioning everything about her that once intrigued me?

Fuck yes. She's an enigma, and while I thought maybe she had some provocative backstory, which made her different from all other women, it turns out that she's just a commitment-phobe who eats rich men up and casts them aside.

More power to you, baby, but that's not the type of game I'm interested in.

And this was probably for the best, as I was leaving to head back to Raleigh in two days to spend time with Zoey. Bri had sent me a text assuring me that they would be back this coming Friday, and when I talked to Zoey last night on the phone, she told me the same.

So I'm going to put Casey out of my mind, and I'm going to enjoy my last few nights here on the coast. Starting right about now as my gaze flicks to the headlights in my rearview mirror of the car that's traveling behind me, which I happen to know holds a beautiful woman that would be easy enough for me to fuck Casey right out of my memories.

This evening is taking an interesting turn of events. After po' boys and a few beers, Kyle was lip-locked with Jenny and I was half expecting he'd drag her into the bathroom to fuck her again. He surprised me, however, when he suggested we head back to Nags Head because he wanted to meet up with Andrea at The Last Call for a few beers.

This idea was fine by me. I had no clue if I'd see

Casey there or not, but after what Kyle had told me, I wasn't all that keen to see her again but I could definitely ignore her if need be.

Okay, that was a fat fucking lie too. I wanted to see her again. I wanted to fuck her again. I wanted to ask her why she was the way she was, and after she told me, I'm sure I'd want to fuck her again after that.

However, that scenario is probably not going to happen, because as we were finishing up our last beer, a friend of Jenny's rolled into the bar. Her name is Mallory, and she's hot. Just hot enough that I can keep my mind preoccupied with something other than Goldie, and Mallory made no bones about being interested in me. This I knew from the way she sat next to me and rested her hand on my thigh. Or the way she giggled and twirled her hair while sucking on her bottom lip when I talked to her. Or, it could even be the way in which she point blank told me that she wanted to fuck me. Yeah, that made it kind of clear.

The next thing I knew, Kyle and I were back on our bikes and Jenny and Mallory were following us to The Last Call in Jenny's car, where I may or may not run into Casey, who may or may not be a good thing or a bad thing, but who most definitely is someone I should stay away from.

We pull into the gravel parking lot, and I can't help the way my eyes quickly scan the lot until they land on the exact thing I'm looking for.

A teal-blue Jeep.

After I park my bike and dismount, I take a quick peek at my watch and see it's closing in on six PM, which is exactly when Casey's shift ended the other night. Part of me considers leaving, staying away for a bit, and giving Casey a chance to leave the bar. Another part of me wants to see her immediately... like right now, to prove to myself that I can give her a glance and not need anything further from her.

And the slightly vindictive part of me... that small part inside of me that actually might be filled with some measure of womanly estrogen, hell bent on making someone jealous, wants to head inside with Mallory on my arm and let Casey Markham know that she's as easily forgotten as I was the other night.

I contemplate my options while Jenny and Mallory exit the car that's parked beside our bikes.

Thirty seconds later, I'm walking through the bar with my arm around Mallory's waist.

CHAPTER 7

Casey

I STARE OUT at the crowd listlessly. It's pretty packed for a Wednesday night, but then again, the summer season is upon us and it will only continue to get busier while the months get hotter.

"Can I get another beer, Casey?" Roy asks as he slides a five-dollar bill toward me.

"Sure thing," I say absently and trudge over to the taps. Pouring the beer, I watch the foam head rise as the golden ale swirls below, round and round, stuck in the same place. I realize my life can be boiled down to this moment… to watching the futility of ale stagnating while foam rises.

Turning the tap off, I slide the beer over to Roy. He gives me a toothless smile and says, "Why so sad, Casey? Had your heart broken?"

I snort and shake my head at him. "Gotta have a heart to break, Roy. I don't think I have one of those."

Before he can lay any pearls of wisdom at my feet,

I turn away and meander over to the register. The clock on the digital display says I can get out of here in five more minutes and then I can go home, put on my rattiest of pajamas, and crawl into bed like I have every night for the past four nights, where I can stare out my window and reflect on how fucked up I'm feeling.

Over Tenn.

Over that amazingly gorgeous biker who smiles like a saint and fucks like the devil.

For all I know, he's not even around anymore. And let's face it... I don't know much. I only know that I gave in to my base desires to have the man, and then he systematically managed to dismantle me in just a few hours' time.

God... the man made me come again... for the fifth time with just a few hard strokes inside of me and even as I was coming down off my high, I knew I wanted him again and again. He pulled up on my hips, practically lifting my feet from the floor as his entire body lurched into me over and over again, hitting me so deep... hitting me in such a remote place, that I knew I'd never be the same again.

When he came, he did it with the force of a hurricane, throwing his head back and roaring out his release. The noise... the noise of his pleasure struck at me hard, because never in all my sexual years have I *heard* a man orgasm like that. I literally felt his release in my ears, and I stared at his reflection in wonder of it all.

When he leaned over me and wrapped his arms around my chest, pulling me up straight so he could hug me from behind, all while his cock was still hard within me, I felt something within me crack. And then he laid his chin on my shoulder and whispered, "Christ, Goldie. I'm ruined."

His voice was so soft… so full of contentment… replete with peace, that a wave of arctic coldness rushed through me and I put my mental walls up immediately. I pulled out of his embrace, mumbled about needing to use the bathroom, and then paced back and forth across the floor while I repeated to myself, *Stay away from him, Casey. He's dangerous.*

So I cut him off at the knees. I was cruel, aloof, and I told him I was done with him, even as my heart screamed at me that I was the most stupid bitch ever to walk the face of the earth.

I left his hotel and sat down on the curb, trying to compose myself before I called Gabby. I hadn't called her like I had told him, but rather told that lie so I wouldn't have to ride on his bike back to my Jeep. I knew if I touched him again, I'd give in. I'd relent to his magnetic pull.

And for the first time since I was eighteen, I sat on that curb and I let tears caused by a man fall from my eyes. I went ahead and let myself mourn for something that I knew I wanted but was too afraid to take. I let it out and when my tears dried, I reminded myself that it was better this way. That this tiny bit of longing and hurt would serve as a reminder of why it could never go any further. I reminded myself that I did what I did for protection. I did it to keep my heart safe.

And so, I plugged along, day after day, continually thinking of my time with Tenn but refusing to let myself wonder what could have been if I had stuck around. I put my friends off, missing out on my weekly Monday breakfast meeting with my girls, Gabby, Alyssa, Savannah and Andrea, claiming a nonexistent sinus infection had kept me in bed. I declined a dinner invitation from Brody one night and then another dinner invitation over to my parents the following night.

I wanted to be left alone.

Alone is what I did best.

"Got big plans tonight?" Kent says from behind me, and I turn to see him stepping behind the bar.

I give a slight shake to my head and offer up a tiny smile. "A frozen pizza and a *Monk* marathon sound big?"

"Sounds interesting," he conceded, and then walked up to the register to begin his nightly ritual.

I turn, grab a rag from the bar, and bend over the sink to wash it out. A generous wiping down of the wooden bar top and I can head home.

"We need a few beers, Casey," I hear from directly on the other side of the bar, and my shoulders tense over that rich, rumbling sound that I know comes from one sexy-as-sin biker.

My head slowly lifts up and Tenn stands there, a genial smile on his face. Immediate warmth floods through me, relief that he's still around, and happiness that he's standing here in front of me, and then comes lust and desire as I look at his pale blue eyes staring at me in interest.

"What do you want?" I ask with a wink, hoping he catches my double entendre, and just that easy, I've thrown out every bit of resolve and common sense where Tenn is concerned.

"Let me see," he says, and then my stomach drops as he turns slightly away from me to reveal a pretty woman standing there with curly, brown hair and large, almond-shaped eyes of the same color. His hand reaches out and touches her shoulder, causing her to turn her head to him. "What do you want to drink, Mallory?"

Stupid fucking name… Mallory.

"A white wine spritzer," she says, and then looks to the woman behind her. "Want the same, Jenny?"

The other woman, who is pretty in a haunted goth sort of way with straight, black hair that comes to her shoulders and several facial piercings, nods.

Kyle steps up beside Tenn and my head turns to him in surprise, and a bit of relief that Tenn isn't here with two women. "We'll take two Buds and two white wine spritzers," he says as he reaches into his wallet. Then he inclines his head toward Tenn and says in a low voice, "And what the fuck is a white wine spritzer?"

Tenn doesn't answer Kyle but turns his gaze to me, and if I'm not mistaken, looks at me expectantly. As if he wants a reaction from me.

"On a double date?" I ask, and then internally wince as I realize how catty my voice sounds.

He smiles big at me, his eyes crinkling with tiny laugh lines at the corner. His lips curve up in a smirk, and he says, "Yeah… something like that."

"Well, you'll have to wait until Kent changes out the register," I say as I jerk my thumb back over my shoulder. "I'll bring your drinks to you."

"Thanks," Tenn says as Kyle throws a twenty on the bar. By the time I snatch it up, he's already turned away, his hand on Mallory's back as he guides her over to one of the empty pool tables. He leans down to say something to her, and I hear her giggle over the music of the jukebox.

Stupid fucking name—Mallory.

In a huff, I turn around and grab two wine glasses from the back bar, proceeding to make the white wine spritzers. I'm proud of myself when I resist the urge to spit in the glasses. I then fish out two Budweisers and as I twist the caps off, my eyes slide over to the pool table. Tenn is bent over it, taking a shot, his tattooed arms flexing and reminding me of the power he holds. Mallory—stupid fucking name—has her hip resting against the corner of the table, and she says something to him that causes those sexy-as-hell lips to lift sexily before breaking out into a full-out laugh.

Ugh. She can't be making him laugh.

I quickly place the drinks on a tray and hand Kent the twenty. "Two Buds, two white wines spritzers."

"What the hell is a white wine spritzer?" he asks as he takes the twenty from me.

"Some stupid drink a woman with a stupid name like Mallory would order," I grumble as he makes me change, handing back three dollars and twenty-five cents.

"Oh-kay," he drawls as he shakes his head at me in confusion.

I take the money, throw it on the tray, and walk out from behind the bar. Kyle is sitting at a small table with Jenny on his lap while Tenn lines up another shot at the pool table. Mallory sees me setting the drinks down and practically skips over to me.

"Yummy," she squeals as she takes one of the wine glasses from my hand to take a sip. She swallow, looks at the glass funny, and then hands it back to me. "Um… it tastes a bit watery."

I stare at the glass, and then raise my eyes to her. "And that's what usually happens when you water down wine to make a spritzer, Sherlock."

She narrows her eyes at me. "That's kind of rude."

"Be glad I didn't spit in it," I say as I ignore the glass and walk past her.

I hear her huff, and she complains to Jenny and Kyle, "I'm going to report her. Didn't you say your sister is friends with the owner, Kyle?"

I snicker to myself. It's true... Andrea is most definitely friends with the owner, but I'm his sister. His little baby sister, in fact, and he'll agree with me. Mallory is a stupid name and a white wine spritzer is a stupid-ass drink.

As I stalk around the edge of the pool table, I run smack into a hard, muscled chest. One whiff of body wash that reminds me of cold mountain air and I know it's Tenn's chest who I'm pressed against. I relish it for a minute and step back, looking up to glare at him.

His eyes are mocking when he murmurs, "Didn't think you were the type to go all meow-meow over me, Goldie. I like this little fit of jealousy."

My jaw drops open, and then snaps back shut as I realize I totally feel jealous of stupid fucking Mallory. "Whatever," I mutter as I drop my face and move to step around him.

He sidesteps, putting himself back in my path. "Now where are you scurrying off to?"

I huff out in frustration and look back up at him. Those blue eyes are piercing straight through me and a completely slappable, yet edible, smirk on his goatee-surrounded lips. "I'm going home."

"Didn't take you for a coward," he murmurs as his head jerks over his shoulder at stupid fucking

Mallory. "If you want my attention, you have it now."

"I don't want your attention," I snap at him and before I can think to move around him, he dips his head lower and whispers to me, "Gonna prove you wrong again."

Those words… so sexy and so reminiscent of the other night when he took great triumph in proving my body wrong causes my heart to start hammering hard. His eyes are challenging me… daring me to step out of my comfort zone and perhaps admit… just a little, that I made a mistake walking away from him the other night.

I take a step back from him, slip my tray under my arm, and reach out to hand him Kyle's money. "Here's the change."

"Keep it," he says without glancing down at it. His eyes rake slowly down my body and then back up again, causing my nipples to tighten in response. When his gaze comes back up to mine, he throws the gauntlet down. "Now… what are you going to do, Goldie? Fight or flight?"

I look at that beautiful mouth and remember exactly how it felt against me the other night. With a flash of anger, I wonder if that mouth will be giving stupid fucking Mallory the same pleasure tonight.

Turning my back on him, I stuff the three-dollar bills in my pocket but slap the quarter on the edge of the pool table, indicating my intention of challenging the winner of the game in progress.

Tenn's eyebrows rise up slightly, and he gives me an amused shake of his head. "You seem sure of yourself. Interested in a bet?"

Now, I watched Tenn take a couple of shots on the table while I was getting his drink order together and he's damn good. But then again, so am I.

"What did you have in mind?" I ask curiously.

"If I win, you have to answer one question for me. And it has to be truthful... no lying."

"That's it?" I ask, almost a little disappointed. I had hoped he would say something that would take the decision out of my hands. Something that would obviate my own stupid barriers I put up. Something like, "If I win, Casey, you're coming home with me and I'm going to fuck you all night long."

"That's all I want," he says assuredly. "And what do you want if you win?"

I consider what I want. I mean... I know what I want. I can't fucking help myself. I want him. I want to be with him and the easiest way to do it seems to lay it right on that pool table in front of me. Stepping in closer to him, I cut a quick glance over to Mallory, of the stupid name, and see her watching me with blazing fury. I stand on my tiptoes and murmur in Tenn's ear, "If I win, I want to give you a blow job."

Tenn's entire body jerks, and he lets out a breath of hot air that fans across my neck. "Fuck, Casey... you know you're all but daring me to lose."

I give him a saucy smile and lick my bottom lip.

"Maybe I am."

Tenn stares at me a moment, and then inclines his head. "It's a bet, then. Just let me finish this game and we'll get it on."

"Oh yes we will," I say with innuendo. "I'm going to get me a beer."

By the time I make it to the bar, order a beer, and pay for it, Tenn is finishing up his game with Mallory. Because her pool-playing skills are as stupid as her name, it didn't take very long.

As the challenger, I rack the balls with a sly grin on my face. Tenn stands over near the table with Mallory pressed in close to him, making sure she garners his attention. He tilts his head her way and smiles at something she says. She shoots me a triumphant look and steps in closer to him, laying her hand on his stomach.

I want to break her fucking wrist, but I refrain. Lucky her.

And lucky me, actually, because since I promised Tenn a blow job if I win, I can guarantee you this game won't take long. I can guarantee you that he'll be walking out the door with me tonight and not Mallory, woman of such a stupid name her parents should be shot.

I release the rack and step away from the table, turning to the wall to grab a cue stick from the holder. By the time I turn back around, Tenn is letting loose and breaks the rack cleanly. Two stripes fall in and he gives me a wolfish grin.

I grin back because I know exactly how this game is going to play out. He might make his next shot, but then he'll start missing them. He'll make a show, of course, but he's going to let me win because he wants my lips wrapped around his dick. I want my lips wrapped around his dick just so I can have another night with him. One more night, I promise myself, and then I'll be done.

"You're going down, Goldie," Tenn says from across the table.

Mallory actually chimes out, "Kick her ass, baby."

I ignore her and give a gracious swipe of my hand toward the green felt. "Then, by all means… take me down."

And much to my utter shock, Tenn proceeds to run the entire fucking table. He sinks shot after shot… striped ball after striped ball falling prey to the corner and side pockets. He doesn't look at me once but concentrates on the game, stalking around the table and calculating his best move. In just a matter of a few minutes, the table is completely devoid of stripes and the only shot left is the eight ball.

He taps the far corner pocket right in front of me, his eyes lifting up to mine. He gives me a hard, appraising stare before he lets the cue stick go. I watch as the cue ball—almost as if in slow motion—hits the eight ball perfectly and it assuredly sinks into the pocket, garnering him the win.

My jaw drops, and this time, my mouth stays open.

He just won.

He just gave up the chance to be with me. He just gave up a fucking blow job, and let me tell you… I give stellar fucking blow jobs.

Tenn casually places the cue stick on the table and walks up to me. I would expect him to have a smirk on his face, but his eyes are deadly serious. "I win. Now you have to answer my question."

"What?" I ask in confusion, because I'm still boggled that he didn't throw the game.

"My question," he repeats. "I want to know the name of the man that hurt you. I want the name of the fucker that made you want to use men and toss them away like yesterday's garbage."

My face flames red with mortification, not because he called me a user of men. But red with embarrassment that he has seemingly figured me all out. That he has managed to narrow down my entire existence to just one small name.

Taking in a deep breath, I let it out shakily. I try to resolve my voice but it quakes with unease as I deny him. "There's no name."

Tenn's eyes flick back and forth between mine, probing deep for a hint of veracity. I hold his gaze, refusing to drop my eyes that are sagging under the weight of the untruth I just told. When it's clear that I won't give him what he wants, his eyes turn sad.

"That's a lie, Casey."

I refuse to acknowledge the truth of that actual statement, so I just lift my chin up higher in defiance.

Tenn looks at me just a moment more, and then tips his head to me. "Well... thanks for the game. You have a nice night, Goldie."

My head swivels to follow him as he steps past me and walks up to Mallory. He touches her shoulder and leans down toward her ear. "You want to get out of here?"

A loud, angry buzzing sound starts in my ears as I realize that Tenn is walking away from me. That he's getting ready to leave with a woman whose name is so stupid, it doesn't even bear repeating. He's going to leave and I'm never going to see him again, and while it scares the shit out of me, I have this feeling deep down inside that I'd be making a colossal mistake if I let him walk away.

Tenn takes Mallory by the hand and holds his other out for Kyle to bump fists. "Later, dude," he says, and then Tenn doesn't even spare me a glance as he turns to head out the door.

He takes one step away from me, then another, and I before I can stop myself, I yell out, "Wait."

Tenn immediately halts in his tracks, drops Mallory's hand, and turns to look at me. I stride up to him, stopping when we're toe to toe. His eyebrows rise in question, and his face is open and accepting.

Taking a deep breath, I let it out slowly and say, "His name is Jeff."

CHAPTER 8

Tenn

THE FUCKER'S NAME is Jeff.

I want to hunt him down and kill him, because whatever he's done, he's taken a beautiful woman and made her lose herself.

Casey stares at me a moment, her eyes wide and vulnerable. I imagine Casey doesn't suffer vulnerability well, so I'm not surprised when she drops her face and pushes past Mallory and me toward the bar. I watch as she runs behind it and grabs her purse. The other bartender says something to her but she ignores him and rushes out, straight down the hall that leads to the front door.

Shit… didn't expect her to run that fast.

"I'm sorry… I gotta go," I tell Mallory as I spin toward the door.

She latches onto my arm, and her eyes narrow at me. "What the hell, Tenn?"

"I'm really sorry," I mutter as I pull my arm away and start weaving my way through the crowd in pursuit of Casey. I've lost sight of her so I pick up my pace, actually bumping shoulders with a few people.

When I burst out the door, I see nothing but cars in the parking lot. I look left, then right, and see a flash of golden hair bouncing as Casey runs toward her Jeep. Thankfully, my legs are longer than hers are and I manage to catch her just as she's reaching for her door handle.

My hand latches on to her elbow. "Wait a minute, Goldie. Where are you going?"

"Home," she says as she tries to jerk herself from my grasp, so I tighten my grip.

"Just wait," I tell her as I turn her to face me.

Rather than pull away from me again, she surprisingly steps into me and lifts up on her tiptoes, her lip curled in a snarl. "Don't ask, Tenn. I'm not telling you another fucking thing about him."

She looks like a wildcat, eyes all wide and feral, her hair streaming over her shoulders in messy disarray, cheeks flushed red. I can tell there will be no reasoning with her, so I do the next best thing by taking her shoulders and pulling her closer to me. I slam my mouth onto hers and kiss the fuck out of her.

Casey struggles for all of two seconds, and then her arms are wrapped around my neck and she's kissing me back.

Desperately.

Her soft body melts into mine, and lust shoots

down to my dick when she moans softly into my mouth.

Only three seconds away from pushing her up against her Jeep and fucking her in the parking lot, I pull away. Her chest is rapidly rising and falling and her eyes are filled with confusion. I bring a hand to the side of her face and cup it, running my thumb over the modelesque swell of her cheekbone.

"I mean it," she says in warning, her eyes looking like a caged animal again. "I won't talk about him."

"We don't have to," I assure her with a reassuring smile. "But let's get out of here... go get a cup of coffee or something. We can talk about something else."

"Like what?" she asks suspiciously.

Leaning in, I kiss her on the forehead and don't miss the subtle sigh that yields from her. Sensing her need for something normal to ground her, I grab Casey's hand and start pulling her toward my motorcycle. "It's a nice night. We can talk about the weather if you want to."

◆

I SIP AT my coffee and look around the diner. It's nearly empty, and the sign on the front says they close at nine PM. Plenty of time for us to sit for a bit and talk.

"Me and my girlfriends do breakfast here every

Monday," Casey says out of the blue, and my gaze slides back to her. It's the first thing she's said since we left the bar.

"Oh, yeah? What are they like?"

Tenderness morphs Casey's face and her eyes go soft, telling me what I've suspected from the start… that she has a big heart. "Well… there's my best friend since I was a kid…. Gabby. She's engaged to my brother, Hunter."

"He's the one that owns The Last Call, right?"

"Yup. And then there's Alyssa. She's engaged to my brother Brody, who is Hunter's twin."

"And he's the one that spent some time in prison?" I ask.

Casey's eyebrows rise in question, so I supply her before she can ask. "Kyle told me. I guess Andrea filled him in on the whole group."

"Did she tell him that Brody went away for a crime he didn't commit?"

Now it's my turn for my eyebrows to rise. "No. Guess she didn't tell him that piece of info."

Casey shrugs her shoulders. "It's not something that people know outside of our family and small group of friends. Andrea probably thought that was too personal to share."

I don't tell her that Andrea apparently shared a bit of personal information about Casey… like her penchant for wealthy men. It's not like Andrea told Kyle anything sordid… just that Casey only dated the rich elite, that she was surprised she agreed to have dinner with me, and that she never had a long-term relationship, seeming to just bounce from guy to guy. I sort of drew my own conclusions from that.

"Then there's Savannah, who used to be my roommate, who is with Gavin, who is this really big-time author, and well, you know Andrea. That's my group of girls," Casey says vaguely.

I want to ask her more about Brody, and I definitely want to hear more about her friends because I'd bet my Harley they're nothing like Casey since they're all in committed relationships. But I don't, because I want to ask her about something else. I promised not to ask her anything more about Jeff, but I'm insanely curious about why she targets just rich men.

And I know that the best way to get information is to share information.

"I have a daughter," I tell her abruptly.

I'm completely blown away when Casey's eyes soften even further, and she gets the sweetest smile on her face that pops out two dimples. "You do?" she asks with delighted surprise.

I grin and nod. "Her name's Zoey and she just turned fourteen. Her mom—my ex-wife—relocated to Raleigh a few months ago. That's the reason I rode out here with Kyle... to see Zoey."

Casey snickers and picks up her coffee cup. She takes a sip and looks at me over the rim with sparkling eyes.

"What?" I ask, curious as to what has amused her so much.

She chuckles and sets the cup down. Leaning her crossed forearms on the table, she says, "It's just… you and I have been very intimate with each other and I don't know anything other than your name and that you're from Wyoming, and now, of course, that you have a daughter named Zoey."

I lean back in the booth and stretch my legs out, caging Casey's legs between my own. Spreading my arms wide, I say, "I'm an open book. What do you want to know?"

"Well, for starters… how old are you? I mean, you have a fourteen-year-old daughter."

"Thirty-three," I tell her. "Had Zoey when I was nineteen."

"And what do you do for a living?"

"Currently, I'm a motorcycle mechanic in between jobs. Prior to that, I was in the Marine Corps and prior to that, I worked on a cattle ranch."

"Wow," Casey says with surprise. "A biker, a Marine, and a cowboy. You like have all the hot guy tropes covered."

Chuckling, I move my legs in closer together so I'm touching hers. It's not much, but for some unexplained reason, I want the physical connection with her. "I think you're romanticizing it just a bit. As a mechanic, I perpetually have grease under my fingernails, as a Marine in the desert, I sometimes went days without showering, and as a ranch hand, I smelled like cow shit at the end of the day."

"Yeah," she huffs, "but you like have all those tattoos and muscles. I could definitely overlook the other stuff."

We both laugh, and I can see most of the tension has lifted from her shoulders. We enjoy a moment of comfortable silence, sipping at our coffees.

"What about you?" I finally ask. "What's your story?"

Casey shrugs her shoulders and lowers her gaze. "Not much to tell. I just turned twenty-six, born and raised here in the Outer Banks. I tried to make a living as a real estate agent but I pretty much suck at that, so now I bartend. Oh, and I flunked out of college after a year, which still pains my mother."

"I don't buy it," I tell her with a shake of my head.

"Buy what?"

"You flunked out of college. You're too smart."

She nods in understanding with her lips quirked. "Let me clarify… I flunked out of college because I was rebelling. Too much partying and not enough studying."

"Rebelling? You?" I ask sarcastically.

Casey laughs, dips her face, and traces the edge of her coffee cup with her finger. When she raises her head, her eyes are sad and serious. "I had a rough senior year in high school… with Brody getting sent to prison and… well, just some other stuff. I sort of went a little crazy when I got out of this town. It was my chance to be someone different. To act without consequences."

"To bury your troubles in alcohol," I guess.

She nods with a sheepish grin. "And pot. Lots and lots of pot."

"Hey… most kids that age go a little crazy. Who you are today isn't who you were back then."

Casey's lips flatten as if I said something distasteful, but she nods her head in agreement. "That's for sure."

The waitress comes to our table with a pot and tops off our coffees. While Casey doctors hers up with a ton of cream and sugar, I take the opportunity to satisfy my curiosity.

"Kyle mentioned something interesting to me," I edge into the conversation. "He said that Andrea was surprised you showed interest in me. Am I so different than other men you've gone out with?"

Casey's eyes snap to mine. She stares at me shrewdly for a minute, and then narrows her eyes. "I'm guessing if Andrea told Kyle that, who in turn passed that on to you, then she also told Kyle about the type of man I normally go out with, right?"

Fuck. Busted.

Before I can even open my mouth to admit that, she continues. "I know Andrea must have said something because of what you said to me earlier. You said I used men and tossed them away like yesterday's garbage."

I groan internally, because I really had not meant to say it that way. I was still pissed that she was able to walk away so easily after that incredible night we shared.

"Casey, Andrea didn't—"

She holds a hand up and waves my words away impatiently. "I love Andrea. She's my friend. I know she never would have said anything that cast me in a derogatory light. So what I'm guessing is she told Kyle the truth. That I don't do relationships. I casually date, and I only date wealthy men. And of those men that I keep around for more than a few dates, I only do so because they understand my boundaries. Now, whether that is what Kyle in turn relayed to you is another matter, but there you have it… I don't go out with men like you. Period. End of story."

I stare at Casey a moment, trying to figure out if she's pissed that she's been the subject of conversation or if she's just matter-of-factly telling me the way things are. Regardless, I ask her instead, "What do you mean 'men like me'?"

She smirks and waves her hand toward me. "You know… men like you."

"No, I don't know what that means," I tell her as I straighten up in the booth and pull my legs back. Leaning forward on my elbows, I murmur, "Enlighten me."

"Dangerous," she says simply. "You're danger-ous."

"I'm a teddy bear," I tell her.

"You're real," she counters. "You're real, down to earth, and there isn't a pretentious bone in your body. That makes you dangerous."

I shake my head in confusion. "I don't under-stand."

Casey smiles at me almost piteously, and I'm surprised she doesn't give me a condescending pat on my head. "I know on the face it looks like I just seek out rich men, and maybe you think that's so because I like to live a glamorous life and I like pretty things. But the truth is... I seek out men that are vain, narcissistic, or self-absorbed. It just so happens that many of those types of men are that way because of what money has done to them. It makes them entitled and it corrupts. It controls their lives and makes them feel more important that what they really are. It gives them the power to hurt people... to destroy. It takes away their capacity to truly care."

"And these are the men you seek out?" I ask dumbly.

"Yes," is all she says, and she waits to see if I get it. When I don't, she continues on, "It's self-preservation at its simplest form."

And then I get it.

I nod, my eyes wide with understanding. "It's easier to keep yourself closed off from those types of people. You aren't in any danger of getting hurt, because you know exactly what you're dealing with. And because these men really aren't of any true interest to you… at least no more than a nice diversion… you aren't ever in any danger of breaking your own boundaries. You're not in danger of falling for them."

Casey grins and stabs her index finger in the air at me. "Bingo. You got it."

Shaking my head, I pick up my coffee cup. Just before taking a sip, I mutter, "You are one complex woman, Goldie."

Casey's voice is whisper soft, full of emotion. "And you *are* dangerous, Tenn Jennings, because you are exactly the type of man that could crumble all of those boundaries."

The honesty of her words and the fact they are said with such resignation about slays me.

My hand drops to my stomach and I rub it gingerly, because those words and the sad quality of her voice just rendered a deep punch to my gut. I want to slide from the booth, pull her out of her seat, and wrap her in my arms. I want to kiss her and tell her she's far more worthy than she gives herself credit for, but I can't do any of those things.

Those are exactly the types of things that would send Casey scurrying away from me. Those are the types of things that make me dangerous in her mind.

So instead, I ask, "What do your friends all think

of this philosophy you have? Why you only seek out those types of men?"

Casey scoffs and rolls her eyes. "Tenn... what I just told you? My reasons for doing what I do? They don't know any of that. They just think Casey wants to drink champagne and the only way to do it on her Coca Cola budget is to target the hotties with the money. I mean... look at me. I don't mean that in any vain sense, but seriously... I can get anyone I want. At least... any man who is so self-absorbed and narcissistic, they don't give a rat's ass that I set boundaries with them. That's all my friends really know... all they need to know. The only reason I told you is because you're fleeting. Just here for a visit."

While I'm not about to disabuse her of the notion that I'm just visiting—since I'm thinking of relocating—I am floored that she's shared something with me that even her closest friends don't know. Which really pisses me off because whatever it is that drives Casey to do the things she does, it comes at the sacrifice of her insulating her friends from whatever pain she's suffered. She doesn't share with them not because she doesn't trust them. She doesn't share with them because she doesn't want them to hurt for her.

Leaning further over the table, I reach out and take one of Casey's hands in my own. I rub my thumb over the peaks and valleys of her knuckles. "You know what your problem is, Goldie?"

She shakes her head, her eyes seeking almost desperately for some truth that she hasn't figured out on her own.

"The men you've been with? They merely stir you and you don't need to be gently stirred," I tell her simply.

One eyebrow drops while the other one rises in skepticism. "I don't need stirred?"

"It's like this. You're not a woman that needs to be treated with kid gloves. You don't need to be coddled or unnecessarily flattered. You're too sharp and savvy for that. In fact, you're almost too sharp and savvy for that. It's made you wary and shielded, which has in turn made you stagnant. You're stuck in a rut of your own making... maybe for self-preservation, maybe not... but your boundaries have stunted the woman you're meant to be. It's like the cocktails you make when you bartend. You need to be shaken, not stirred."

Casey just stares at me as understanding of what I just said starts to take root. Her eyes flare round and her mouth parts slightly. Just as I think she's getting ready to tell me that I am the wisest of all creatures she's ever encountered, she leans over to the side and slaps her free hand on the tabletop while she lets out a bark of a laugh. She peals out uncontrollable chuckles and then wheezes. When she finally sucks in a deep breath of air, she wipes her eyes and says, "That is the biggest crock of shit I've ever heard in my life, Tenn."

I smirk at her as I release her hand and slide out of

the booth. After fishing a twenty out to cover the coffee and an extremely generous tip, which I throw down on the table, I hold my hand out to her. Still snickering, she places her hand in mine and looks up at me with amusement.

"Come on, Goldie," I tell her as I pull her from the booth. "You can laugh all you want, but I'm right about that. I'm going to prove it to you."

"Oh yeah?" she asks with a giggle as we start to walk out of the diner hand in hand. "How are you going to prove it to me?"

"I'm going to take you back to my hotel room and I'm going to fuck you hard into submission," I growl at her in a low voice so as not to distress the waitress who waves goodbye to us.

"Mmmmm," Casey moans dramatically as we hit the parking lot. "That sounds nice."

"You'll be walking funny tomorrow," I warn her ominously.

"Even better," she chirps and starts pulling me faster through the lot to my bike. When we get there, I reach out for her helmet to put it on her, but she grabs ahold of my wrists. "But I have a better idea."

"Oh yeah… what's that?"

"You come to my house instead," she says quietly, and my body goes still.

This, I know, is huge. Given the boundaries that Casey sets with men… the fact that she doesn't let them in personally at all… there's no way in hell she opens her house up to them.

"Am I the first?" I ask her gruffly.

She nods her head as she nibbles on her lower lip.

Pleasure and an odd sense of accomplishment rushes through me. Actually, it's euphoric.

I jerk Casey into my body and crush my mouth down on to hers, showing her how much I appreciate the tiny bit of trust she's placed in me. I know this is a monumental moment for her, and I want her to see how special it is to me.

Christ… I feel like she just awarded me her virginity or something.

CHAPTER 9

Casey

OH, BOY… THIS was not a good idea. What was I thinking inviting Tenn into my home?

Stupid, stupid, stupid.

I opened the door to my house and metaphorically opened up a boundary that had been sealed tight.

Wringing my hands, I nervously walk through my small living room. "Um… not much to it. Just a small living room and kitchen. Two bedrooms and two baths."

"It's nice," Tenn says as he looks around and then walks to the back sliding glass door. "Cozy in fact."

I watch as he opens the door and steps out onto my minuscule deck. My tiny beach house sits two streets off the ocean, so most of my view is of other beach houses with just a tiny glimpse of the Atlantic. My house faces south so from the back deck, you can actually see not only a little bit of the ocean to the east but also a tiny bit of the sound to the west. It's all I could afford as beachfront is definitely not within the budget of a down-and-out realtor turned bartender.

Tenn puts his hands on the deck railing and leans over it, craning his neck slightly to the left to look toward the ocean. A soft breeze filters in through the door, but my skin feels chilled.

I kind of thought Tenn would jump on me the minute we walked in. I didn't expect him to ask me questions or look around with interest. I certainly didn't expect him to mosey on out to the deck and check out the scenery by moonlight.

This is not good. This is all too friendly and intimate. It's all just too much, especially after the way I prattled on to him at the diner... letting him in on a secret not one other person knows about me.

I feel itchy and tense and fuck... now my palms are sweating. I rub them furiously on the hem of my shorts and realize that I need to get this turned around. Quickly trotting over to my stereo, I put on some music and completely luck out with R. Kelly's *Bump N' Grind*.

Straightening up, I turn toward the back door and see Tenn standing just inside of it. I get a sinful pull of his lips upward as he gives a nod of his head toward the stereo. Sliding the door shut behind him, he says, "That's some pretty sexy music you got on there, Goldie."

Taking a deep breath, I let it out. I also let out all the warm and fuzzies I've been feeling for Tenn this evening. The friendship and bonding. I empty it all out and as I suck in a deep breath to replace it, I fill myself up with sensuality. I think about all the things Tenn has done to my body, and I let the need to feel it all again cram the void. I turn myself into the sexual creature that has sustained my need for touch by questing for an orgasm. I'm Casey Markham... the woman who only cares about physical pleasure, leaving the joys of the heart to other poor saps.

As Tenn takes a few steps into the living room, I start to prowl my way to him, sexily rolling my hips as I let my fingers flirt with the edges of my shorts. He comes to a stop and watches me, his eyes running down my body appraisingly. He even mimics my patented move—pulling his bottom lip in between his teeth while he imagines all the dirty things we'll do to each other—and fuck... that's really, really hot when he does that.

No wonder it works so well.

Stepping up to him, my fingers dip down into the waistband of his jeans. I crane my neck to look up at him and my breath never fails to get robbed by his sky blue eyes, those provocative lips, and that kick-ass goatee.

"Something occurred to me," I tell him with a throaty purr.

"What's that?" he asks, his eyes heating up over the promise in my voice.

"You bestowed all kinds of oral pleasure on me the other night, and I never even got to return the favor." For good measure, I stick my lower lip out into a pout as my hands reach for his belt buckle. My head dips down but I raise my eyes up in coy flirtation, knowing my long lashes framing my eyes will look spectacular to him from that angle.

As I unhook his belt from the buckle, I lower my eyes to my task and whisper just loud enough for him to hear, "You have no idea the things I can do with this mouth."

A low growl thunders in Tenn's chest, and I smile inwardly. When I pull the black leather free from the loops, I look up at him directly as I drop the belt to the ground. "I bet Mallory—which is a stupid name by the way—could never suck you down the way I'm going to do it."

Hot breath rushes out of Tenn's mouth and gusts over the top of my head. My fingers deftly maneuver the top button of his jeans open but before I unzip him, I press my palm to his erection, pushing hard against the denim. "Oh, baby," I murmur. "Trust me… this is going to be the best you've ever had."

Tenn reaches a hand up, threads his fingers through my hair at my temple, and curls them around my head. "Wait a minute, Casey," he murmurs, but surely he doesn't mean it. There's no way in hell he wants me to stop.

I pull his zipper down, peel the fly apart, and my mouth actually waters as I get a glimpse of the mushroomed head of his cock sticking up past the edge of his boxers. Odd… never had my mouth water to get a taste of a man before, but right now, saliva pools over my tongue.

"Be warned," I say with a soft moan as my fingers graze over the tip. "I'll bring you to your knees."

"Casey… stop," Tenn says as his fingers dig slightly into my scalp.

I ignore him and push my fingers past the elastic of his underwear, curling my hand around his length. "You'll be begging me to finish you off—"

"Just stop, Casey," Tenn growls and pulls away from me completely.

Feeling like a wave of ice-cold water just doused me, I look up at him and blink in surprise. His jaw is hard and his eyes are frosty.

"What's wrong?" I ask as an empty pit starts forming in my stomach.

Tenn huffs out a breath of frustration and holds his arms out to the side. "What's going on here, Casey?"

Hmmmm. I thought I was being obvious, but apparently not.

I step back up to him, and my hand reaches toward his dick. "I'm going to make you feel good, baby," I say, and then I'm stunned when he bats my hand away.

"You can suck my cock later," he snarls at me. "But I want to know what the fuck you think you're doing? What's with the act?"

"Act?" I ask, dumbfounded.

"Yeah… act," he says with exasperation, and then he mimics me, "Oh, baby… I'm going to have you begging. Oh, baby… you've never had it this good. Blah, blah, blah."

My mouth drops open in stunned surprise. "I don't understand. Don't you like dirty talk?"

"I like dirty talk just fine," Tenn says quietly. "But only when you mean it. When you do it to ramp up both of our pleasure. But just now… what you were doing? You sounded like a robot. It sounded rehearsed. Christ, Casey… is that what you do to get all your rich men hot and horny?"

I just stare at him, so completely shocked to hear this revelation about myself.

"I'm not into playing games, Casey. I want *you*. You," he emphasizes again by placing a finger gently in the middle of my chest. "Not some shell of a woman that operates on auto pilot because she's afraid to feel."

"I don't—" I start to say, but he cuts me off quickly.

"You do," he rolls right over me. "You're problem is you've never had anyone tell you the truth, but I'm fucking telling you right now… this shit you're doing? It ain't fucking sexy to me at all."

Oily, black, sludgy shame rolls through me, and my stomach actually pitches sideways. Is this what I've become? Have I been reduced to someone who operates on a nonexistent plane just to keep myself untouchable? Have I done this with my friends? My family?

My face lowers to the ground, and all I can do is whisper, "I'm sorry."

Strong arms immediately wrap around me, one around my upper back and the other cradling my head. Tenn pulls me into his chest and his lips come to the top of my head. "It's okay."

Shaking my head, I manage to mutter in to his chest, "I'm not sure I know how to be any other way."

Tenn squeezes me gently. "Not true, Goldie. You know. You're just too afraid to try it out."

He's right. I'm a fucking coward for sure. It's so easy to be that other Casey... keeping everyone at a distance, completely shielding myself and depending only upon myself to fulfill my own desires.

Unfortunately or fortuitously, I'm not sure which at this point, but Tenn has pointed out some ugly truths about me and I have to decide if I want to continue to be an ugly person.

Pulling gently out of his embrace, I screw up my courage and lift my eyes to his. "I'd like to try this again," I say softly, and he gives me an accepting smile in return.

Taking him by the hand, I lead him all the way into the living room and over to a small corner chair that I got at a garage sale. I turn him so his back is to the chair and bring my fingers up to the edge of his boxers again. His erection hasn't diminished a bit, and that gives me heart.

"Can I try again?" I ask him hesitantly as I look at my fingers hovering right over his hardness.

Tenn slips a finger under my chin, and he raises my face to his. His eyes are soft and his smile is tender. "Yeah, Goldie... try it again."

Giving him a smile of my own, I take a deep breath. I let my fingers settle in over the tip of his cock, lightly stroking it. "Okay... so, this might not sound very sexy but the truth is... when I first opened your jeans up and saw your erection, my mouth actually watered."

Tenn lets out a hum of approval and his eyes start to glitter.

"Truth is," I say quietly. "I've never, ever had my mouth water for a man before. It was always just... an act. A way to control."

"Casey," Tenn whispers, and his fingers thread once again into my hair to cup my head.

"And I'm really, really dying to get a taste of you," I say hesitantly, hoping that I'm doing this right. "I feel starved and the only way I can get filled up is by sucking your cock. Just your cock will do though."

"Jesus," Tenn mutters, his eyes sizzling now with lust. "Now that may be the sexiest thing I've ever heard."

Joy courses through me because I hear the truth in his words. "Really?" I ask hopefully, not daring to believe it's really so, because I thought I sounded awkward and amateurish.

"Goldie," Tenn breathes out in a rush as his fingers tighten their hold on my head, "if you don't get on your knees and put my dick in your mouth soon, I'm going to die here, okay?"

I grin at him, give him a wink for good measure, and say, "Okay. I'm on it, Chief."

"That right there," he mutters. "Not sexy."

Chuckling, I slide my hands into the waistband of his boxers. I push them and his jeans down over his hips, gently freeing my target. Giving him a sly smile, I graze my fingers up his chest, flatten my palms there, and then push him backward until he falls down into the chair.

I step up confidently in between his legs, and this isn't robot Casey talking, but the woman whose mouth is still watering for this man. "It's better if you sit down for this. I wasn't joking when I said it could bring you to your knees."

Tenn laughs, his eyes squinting and bringing out thirty-three years of laugh lines at the corner. He stretches his legs out confidently, one on either side of me, and takes his cock in his hand. With a languid smile, he starts stroking himself, and I'm mesmerized to watch him do so. He's so sexually confident in himself, which is something that I have absolutely no experience with. All the men I've been with have been so wrapped up in themselves that they would never think it would be sexy or pleasurable to me to watch a man masturbate.

But this… watching Tenn move his hand roughly as he jerks himself… I could get used to this.

"What you waiting for, Goldie?" he asks, now moving his other hand down to fondle his balls.

I blink hard and shake my head. "Sorry, but damn… that's really hot watching you doing that."

"Get on your knees, baby," Tenn commands, although I can see the amusement in his eyes over my admission. "Let me see what you've got."

I drop to my knees and as my hands reach toward him, his own drop away to give me access. I take him firmly by the base, my hand coming nowhere close to even being able to wrap fully around him. His skin is so warm and soft, yet when I contract my fingers, he's as hard as concrete underneath.

Leaning forward and dipping my chin, I run my tongue up the base of his cock, wiggling it back and forth under the sensitive tip. Tenn hisses in pleasure.

So velvety soft. Warm. Salty.

"You're delicious," I whisper reverently and then I lick him around the tip, lapping at the wetness seeping out. Tenn grunts and both hands come up to fist my hair, one at the side of my head, the other at the back.

"Suck it," Tenn groans as his hands push down on my head. "You're driving me fucking nuts, Goldie."

"Don't want that," I murmur as I graze my lips down the side of his shaft.

"Casey," Tenn murmurs, and it's my name said as a prayer as much as it is a plea.

No man has ever said my name like that before... with such raw need.

I lean up on my knees and bend my head further, taking him from the top and pulling him all the way back into my mouth. What part of his cock I can't fit in my mouth, I make up for with strong strokes of my hand. I hollow my cheeks and suck just as he told me to do.

"Fuck. Christ. Fuck," Tenn groans as his hands tighten on me hard and his hips start thrusting upward. "Going to come in that hot, sweet mouth of yours, Goldie."

I moan my agreement and move over him faster, jerking at him roughly from the bottom. Tenn's hips move in shallow thrusts, and I'm not sure who's fucking who at this point but knowing that I'm driving him this crazy causes that space between my legs to clench hard. God, I'm so turned on right now by what I'm doing to him that I drop my free hand to my shorts and slip my fingers into the waistband. Straight into my panties. Right down between my legs where I start to rub at myself.

Tenn shifts, I hear him groan, and then he says, "Holy fuck. Are you fingering yourself?"

On an upstroke, I raise my eyes to peek up at him

and see he's leaning over the side of the chair to get a look at what I'm doing. His pupils are dilated and his irises are so dark, they're almost the color of denim.

"Yes, baby," Tenn murmurs urgently while he stares at my hand working in between my legs. "Make yourself come."

Oh, my God, that's so freakin' sexy that I falter. His cock slips free of my mouth, and my fingers go still against my wet flesh. Tenn drags his fevered eyes slowly over to my face and blinks at me hard.

A slow smile creeps over those lips, and Tenn gently pushes on my head. "Get those lips back on my cock, Goldie."

What? Oh, yeah… stellar blow job in progress. I grin at him and start to bend back over his lap when he pulls on my hair to stop me. As I raise my eyes back up, his eyes cut downward. "And get those fingers moving again. I want to watch you make yourself come while you blow me."

Oh, God. Oh, God.

He's a master at dirty talk. A complete genius. I'm truly humbled by his greatness.

I swallow Tenn's dick back down—he groans loudly—and my fingers start to circle and rub. I'm so wet right now that my fingers glide sinuously over my clit, making it over-sensitized.

My fingers fly, Tenn's hips buck his cock to the back of my throat, and the room is filled with lust and heavy breathing.

A soft chant starts from Tenn. *Yes, yes, yes, yes.*

My blood rages through my veins, and my spine starts to tingle with an orgasm. I rub harder against my clit and wrap my lips tight around his shaft as I suck.

With a massive push upward, Tenn surges into me, then he goes absolutely still while he roars out, "Oh God."

Just as he starts coming in my mouth, my own orgasm breaks free and I whimper against the warm, salty fluid that I drink down as soon as he gives it to me. My body shudders, I give another strong pull against his cock with my mouth, which causes Tenn to groan again, and then I'm collapsing onto his lap.

I'm barely cognizant, depleted of strength and completely malleable. Tenn reaches down and gently pulls my own hand from my pants, causing another tiny whimper to escape me as my fingers graze over my clit. He lifts me up onto his lap, shifting me onto one leg so I don't crush his half-hard dick, and presses my face into his chest. I try to raise my arms to loop around the back of his neck, but I don't have the strength and they flop uselessly down to rest on the tops of my legs.

When our breathing evens out, Tenn grasps my chin with his hand, pushing me away from his chest just far enough to give him room to bend down to kiss me. His lips are soft, his tongue taking a gentle swipe at mine before he pulls away.

"You okay, Goldie?" he murmurs through a knowing smile.

"Never better," I mutter with a dopey smile of my own.

He chuckles and kisses me again… swiftly this time. When he pulls away, his eyes are serious. "I have to leave day after tomorrow to head back to Raleigh. I'm going to see Zoey for a few days, and then I have to head up to New Jersey to visit a buddy of mine."

Suddenly, the vague haze of post-coital bliss starts to dissipate and disappointment starts welling up. For the first time ever, I don't want a man to go. I want him to stay.

"So, this is it, huh?" I ask, not liking at all the feelings that are battling inside of me. One part relieved, because I know just how dangerous my involvement with Tenn is, and the other part disappointed, because he makes me start to consider that I might want something more.

"I'm coming back," Tenn says softly. "I mean… to North Carolina. I want to spend some time with Zoey over the summer before she starts school. I'm actually thinking of relocating so I can be near her."

"Oh," I say thoughtfully, wondering what that all means.

"And I'd like to come back here to visit… to see you again," he adds on.

Yes, I'd like that very much.

I think.

I mean... just for some hot-as-hell sex, nothing more. Because I can't continue to open up my boundaries to him.

Presumably taking my silence as reticence, Tenn gruffly asks, "Want me to get going?"

I immediately shake my head and wrap my arms around his neck. Laying my head back on his chest, I say, "I want you to stay here... until you have to leave, that is."

That's all I'm willing to commit to at this point.

I can't see his face, but I can hear his smile in his voice. "Sounds good, Goldie. Real good."

CHAPTER 10

Jenn

I KNOCK ON the door and hear a loud squeal inside, followed by pounding footsteps that get closer and closer. Then the door is thrown open and Zoey is launching herself into my arms.

Best. Feeling. Ever.

Wrapping my arms around her frame, I squeeze gently but firmly… kiss the top of her head… tell her how much I miss her. She's a tiny thing… just like her mom, but she got my dark hair and blue eyes, and I'm going to have to fight the boys off soon.

"I'm so glad you're here," she mumbles into my chest, and something about the tone of her voice sets me on edge.

I pull her away from me so I can look down into her eyes. "Everything okay?"

She nods quickly and smiles. "Yeah… sure. Just… we'll talk later, okay?"

"Sure thing, baby girl," I tell her as I pull her back in for another hug, closing my eyes and resting my cheek on the top of her head.

"Hi Tenn," I hear from behind Zoey, and my eyes open to see Brianna hovering a few feet away. She's trying for sexy-aloof while she stands there with a hip cocked out and watches with jealous eyes as I hug my daughter. Bri could never stand how close Zoey and I are because as sick as it is, she's jealous that my attentions were always more focused on Zoey than her.

I jerk my head up in greeting and Zoey steps back from me, looking up at me in adoration.

This.

This right here.

This is why I'd relocate to the ends of the earth to be near my daughter.

"What do you want to do today?" I ask her, ignoring Bri as she comes closer to the door.

"Definitely want to ride," she says eagerly.

Yup… my little girl loves Harleys as much as I do.

"Okay," I say as I turn her toward the inside of the apartment and give her a push. "Go get whatever you need and we'll play it by ear, but whatever we decide to do, it will be on the bike."

"Sweet," Zoey chirps and pushes past Brianna back into the apartment.

Brianna inches closer toward me until she leans against the doorframe, crossing her arms under her chest so her breasts push up. I don't even spare them a glance. Not that they aren't great, because they are, but first, Bri fucked our marriage up so badly that I have absolutely no attraction left for her, and two... they are nothing compared to Casey's tits. Now those are spectacular and so vivid in my imagination, I don't need to look at another set.

"That shit wasn't cool," I tell Brianna as I level a hard stare at her.

"What?" she asks innocently, batting her lashes.

"Taking Zoey to Florida last week when you knew I was going to be here for her," I growl with frustration, because she knows damn well what I'm talking about.

"Sorry... it was too good an opportunity to pass up." Her petulance makes me grind my teeth together.

Leaning in toward her and lowering my voice, I say, "What was too good to pass up? Taking advantage of your newest fuck and his money or making me suffer?"

Bri's eyes narrow at me, and she hisses, "Both."

I lean back away from her and mutter, "Selfish bitch. Always looking out for yourself."

She's completely unfazed though and as if I hadn't just called her a bitch, asks sweetly, "So... are you going to move here to be near us?"

"Are you going to stay put here?" I ask her skeptically. "Because I'm not chasing you all over the fucking country just to be with my daughter."

"You'll go wherever we are," she asserts confidently. "You can't stay away."

I nod at her in agreement and then lean back in toward her. My voice is steely and dead fucking serious. "You're right. There's no way in hell I can stay away from my daughter, but I'll fight you for custody if you keep playing these sick games, Bri. Take a fucking hint… we are done and I am never going to be with you again."

And once again proving why I couldn't stay married to her crazy ass, she waves her hand at me impatiently and says, "You'll change your mind and I'll be here waiting."

I want to punch the wall in frustration, but I don't. I never do anything outwardly actionable that lets Bri know just how much she gets to me. I'm ultimately saved from further maddening conversation with my ex when Zoey comes running back through the living room. She put her hair in a long braid and has an army-green satchel looped across her chest.

"I'm ready," she says. She bounces right past Brianna without a backward glance and heads for the stairs.

"What time will you be back?" Brianna asks with eager anticipation. "I'll have dinner ready for all of us."

Crazy bitch.

I turn to follow Zoey but swivel my head slightly to look at her over my shoulder. "I'll have her back *after* dinner."

♦

"So what's the deal?" I ask Zoey as we munch on blue corn chips and spicy salsa. We chose a Mexican restaurant with outdoor seating for lunch.

She shrugs her shoulders and won't meet my gaze. Her hand reaches for another chip, but I reach out and grab it. Her eyes come to mine.

"I can't fix it unless I know what the problem is," I tell her softly but firmly.

Zoey pulls her hand away and then a fountain starts gushing. "I hate it here. I miss you and Wyoming. Mom's always working and when she's not working, she's always with Kip. And she's doing the same shit—"

"Language," I warn.

"—sorry, crap that she did with you. Gets pissed if Kip shows me any attention."

"And what type of attention is he showing you?" I growl menacingly.

"Eww… gross, Dad," Zoey says with a huge eye roll. "He's a nice guy. He shows an interest in my schoolwork and my activities. It was his idea to go to Disney, but he said we should wait until after you came to visit me. It was Mom who insisted we go right then… said it was the only time she could get off work, but we both know that's bullshit."

My hackles immediately flatten out, and I disregard her curse word. I personally had thought Kip was an okay dude… an idiot for putting up with Brianna's shit, but he seemed cool. Brianna has been dating him for almost a year and after he got a job here in North Carolina, she used that as the perfect excuse to pack my daughter up and leave with her. As a nurse, Brianna was highly employable, and it was nothing for her to relocate. She easily got a job that paid her way more money than she ever made back in Wyoming.

Placing my forearms on the table, I lean toward her. "Listen, honey. Your mom is… well, your mom has some issues."

"She's nuts," Zoey huffs.

"She loves you," I maintain, because that's true enough. Despite Bri's petty jealousies and mind games, I know she loves her daughter. "We have to accept the way she is."

"I want to go back to Wyoming and live with you," she whines, those big, blue eyes filling with tears, and aw, fuck… that gets me every time. "It's not fair."

"Listen," I say as I reach across the table and grab her hands. "We are going to be together. I'm looking at some options to move here. I have an idea on a business I want to start."

"I bet Grandpa loved hearing that," Zoey says sarcastically.

I laugh and squeeze her hands before I release them. "Well, I haven't told him that part yet, but I'm sure he'll have something to say about it."

My father always had something to say about the direction I chose to move my life, especially since it wasn't aimed back at the ranch.

"I miss my horse," Zoey blurts out. "I miss riding every day."

"Aren't you going to a riding camp next week?" I ask as I reach for another corn chip.

"Yeah… Kip found a great one just north of Raleigh," she says excitedly.

And as only a fourteen-year-old can do, she immediately changes subjects again. "I want to live with you once you move here."

A wave of pure, unadulterated joy sweeps through me, because there is nothing I would want more in this world than to have Zoey with me full time. But I proceed cautiously. "Are you sure about that, honey? I mean… I work too. Or, at least I hope to be working if I can get this business idea launched off the ground. Could be long hours."

"Dad," Zoey says earnestly as she looks me dead in the eye. "No matter how hard you worked before, you always had time for me. You always helped me with schoolwork, went horseback riding with me, and took me on bike rides. You spent all your free time with me. You've always been there for me."

And fuck… getting a little choked up now. I clear

my throat and give her a tentative smile. "Okay… got it. I'm a pretty cool dad."

"So can I live with you?" she presses.

"I'll talk to your mom about it once things get settled with me," I promise her.

"She won't agree," she mutters sulkily. "She won't agree just to punish you."

While I don't voice this to Zoey, I know without a doubt that if she really wants to live with me and Bri won't allow it, I'll fight her in court. Zoey's old enough now that a judge will listen to her preferences.

"Don't worry about it, baby girl. I'll handle it, okay?"

"Okay," she says happily and then launches in to telling me about the riding camp she's going to attend.

♦

I FUCKING HATE doing laundry. I hate it even more when I'm out on the road because there is nothing worse than sitting in a laundry mat and watching all the other pathetic fools folding their underwear and socks on a Friday night.

Throwing my laundry bag complete with freshly washed clothes on one of the hotel beds, I flop down on my back on the other. Laundry aside, today was a moderately successful day. I had a blast with Zoey, and I even got Brianna's agreement to let me take her to the beach when she gets back from riding camp.

Of course, I want Zoey to have a great vacation on a sunny beach, but my idea to bring her there is completely self-serving as well. It means I get to see Casey some more, which is a very good thing because I can't get her out of my fucking head.

As per usual, Brianna put up a huge fight about it, maintaining that Zoey needed to stay in Raleigh because she couldn't be parted with her for that long. For Christ sake, it's just a week or two, but luckily for me, I didn't even have to enter the argument. Kip happened to be there and yeah… he's a cool fucking dude because he stepped in and got Brianna to agree to it with a lot of cajoling, of which, I'm sure she'll make him suffer for later.

My phone rings, and I turn onto one hip to retrieve it out of my back pocket. When I see the Caller ID, my smile breaks out as I answer, "About time you called me back, asshole."

My buddy, Nix Caldwell's, deep voice booms through. "You left a message just two hours ago, asshole."

Yeah… when you serve in the Marine Corps together, forever spitting sand out of your mouth and sweating buckets a day in a war zone, you tend to get away with affectionately calling each other "asshole".

"How are you, man?" I ask as I push myself up on the bed to rest my back against the headboard.

"Fucking fantastic," he says, and then in a lower

voice he whispers, "but I have to say, planning this wedding sucks donkey dick."

I hear a feminine voice in the background say, "I heard that, and you'll pay."

Snickering, I try to call upon an image of badass Nix Caldwell tasting wedding cakes and picking out flowers. "It will be worth it, dude. Keep your honey happy."

"That's what my life is all about, man. Keeping Emily happy."

I saw Nix about six months ago out in San Diego when we had a battalion reunion. He brought his fiancée Emily with him and holy fuck... the guy scored big time with that one. She's bright, funny, and scorchingly hot, so yeah... I'd see why he'd want to marry that woman and lock her ass down.

Also got to see our buddy, Paul, who served with us. He's walking great on his prosthetics and was starting to do some motivational work with other wounded warriors. While I don't know all the details because the mission was beyond my secrecy clearing, Nix and Paul got caught up in a green-on-blue attack and both of them got pretty fucked up. Nix took a bullet to the chest, and Paul lost both his legs. Would have lost a whole lot more the way he tells it if Nix hadn't pulled him out.

It was during that get together that the three of us went out for beers one night, and I became extremely interested in what Nix has been up to since he got out of the Corps. He works as a metal artist but one of his specialties is custom-built motorcycles. It got me thinking and I haven't been able to let it go since.

"So… you up for a visit?" I ask him.

"Dude… door is always open," he says. "When can you be here?"

"Two days," I tell him. "I'm going to fly rather than ride my bike. I have to be back in Raleigh by middle of next week."

Because I want a full week back on the Outer Banks with Casey before Zoey comes back from riding camp. I want at least a full week to immerse myself in her hot body and hopefully continue to chip away at her walls. It wasn't until Zoey told me that she wanted to live with me that I seriously started realizing that I'd be making North Carolina my home. Casey and me in the same state? Yeah… that was all right by me.

Nix and I iron out the details for my arrival. He knows I want to discuss a business idea with him, but we didn't get into the specifics. After we hang up, I take a moment to flip through my email. I'm not a big electronic communicator, but I try to make it a habit to check it every few days.

As expected, there's a long-winded email from my father, giving me a chatty update about the ranch and reminding me of my heritage and legacy. God love my father… he's a wonderful man, truly. But he's a bit rigid in his ideas over what his sons ought to be doing with their lives.

I forward the email on to Woolf with a short but blunt statement, "Dude... you need to step up."

If only my baby brother would grow up and take the helm, then I'd be released from my obligation to the family and the ranch. And it's not like I'm pressing upon him something he doesn't want. He loves that ranch more than anything but he refuses to grow the fuck up, instead intent on spending all of his free time partying and chasing tail. Running the ranch requires he settle down... man up... pay attention to what's important, the way my father has his whole life.

I really wish it was something I wanted. I really wish I had some desire to fulfill my father's legacy, but I don't. I've never been built that way. As long as Woolf will eventually get his head out of his ass, I'll be free to do what I really want with my life, which is to work in a career I love, have my daughter by my side, and some day... the fates willing... have a good woman by my side to share in it.

That, of course, makes me think of Casey. The woman I know virtually nothing about, yet share knowledge of one of her most intimate secrets. The woman who I have no clue whether she likes red or white wine, yet I know she sucks my cock like she owns it.

Yup... she pretty much owns it, and just thinking about that wet mouth wrapped around my dick starts to get me hard.

I made Casey give me her phone number before I left. She fought me on it, insisting that was a little too close for her comfort. So I pushed her down on the bed, stripped her bare, and ate her pussy like a mad man. And when she'd get close… I'd withhold her orgasm from her until she promised me the number.

She obviously relented, she came fantastically hard, and now I feel like calling her.

But this being Casey, I expect she might ignore me.

One, two, three rings and I'm shocked. She answers, "Hey stud. Missing me yet?"

It's maddening, but I do miss her. I also know she really doesn't want to know that, so I keep it more on a level she understands. "Miss fucking that beautiful body."

And Christ… I fucked that body a lot in the two days I had with her before I left. I thought we might burn ourselves out or even get a little tired of being around each other, but it never happened. We were insatiable… unstoppable… completely ravenous for one another.

"Mmmm," she murmurs into the phone, and I can hear the playfulness in her voice. I caught her at a good time. "I miss that big cock of yours."

That right there makes me go fully hard.

As I start unbuttoning my jeans, I ask her, "Feel like talking dirty to me while I jack off?"

"Only if I can play with myself at the same time," she says with a hoarse laugh, causing me to groan and go harder yet.

Goddamn, I fucking miss her.

"Get naked," I tell her. "It's on."

CHAPTER 11

Casey

"**S**ERIOUSLY, CASEY... WILL you just look over there once and put those men out of their misery?" Gabby grumbles at me.

Ignoring her, I tilt my head back so my face gets the maximum exposure to the hot Carolina sun. I push my feet further into the sand, wiggling my hips a little to settle deeper into my beach chair. My eyes are closed and I want to get into a nice, hot daydream about Tenn.

The slap on my thigh gets my attention though, and I surge up into a sitting position to glare at Gabby. "What the hell, Gabs? I'm trying to relax here."

"I don't like being ignored," she sniffs. "Besides... I'm tired of those guys over there with their lame attempts to play Frisbee just so they can get your attention. They keep throwing it closer and closer to us, so just freakin' look over there and give them a smile or something to appease them."

Turning my head to the right, I watch as two guys look at me with their tongues hanging out of their mouths and unbridled hope in their eyes. I shoot them the bird and then lay back down in my chair, closing my eyes again and conjuring up an image of a naked Tenn Jennings.

Slap.

"For fuck's sake, Gabby," I yell as I sit back up again and rub my stinging thigh. "I'd like to spend a few hours on my day off relaxing in peace on this beach, and you're ruining it."

"What the hell is wrong with you?" she asks me with narrowed eyes.

I blink at her and take note of the eyebrows drawn severely in and the flat line to her lips. She's seriously dismayed with me. "What do you mean, 'what's wrong with me'?"

She flicks her hands at the men over my shoulder who I just flipped off. "You're acting strange. Those dudes have money... I can tell by the amount of gold hanging off them, their fancy haircuts, and their designer beachwear. Granted, one has a bit of a pot belly, but the other is kind of cute."

"So?" I ask, not even bothering to look back over my shoulder at them. No sense in giving any false encouragement.

"So," she drawls out as if she's getting ready to reveal the secret to world peace, "that's not like you to ignore that. That's your modus operandi. Those guys are right up your alley. The Casey Markham I know and would love to kill on any given day would have sauntered her lovely ass up to them and had a date within about three minutes flat. So I repeat… what the hell is wrong with you?"

I open my mouth to try for some reassurance but apparently, Gabby hasn't run out of steam yet.

"And on top of that, you've been withdrawn… hiding out. You don't hang with me anymore. So something is up," she proclaims.

"I'm hanging with you now," I counter.

"Only because I dragged your ass out of your house," she counters back. Narrowing her eyes further, she then one-ups me. "Plus… I saw a used condom in your bathroom trashcan when I peed so I know you've had a man at your house, and you never have men at your house. Never."

"Eww. Gross," I mutter. "How'd I miss that?"

"Casey," Gabby barks at me to get me focused and back on track.

"Is it time for lunch yet?" I hear and turn my head to see Hunter jogging up to us with his surfboard under his arm. He starts to jam the end down into the sand, but Gabby points back out to the ocean.

"Get back in the water, baby," she says sweetly.

"What?" he asks in thorough confusion.

"I'm in the middle of berating Casey. She's on the verge of spilling some juicy secrets to me. So get your ass back in the water and give me a few more investigative moments."

Hunter just stares at Gabby a moment. Then he starts muttering curses as he jerks his surfboard back under his arm and heads back to the ocean.

True love at its finest.

"Now—" Gabby says as she flips her legs to the side so she can face me.

"You really have him pussy whipped," I observe thoughtfully as I watch Hunter running back in to the water.

"Focus, Casey," Gabby says, snapping her fingers in front of my face.

I turn to face her and with a sigh, I tell, "There's nothing wrong with me. You're imagining things."

"I am not," she says confidently. "There is something going on with you, and I want to know what it is right now. Tell me about the man you had at your house."

Mmmmmm. Tenn.

The corners of my lips tip upward and my eyes flutter closed, remembering what he looked like just before he left a few days ago. When he kissed me so thoroughly, I knew I'd be feeling him on my lips for some time to come.

"Casey… so help me God, if you don't let me in, I'm going to schedule an intervention with the entire crew," Gabby warns.

And that really gets my attention because I totally don't want the gang sniffing around in my business.

With a huff, I turn around in my chair to face her and say, "Fine. What do you want to know?"

Gabby blinks in surprise, completely thrown off by my sudden capitulation. When she stays mute, I smirk at her and start to lie back down on my chair again.

"What's his name?" she blurts out, and my reprieve is gone.

I sit back up and face her. "Tenn."

"Like the number?" she asks curiously.

"No, like the poet, Tennyson. He's thirty-three, from Wyoming, visiting the area with Andrea's brother Kyle, and he's hung like a porn star. He fucks better than a porn star."

"What does he do for a living?" she asks me, resting her arms on her knees as she leans forward.

"Used to be a mechanic, but he said he's in between jobs right now."

"A mechanic?" she asks in disbelief. "An unemployed mechanic?"

"Yes, a mechanic. He's also been a Marine and a cowboy," I tell her, and then I imagine what Tenn would look like naked in chaps.

"But you don't date mechanics," she says dumbly. "Or Marines or cowboys for that matter."

"I'm totally diverse," I grumble.

"Not when it comes to money, you're not," she points out. "And I don't think mechanics make the dollar range you aim for. I know for sure unemployed ones don't."

"Well, maybe my tastes are changing," I tell her, and then immediately regret it. I've just invited her to start really nosing around.

I expect a barrage of questions now, but Gabby does the unexpected. "Look, Casey... I love you. You're like my sister, and there isn't anything you can't tell me. But I also don't pretend to fully understand you either. I think there are things that are driving you... things that make you uniquely you. I can't say I'm not worried about your choices sometimes but one thing I do know... you're an immensely smart and loving woman. If you're changing, then it's only because you want it to be so, and you will find what you're seeking. That's how much faith I have in you."

My eyes get a little moist and I have no clue what to say, so I instead lunge forward and wrap my arms around her, squeezing her so hard she gasps in my ear. As she squirms out of my hold, I whisper, "I love you too."

When I release her, we give each other grins and then settle back in our chairs.

"So, when do I get to meet this guy?" Gabby asks conversationally.

"Not sure," I tell her. "We're not dating or any-thing. You know I don't do that."

"Then what are you doing?"

I shrug my shoulders and tilt my face back again.

"Lots and lots of sexing for sure. He's coming back into town in a few days."

"Well, bring him to Andrea's birthday party," Gabby says. "I promise I won't make a big deal of it."

"Whatever," I scoff and to change the subject, I ask, "Anything else I need to do to help with the party?"

"I've got it covered. I stopped by the bakery yesterday to order her cake."

"Sweet," I murmur, feeling the sun start to make me drowsy.

"Oh," Gabby exclaims, and she slaps me on my thigh again. "You'll never guess who I ran into at the bakery."

I turn to glare at her. "Who?"

"Jeff Parkhurst," Gabby says, and my insides clench violently. "He's visiting with his fiancée, and they were there checking out wedding cakes. They're apparently going to get married next summer on the island. His fiancée was heading back to New York today, but he's apparently staying for a while to visit with his parents. She's really nice too… and pretty, but I mean… hello, this is Jeff Parkhurst we're talking about."

Gabby's voice drones on and on while bitter rage wells up inside of me. Rage for what he did to me and bitterness for what he's made me into.

"Didn't you like date him for a little bit in high school?" Gabby chatters on and then giggles. "I mean... I think it was all of like two weeks or something. That must have been when you decided to become a man-eater, right Case?"

Yeah... that's when I decided to become someone different. That's when I decided that open and trusting did me no good. That's when I realized that love was stupid, overrated, and most likely a lie.

Gabby has no clue what really went down with Jeff and me. No one does for that matter, unless you count Tenn. He knows Jeff's name, and he knows he had something to do with the way I am.

I think of Tenn... gorgeous, smiling face, carefree ways, down-to-earth nature. All things that I really started looking at and appreciating. All things that I knew were treacherous to a woman like me and so treated my interest with a measure of caution. I've certainly enjoyed replaying the memories of my time with him, and I'll admit I've been eager to reconnect with him.

But now, with Gabby's innocent mention of Jeff Parkhurst, it all comes flooding back to me. The sour memory of having my first taste of love destroyed in a very humiliating way, and at a time in my life where I needed love and stability.

Brody had just been sentenced to prison, and my world had been shattered. Prior to that, high school had been one endless and glorious event for me, and I was halfway through my senior year riding high on happiness. I was popular, fun to hang around, had amazing friends and I was dating the best-looking guy.

Jeff Parkhurst had it all. Sandy blond hair, gray eyes, and a winning smile. His body was to die for, and every girl wanted the captain of the football team. His parents were loaded, and he drove a hot sports car. To a girl on the verge of womanhood, these were the most important things ever. It's what defined my life.

Gabby is a little off in her recollection though. We had been dating almost a month when Brody became a sentenced felon, and Jeff was everything I could ever want in a boyfriend. He was sensitive and let me cry on his shoulder... I mean, like all the time. He put a stop to ugly rumors that started swirling around school about me... the baby sister of a murderer. He treated me reverently and with care. He told me he loved me and would love me forever.

On the night that Brody was taken away to serve his time, Jeff took me out to the beach and held me while I cried some more. Then he kissed me sweetly and murmured all the things that a girl as lost as me was desperate to hear. That I was beautiful, that he would offer me up the world, that he would take care of me, and that he would love me no matter what.

His kisses went from sweet to hot.

Jeff was skilled and he was not a virgin the way I was. He touched me in just the right way and then fed me more promises that made my heart fall further slave to him.

So on that moonlit beach, when he asked me for my virginity, I gave it up to him without another thought. I gave it willingly and blindly and I didn't regret my choice in the slightest.

Not until about a week later when everything I thought I knew about love came crashing down.

I snuck out of my parents' house late one night to go to a party that Jeff was throwing at his house. His parents were out of town, but my parents wouldn't let me go. Jeff assured me it was fine and it was okay if I couldn't come. He'd miss me and all that, but that we'd hook up the next day at the beach.

He was completely cool with hanging without me but as a young woman in love, I wanted to be by his side all the time. So I snuck out and I went to the party.

I think it would have been easier on me if I had found Jeff in some compromising position. Maybe in that respect, I could at least rationalize a man's baser instinct and capacity for infidelity. But that's not what I found.

Instead, I came up on Jeff while he was standing in the kitchen with a group of his rich buddies. They were all standing around and laughing with beers in their hands. Jeff's back was to me, and I remember taking a moment to appreciate his stylish hair and the cut of his clothes on his well-muscled body. I thought about surprising him with a small pat on his ass or something equally sassy.

When I walked up behind him though, I was stopped dead in my tracks when I heard him say, "I think I'm going to ask Tory Capps to the prom. Her dad does some investing with my dad and it's a good connection to have."

One of his buddies whistled low and shook his head, "She is one hot piece, but seriously dude... you've got Casey Markham. Why do you want to mess with Tory?"

As if they were discussing the stock market, Jeff got all serious. "Man... she is one seriously fantastic fuck. I mean, the hottest, tightest fuck you can imagine. But get real... she's not marriage material. She doesn't have the credentials, and you know she doesn't fit into our world. Her dad's a fisherman and her brother is a murderer, for Christ sake."

I remember that my head started spinning as I listened in disbelief to his cruel words. And then I'll never forget the last words I heard him say before I ran out of there.

"She's not marriage material, gents," Jeff said with a laugh and raised his beer in salute. "Casey Markham isn't good enough for someone like me. She's the one you want to fuck behind your wife's back."

Crushed. Devastated. Depressed.

I was all of that and more.

Brody had abandoned me, and now Jeff had humiliated me and abused the love and trust I gave him.

I ran out of that beach house in tears, but no one saw me. No one ever knew I was there and had overheard Jeff.

I was absolutely despondent.

For about a day.

Then I realized something about myself. I had an epiphany.

My parents had raised me to be proud and strong. They raised me to be independent. They taught me that I could be anything that I wanted to be. It was all within my control.

So that is when I decided to take control of my life… most in particular, my love life, and I was never going to let another man hurt me again.

I called Jeff up the next day and just politely told him I couldn't see him anymore. He asked me why, but I just graciously told him that things were too crazy in my life to be involved in a relationship. He acted a little put off, which I found to be heavily ironic given the way I knew he viewed me.

And from then on, I became the Casey Markham who called all the shots. I was the one that decided who was good enough for me. I was the one that made men fall to their knees and beg to have a chance with me. I was the one that targeted a certain type of man… one that could be easily manipulated and controlled, so I would never have to worry again about someone taking advantage of me.

I've used my face and my body to that advantage.

I've ramped up my sexuality, and I've become very good at getting a man off so beautifully that he would never want me to leave his side. I became a woman that loves and appreciates sex... revels in the feelings and the release of it all. I use it to get what I want, and I do it all from deep within the safety of the walls I've built up around me.

I only see men who think they are better than everyone else. I target men just like Jeff Parkhurst, and I use them as my surrogates. I play the same game over and over again, figuring every notch in my bedpost is another vain, narcissistic asshole who isn't getting one over on Casey Markham.

I do all of this playing by my rules and my rules only.

"Casey... have you been listening to a thing I've said?" Gabby grumbles.

"Yeah... sure. Jeff Parkhurst back and all," I say absently, and my head swivels back to the right to look at the two men who were ogling me just a bit ago. I appraise them. There's money there no doubt. By the fake tans and expensive jewelry both are sporting, I'm betting their vanity runs amok.

Just my type of men.

I push up out of my chair, a small feeling of guilt and emptiness settling into the pit of my stomach when I think about Tenn and all the ways in which he's wormed his way inside my walls.

Too fucking perilous. I knew it from the start and

was fool enough to break my own rules.

But I can't let a man like him continue to occupy my thoughts. I can't let him manipulate my actions. Gabby has done me a solid today and reminded me the type of woman that I am, and it's time to get back to what I do best.

"I'll be back in a bit," I tell Gabby and then I start walking down the beach, swaying my hips and heading right for the two men who are staring hungrily at me.

CHAPTER 12

Tenn

I'M EXHAUSTED YET determined to find Casey tonight. I flew into Raleigh this morning, had a quick lunch with Zoey, then hightailed it to the Outer Banks where I checked into a hotel, took a shower, and then went on the hunt.

I'm on the hunt because Casey seems to have dropped off the face of the earth the last two days. We've gone from dirty talking phone calls with a few witty texts in between to nothing for almost forty-eight hours.

Without a doubt, I know something has happened to her. Oh, not anything ominous, because Kyle reassured me that he hadn't heard anything bad from Andrea. But something caused her to go abruptly cold on me, and I'm going to find out what the fuck it was.

Then I'm going to kiss some sense in to her.

If that doesn't work, I'll fuck some sense in to her.

I pull up outside of The Last Call. It's the only

place I know to try as I completely bombed out when I went to her house. It was locked up tight, the lights were all off, and her Jeep was gone. While cruising for a parking spot since the lot is packed, I keep my eyes peeled for her Jeep but I don't see it. This is disappointing because I figured best-case scenario is she'd be stuck working behind the bar and wouldn't be able to escape me.

I finally find a spot and pull my bike in at an angle. After taking my lid off, I run my fingers through my hair and buck up by taking a deep breath. *It will be fine*, I tell myself. Casey is fine.

Why a woman I barely know outside of the intimacies of fucking is playing havoc with my mind is beyond me, but damn if I can just let this go. There's something about Casey that is just begging me to latch on, and that is not something I've ever felt for another woman in my life. Didn't feel it with Brianna, who trapped me into marriage with an "unexpected" pregnancy, nor in any of the women I dated after we divorced.

Just Casey.

Beautiful, pigheaded, and broken Casey.

I have to have her.

I walk into the bar, my eyes sweeping the place for golden hair. Coming up empty, I walk into the back bar area which is packed shoulder to shoulder with people. Luckily, my height gives me immediate advantage over the field and I quickly discern she's not behind the bar working, but that doesn't surprise me since her Jeep's not here.

I do see the blond male bartender that I've seen come on duty when she gets off shift behind the bar, so I weave my way in between people until I make my way up to the edge. It takes a moment to get to me but luckily, the guy is efficient at his job.

"What can I get you?" he asks as he swipes the bar with a rag, before throwing it casually across his shoulder.

"Looking for Casey," I tell him. "You know where she is?"

"Nah, man. She's off today," he says apologetically.

"When does she work again?"

"Tomorrow… twelve to six PM."

"Thanks," I say with a nod and then as an afterthought, "let me get a Budweiser."

No sooner is the bartender's back turned on me when I feel a light touch on my arm and a voice that says, "You're looking for Casey?"

I look down to my left and see a woman sitting on a bar stool with a pint glass in front of her. She has long, dark hair and cat eyes, along with cheekbones that sit even higher and more prominent than Casey's.

"Who wants to know?" I ask evasively.

"I want to fucking know," the guy sitting beside the woman says as he stands from his bar stool. I hadn't noticed him before, but I notice him now as he rounds the pretty, dark-haired woman to come stand before me. "I'm her brother."

"Hunter or Brody?" I ask, and the dude's eyebrows raise high.

"Hunter," he says guardedly, eyes filled with suspicion.

"Oh, my God," the dark-haired woman says with delight. "You're Tenn, aren't you?"

Now I'm all charm and I push past Hunter to stick my hand out to her with a smile. "Yes, I am. And you are?"

She shakes my hand exuberantly and says, "I'm Gabby. I'm her best friend. And of course, you just met her brother, Hunter, who happens to be my fiancé."

"Casey's told me all about you and Hunter, as well as the rest of the gang," I say warmly, not offering my hand to Hunter. Truth is… she hasn't told me much, but they don't know that and I want to get information.

"What the fuck?" Hunter says in exasperation. "Casey doesn't talk about us to men. At all. So seriously, dude… who are you?"

Gabby makes a backhanded slap against Hunter's chest and rolls her eyes at him before turning her attention back to me. "Casey told me about you… the other day when we were hanging out at the beach. I think she was quite smitten with you."

Yeah, I don't think smitten is a word I would ever use to describe Casey, but I have to appreciate Gabby's enthusiasm. I'm also filled with a jolt of happiness as I realize that Casey has mentioned me to her best friend. That surely has to mean something, right?

"Any idea where she is tonight?" I ask casually, and then place a ten-dollar bill on the wooden countertop as the bartender sets my beer down.

Hunter shakes his head no, but Gabby's eyes dart to the floor and then back to Hunter nervously. I don't like that... not at all.

"Did something happen to her?" I ask with no small measure of dread in my voice.

"No, no," Gabby assures me with an apologetic smile. "She's fine."

"Then where is she?" I ask again, now starting to run out of patience. "We had plans to get together when I got back in to town."

"She, um..." Gabby starts to say, but then Hunter intervenes.

"Stay out of it, Gabby," he warns in a low voice.

This causes him to get another backhanded slap to his chest as she gives him an icy look. "I will not stay out of it. Casey's my bestie and she likes Tenn, and I think she may be making a really stupid mistake right about now."

Now my blood pressure starts to skyrocket and heat creeps up the back of my neck. "Where is she?" I grit out.

"She went out on a date with some guy she met the other day on the beach," she blurts out as Hunter throws his hands up in the air in defeat and plops back down on his barstool. "They're at dinner right now."

Motherfucker.

My hands clench tightly and I war with myself between the need to walk away and leave Casey and her fucked-up head behind, and the need to potentially rescue her from a life I know she's not destined to lead.

"Tell me where the restaurant is," I say to Gabby, wondering if I'm about to make a mistake by going after her.

♦

OF COURSE, CASEY would be on a date at a restaurant that looks like you can't get out of it without at least a two-hundred dollar bill. It's a French restaurant in the downtown area of Nags Head and because it's apparently very popular, it takes me forever to find a parking spot. I finally give up and ease my bike into the back alley behind the restaurant, not keen to leave it here, but my anxiety in reaching Casey outweighs my concern for my Harley.

When I walk into the restaurant, I'm immediately stopped at the door by a tuxedoed maître'd who looks me up and down with distaste. "Can I help you, sir?"

"I'm looking for someone," I say, leaning right around the man to look into the restaurant. It's all dark with candles on each table, romantic music in the background, and the smell of foie gras penetrating my nose.

It doesn't take me two seconds to spot Casey's golden hair, and I'm flooded with desire over how beautiful she is and white-hot anger that she's sitting at a table having a romantic dinner with another man. Her hair is long and draped over her shoulders, but doesn't do a damn thing to conceal the deep cleavage from the low-cut black dress she's wearing.

She's facing me with her elbows on the table and her chin resting on her clasped hands. It's the posture of someone that is paying rapt attention to whatever her dinner partner is saying. The posture of someone who is immensely enjoying the conversation.

But upon closer inspection of just her face, I see something different and it heartens me.

Absolute boredom.

Complete indifference.

Maybe even a bit of regret.

This boosts my resolve over what I had originally planned to do... which was fucking drag her out of this restaurant.

I step by the maître'd, but he attempts to halt me with a hand on my forearm. "Sir... you can't go into the dining room without a coat and tie."

I don't want to make a scene, so I dip my head down and speak in a low voice. "Get your hand off me before I fucking break it."

The little tuxedoed man jumps backward as if I'd scalded him with boiling water. Just to alleviate his anxiety a bit, I add on, "I'll just be a minute and then I'm out of here."

"Of course, sir," he says with a quavering voice.

I spin on my heel and enter the dining room, winding my way through cozily placed tables and sidestepping some dude playing a violin. I come up behind Casey's date and watch as Casey finally lifts her eyes and sees me approaching.

I wish I could put into adequate words the expressions that cross her face, but they all happen so briefly, I'm not quite sure what I'm looking at. Happiness, desire, joy, sadness, regret, and shame.

Fuck... that's a lot of damn feeling for one woman to have.

Walking up to her chair, I vaguely hear her date say something like, "And then, I quadrupled my portfolio and reinvested in Chinese agribusiness."

Eesh. Fucking boring.

Casey's eyes remain pinned on me. I reach out, take her gently by her upper arm, and pull her from the chair. "Come on. We're going."

I don't spare a glance at her date... not at first, but then the dude makes the mistake of standing up and stepping into my path. "What's going on here?"

"Casey's leaving… with me," I tell him simply.

He looks past my shoulder to Casey and says, "Casey? Shall I have security escort this man out?"

I lower my face to account for about the five-inch difference in our mutual heights and tell him quietly, "How about I escort you out of here and kick your ass up and down Main Street?"

The man starts stuttering, but then he's forgotten. I turn to Casey and ask her, "Do you want to stay here?"

Her eyes are wide, a tiny bit fearful, but also sparkling with a vague bit of relief. She shakes her head at me.

"Then let's go," I say and start pulling her out of the restaurant.

I'm immensely relieved and gratified she's leaving with me, but every step I take through the restaurant, my anger starts building again. Anger at her for even considering that douchebag sitting in there. Fury over the possibility that she may have already fucked him. Rage over the fact that she continues to seek out things that are not good for her.

By the time I make it out onto the sidewalk in front of the restaurant, my strides are so long and fueled by my acidic thoughts that Casey is practically running in her heels to keep up with me. It doesn't slow me down though, and I steer her down the block and into the back alleyway where my bike is parked.

It's dark and the air is humid, the alleyway lit by a

single yellow bulb beside the back door to the restaurant. It casts a sulfurous tinge to the immediate vicinity, but the rest of the area is layered in heavy shadows.

We walk past the door and just before we reach my bike, I spin Casey and back her up into the brick wall. I step in toward her, bringing my body up against hers and holding her captive against the wall with my pelvis. She lets out a startled gasp, and I can barely make out the blue in her eyes from the thick darkness blanketing us.

Placing my fingers at her jaw, I grip her firmly and ask, "Did you fuck him?"

She vehemently shakes her head. "No. It was our first date."

"Have you fucked anyone else since you've been with me?" I ask her, my breath clogged in my lungs until I can hear the answer.

"No," she whispers, and I hear the truth in her words. I have no clue what she was trying to accomplish tonight, but I know it didn't involve sex with another man.

"Good," I tell her and then lean in to bite her lower lip. "Because I need to fuck you right now."

I bury my face in Casey's neck and drop a hand down to pull the hemline up on the little black dress she's wearing. My fingers immediately snake their way under the wet lace between her legs, and I groan my approval over how slick she is already.

I remove my hand and with jerky movements, pull her dress all the way up past her hips, and then dive into my back pocket for my wallet. My fingers fumble... grab onto the condom, and then drop the wallet to the pavement because it's forgotten.

My button and zipper is opened in a flash, and I push my pants down my hips a bit until my cock is freed. I'm practically shaking with unbridled lust and a need to dominate Casey as I tear at the condom wrapper.

"What are you doing?" Casey asks breathlessly.

I glance up at her, and her eyes are pinned to my dick in fascination. "Getting ready to fuck you," I tell her simply as I roll the condom on.

"Right now?" she asks in disbelief.

My hands go around to her ass where I squeeze the tight flesh a moment and then lift her up. "Right now," I affirm. "Legs around me, baby."

She wraps those long legs around my waist like a good girl even as she says, "But we're in public."

"Don't care," I say as I support her under the ass with one arm and reach my other hand down to grab my cock.

"We might be seen," she says, not a real ounce of worry in her voice.

"Don't care," I tell her as I surge up into her body, and fuck... fuck that feels good.

Casey lets out a long, strangled moan and her legs squeeze me tight. "Someone might call the cops," she breathes into my ear before she nips at it.

I pull out and slam back into her, causing Casey to give the most unladylike grunt I've ever heard.

"Oh, Tenn," she whimpers. "We really, really should not be fucking in a back alley."

"Shut up, Casey," I mutter as I start thrusting into her frantically, pressing my cheek against hers. "I'm still mad at you."

She's silent a moment… well, unless you count the moaning and heavy breathing on her part. As for my part, I surge over and over again into her tight, wet pussy, trying to pound away every bit of anger and confusion this woman causes in me. Casey's fingers dig into my shoulders and her hips gyrate against me.

She catches me totally off guard when she suddenly starts coming, and I know this by the way her muscles clamp down hard against my dick and she screams out into the night air. That fuels me on harder and I start thrusting faster into her, my entire body lurching upward in a vain attempt to catch up to her.

Always feels like I'm trying to catch up to her.

Casey's hands come to my face, and she pushes slightly at me so she can look me in the eye. My pace falls a bit, but I still aim as deep as possible.

She leans in, gives me a light kiss on my lips as I press her body tight against the brick wall.

"I'm mad at you too," she whispers and my body

goes completely still, lodged deep inside of her. My heartbeat is pounding madly, my blood is still firing, and my chest clenches over the uncertainty I see in her eyes. Then she kills me when she says, "I'm mad at you because you make me feel things that scare the shit out of me, but I'm just really glad you came in there and got me, Tenn."

Her words cause my pelvis to tilt and grind against her hard, and I immediately start coming inside of her. My head drops to her shoulder, and I see stars for a moment as I unload drop after hot drop.

Fuck. Goddamn. Fuck.

What this woman does to me.

What this fucking woman does to me.

CHAPTER 13

Casey

M Y INSIDES ARE all twisted.

The more I learn about Tenn, the more I like him.

The more I like him, the more I have to start considering major changes in my life.

The more I consider major changes in my life, the more I might have to admit to myself that I've wasted a good portion of it.

All of this produces anxiety. All of this stresses me out. All of this makes me feel ashamed of my choices in life.

And yet… the view before me does tend to alleviate some of that anxiety. It tends to make me forget about stresses and poor choices.

Tenn Jennings.

Naked on my bed, the early morning sunlight pouring through the windows and bathing his skin golden. He's sleeping on his stomach, tattooed arms in green, black, and red ink wrapped around a pillow with his face turned my way. One leg stretched out, so long his foot hangs off the end of my bed, the other bent at an angle that makes his ass look positively amazing.

With his eyes closed, I can see just how long his lashes are. Dark like his hair and just as thick. So thick it looks like he's wearing eyeliner against those pale blue eyes. That goatee... I just want to lick at it, and I love the way it rubs against my skin when he's going down on me.

He's perfection. Simple male perfection.

Add on to that that he's kind, unpretentious, and wise, which I respect immensely. Add on to that he's also alpha and domineering, which strangely, I also like.

He's the perfect blend of everything that could ever make me want to change my life and open up to a man. But I'm not about to go there. Not fully.

After Tenn fucked me against the back wall of La Papillon, he immediately ordered me to get into my Jeep and follow him back to my house. I didn't think to argue... not with the way he was still looking like he wanted to wring my neck.

I know it was stupid to go out with that guy. It was stupid, reckless, and I knew it would probably hurt Tenn's feelings if he found out about it. I certainly didn't want to go out with that prick. He certainly wasn't as self-absorbed as many men that I'd gone out with, but damn... he was so freakin' boring that I almost fell asleep while he was talking.

No, I didn't want to go out with him, but I made myself do it.

I made myself take an action that I knew would center me once again and would make me remember all the things about my dating lifestyle that were safe and secure. I did it not only because thinking about Jeff Parkhurst back in my home town conjured up some very bitter feelings, but I did it because I had to prove to myself that I was immune to men like Tenn.

Which... apparently... I'm not.

Reaching a finger out, I gently trace the edge of his lashes laying against the skin under his eye. The corner of Tenn's mouth curves up, making me want to nuzzle along his goatee. Instead, I trace my finger over his cheekbone, down his neck, and over his shoulder. I push up on my elbow to get me closer to his body, and gently stroke my finger down his back.

"What are you doing?" Tenn mumbles sleepily.

"Touching you," I say simply. "You can't lay like that... all sexy in my bed, and expect me to keep my hands to myself."

Tenn chuckles and buries his face deeper into the pillow. Moving my finger lower, I watch the muscles on his back jump under my touch. I cruise right down the middle of his spine, lightly run my finger through his ass cheeks, and then right down in between his legs, where I flutter my fingers against his balls that I have easy access to with his leg cocked up.

Tenn groans and presses his hips into the mattress. "Stop, Casey. You're giving me a hard-on."

"That may have been my sinister intention," I murmur, and then tilt my hand to cup his balls so I can massage them.

"Mmmmm," Tenn groans and his hips gyrate, humping the mattress.

I expect… at any moment now, for Tenn to roll over, shoot me a lethally sexy smile, and command me to suck his dick. Which was my ultimate goal when I started touching him.

Instead, he surges up from the bed, launches himself at me, and wraps his arms tightly around my waist. He rolls onto his back, taking my body with him until I'm laying completely flush against his muscled hardness, with another hardness pressed into my belly.

"Christ woman," he grumbles before leaning up to give me a swift kiss. "What do you have against sleeping in?"

"I can't help it," I whine dramatically as I push up into a sitting position to straddle him. "I'm horny."

To prove my point, I tilt my hips, rubbing myself over his hard length. "See," I murmur huskily. "I'm wet for you."

Tenn's eyes flare hot and his hands come to my hips, trying to push me down to grind on his cock. "Sleeping is totally overrated."

"Yes it is," I agree, and then lean forward to run

my lips along his neck.

"Casey?" Tenn whispers.

"Hmmmmm?" I move my lips from his neck, sliding up to the area behind his ear that I know drives him crazy. I learned that fortuitously last night.

"Ever fucked bare?"

I jerk in surprise over the question, but I also can feel wetness seeping out of me over the idea. Lifting my head, I look down at him. "No. Have you?"

"Yup," he says with a knowing smile. "With my ex-wife."

"Oh," I say, not prepared for the surge of jealousy that flows through me.

"Of course," he says with a careless shrug of his shoulders, "she fucked around on me so I had to get tested, but I'm all clean and spiffy, and I've always wrapped up since then."

"She cheated on you?" I asked with wonder. Because why, oh why, would a woman ever go looking for something else when she had a man like this in her bed?

"She's a bit fruity," he says with a grin. "Still holds aspirations I'll come back to her one day."

I wrinkle my nose at the prospect. "I don't think I like her. Granted... I don't know her, but I don't think I like her."

"Well, that makes two of us," he says affably. "I tolerate her because she's Zoey's mother, but that's about all she gets from me."

"Speaking of Zoey," I say, my thoughts of his hard cock between my legs momentarily forgotten, "how was your visit with her?"

Tenn's face breaks out into a huge smile. He then proceeds to talk for ten minutes about everything they did for the few days he was in Raleigh and how he's going to bring her here next week. Of course, I went ahead and sat up straight so I could listen to him, and of course, since we were talking about his daughter, his hard-on waned, but that would be expected.

"I'm going to bring her here next week when she gets back from riding camp," he says. "Let her spend a few weeks here for summer vacation."

"Don't you have plans to get back to work or something?" I ask hesitantly.

"No immediate plans," he says. "I'm thinking about starting up a business with a buddy of mine I served in the Marine Corps with."

"What kind of business?"

"A custom bike shop. He does custom work right now but not on a large scale and only through word of mouth. Figured he could do the body work and I could do the engine work."

"Where would you do that?"

"Somewhere in North Carolina," he says, and I immediately experience a jolt of pleasure over the fact that Tenn will be living in the same state as me. "Somewhere close to Zoey so I can see her. And speaking of Zoey... think you can use your realty connections to find me a place to rent here for a few weeks? I don't want to have to get two hotel rooms when she comes, and given that she's a fourteen-year-old girl, I know she doesn't want to be bunking down with her dad."

Shaking my head, I say, "It'll be hard. We're in high season now, but I'll look around for you this morning."

"Cool," he says and then his hands come up to my thighs, where they stroke upward past my hips to my ribs, and from ribs to the front of my breasts. I arch my back, pressing into his touch, and feel him start to grow hard underneath me again.

Then I'm struck with an insane idea. "But what if you two just stayed with me? I have two bedrooms."

Tenn's hands stop moving, but they squeeze reflexively. "Here? With you?"

"Well, yeah," I say hesitantly, now wondering if that was a completely stupid idea. "I mean… if that's a problem, I could always go stay with my parents and let you two have this place. That would solve your problem, and seeing as how you're unemployed right now, it will save you money."

"Yeah, wasn't really worried about the money, baby," he says offhandedly, and then his eyes narrow. "I was more thinking about the fact that you're a bit skittish when it comes to men in your territory. This offer wouldn't have anything to do with the fact that you're just trying to keep my big, muscular body in your bed for a while, would it?"

My eyes go wide, and I flutter my hand against my chest. In my best southern yet affronted voice, I say while batting my eyelashes, "What? Me? Want to take advantage of this big, beautiful body?"

Tenn chuckles and his hands squeeze my breasts again before pinching my nipples gently. "You're the one with a beautiful body. I could just stare at you for hours and be completely satisfied."

My spine turns in to absolute mush, and I start to sag against him. His words... so reverent... so filled with hunger for me. It's almost disorienting to my senses.

"You okay?" Tenn asks quietly, his eyes pinned to the way his fingers are working at my nipples.

I nod at him with a smile and press my hips down to rub against his erection. "Perfect."

"Yes, you are," he murmurs, lifting his hips up to meet my movements.

"So... about this idea," I press him since things are heating back up.

"Yes," Tenn says quickly. "Zoey and I would love to stay here with you."

I shake my head and give him an admonishing look. "That's not what I was talking about, although I'm glad to hear you'll stay here. I plan on sexing you to death, just as FYI. But quietly and discreetly so Zoey is none the wiser."

Swiftly rolling to bring me underneath him, Tenn

hovers over me and flexes his hips to grind his cock against me. "What idea are you talking about? And I'll take you up on the sexing to death promise and one up you by promising you lots of orgasms in return. Discreetly, of course."

Yes, that sounded nice indeed. "I'm talking about your idea about fucking bare."

"That was an idea?" he asks teasingly. "I was just making conversation."

Just so he knows how serious I am and not in the mood to tease, I reach my hand down and circle it around his erection. I maneuver it between my wet folds and place the tip right at my center. "Do you want to fuck me bare, Tenn? Yes or no? If it's a yes, just give a push. If it's a no, get your ass up and get a condom on."

He doesn't answer me. He just thrusts into me deeply… one stroke… straight to the hilt. My back bows upward in pleasure and my hands grip onto his biceps hard.

"Answer your question, Goldie?" he taunts.

"Yes," I manage to gasp, still feeling my body adjust to his length and girth.

"Are you on the Pill?" he asks before he makes another move. "And please say yes, because I seriously don't think I can leave you right now to get a condom."

"Yeah baby," I say softly, moving my hands up behind his neck. I pull on him so he lowers his face toward me. "I'm on the Pill, so you can go ahead and start fucking me now."

Tenn's mouth comes down onto mine, and he kisses me slowly. He kisses me deeply, all tongue and soft lips, his goatee scratching at my face. I raise my legs, bend my knees, and tilt my hips to take him in deeper.

He moves in and out of me slowly… hips rolling at a deliberately slow pace… kissing me the entire time. He kisses me so thoroughly that I'm not sure where his tongue ends and mine starts. Between the movement of his cock tunneling in and out of me and his mouth possessing mine, I start to get overwhelmed with sensations.

I take stock of the way our breaths come out in long, harsh pants, listening intently to the grumbling inside his chest that every stroke produces. I feel my pulse pounding frantically within my veins. All while he moves with measured, slow strokes that seem to cause every nerve within me to burst in pleasure.

I realize all of a sudden… Tenn is making love to me.

A brief moment of panic inundates me, robbing me of my breath, but I refuse to succumb to it. I push it away and forbid it from coming back.

I'm changing, damn it, and I like these feelings far more than I'm afraid of them.

I listen.

I feel.

I reciprocate.

Tenn pushes in and out of me for what seems like hours and builds me up to a slow orgasm. When I start to come, I wrap my arms around his neck tight and cry out his name.

Then Tenn follows me over the edge with one hard push deep inside, and he starts pulsing jets of his pleasure into me. His face buries into my neck, his fingers grip my hair, he collapses on top of me and groans, "Casey... fuck... I'll never get enough of you."

And I realize that this is okay with me.

I'm completely fine with a man proclaiming some type of dependence upon me.

I'm absolutely and utterly at peace with the fact that I don't want to run and hide from these emotions.

So very fucking weird, but there you have it. This amazing man fucking broke my boundaries... and now I have to figure out what to do with all the pieces.

Tenn rolls to the side while wrapping his arms around me. Rolling with him, I keep one leg wrapped tightly around his hip so that he doesn't slip free of me. I like the feel of him inside of me bare. I want to prolong that feeling.

Palming the back of my head, Tenn pushes my face into his neck where I can feel the pounding of his heartbeat through his jugular right at my cheekbone.

With every beat, it starts to slow and become more relaxed.

"Let's cuddle just a moment," he says sleepily. "And if we happen to fall back asleep, that would be cool too."

"Cuddle?" I ask with mock confusion. "I've heard of that concept but not sure I really understand what it means."

I can feel the rumble of laughter in his chest, and Tenn embraces me affectionately. "Oh, Goldie... I have so much to teach you."

Smiling, I burrow in deeper to him... press a kiss to his neck... wrap my leg tighter around his hip. This isn't so bad. This isn't nearly as terrifying as I thought it would be.

Am I at risk now to get hurt?

No, not really.

Because as much as I enjoy Tenn and his affections, as much as I have come to crave him physically, I'm not ever going to let my heart get tied up in this. I'm going to keep it removed... locked deep in an area that I keep reserved only for my family and close friends. Tenn may have busted my boundaries but there's no way I'm ever going to let him bust the walls I've put up around my heart. It's just too precious to me to trust it to him or any other man.

"You're not relaxing, Casey," Tenn mumbles. "I can feel your body stiffening, and I'm sorry... but cuddling requires absolute relaxation."

I force my muscles to unclench… I melt in a little closer to him.

"That's better," he praises me, and then starts stroking my lower back with his hand. And wow… this cuddling sure feels good. "What do you want to do today?" he asks.

I give a little shrug. "I have to go in to work at noon, and then I'm off at six."

"Then how about this?" Tenn says in a soothing voice. "As soon as I regain feeling in my legs, because damn, woman… that was the fucking bomb coming inside you like that, we go take a shower together. And in that shower, I'm feeling so generous that I'm going to eat you out until you come on my face. Then you may or may not choose to suck my dick, but I'll leave that up to you, because I'm not one that necessarily believes in quid pro quo. Then we'll go out to breakfast, my treat, and yes… that would be considered a date so suck it up and get over it. Then you go to work and when you get off, I'll take you to dinner, and yes… that also would be a date. If you're good, and you don't complain, we'll come back here and I swear I'll give you at least four orgasms before we go to bed. Five if you're a really good girl and beg for it. Sound good?"

Fuck, fuck, fuck. I will not let my heart get tied up with this man. I will not let my heart get tied up with this man. I will not let my—

Crap. I'm doomed.

CHAPTER 14

Jenn

I FUCKING LOVE the feel of Casey on my bike behind me. Her body pressed in tight, her arms securely around my waist, and sometimes, she lays her cheek on my back... yeah, that's the shit.

We're heading to The Last Call for Andrea's "surprise" birthday party that ended up not being a surprise at all because she stopped by for a visit to Gabby and Hunter's house and saw her cake on the table. And because it's not a surprise anymore, I don't feel guilty in the slightest that Casey and I are going to be a little late since I had the overwhelming urge to play around with her while we took a shower together.

It's not my fault really. I would have left her alone except while I was rooting around underneath her sink for some shaving cream since I'd run out, I found her handy-dandy waterproof vibrator, and there was absolutely no way I was going to pass up the wet opportunity to use it on her. So instead of shaving, I crawled into the shower behind her and put it to good use on Casey. And what do you know? She wasn't upset in the slightest that we were going to be running late.

Even though it's nearing seven PM, it's still plenty light out with the high summer sun. It's really warm... unbearably hot actually because of the humidity, so the wind blowing over us is welcome on the ride. I'm finding I really like this area of North Carolina and the small community of Nags Head in particular. While the differences between coastal North Carolina and the Teton Mountain range where I'm from are like night and day, there are a lot of similarities between small town life, no matter where you're located.

On the left up ahead, I see a large, white sign with big, block, red letters that says "Commercial Property – For Sale". I've been down this road several times since The Last Call sits on it, but I hadn't noticed that sign before. It draws my attention now and as we pass by, I see a huge, abandoned garage with four bays.

I immediately slow my bike, feeling Casey's body press in closer to me with the loss of momentum. A quick check of my rearview mirror and I make a controlled U-turn.

When I pull into the parking lot of the garage, I can immediately see the metal building is fairly new. To the right of the garage bays sits a windowed office.

I pull my bike up close to the office portion, turn it off, and place the kickstand. Reaching a hand back over my shoulder, Casey automatically grabs it. I help her swing a leg over to dismount, and then I do the same.

"Why did you stop here?" she asks as I start walking up to the office. I put my face to the glass, cup my hands around my eyes, and peer in.

"Just thought I'd check it out," I say distractedly. The interior is furnished with a built in u-shaped reception desk, shelving, and seating for about five people.

Casey walks up beside me and looks in, but I'm already turning away to walk around the building. I estimate it's about eight-thousand square feet, seventy-five hundred of which is easily devoted to the garage bays. There's a back door that leads to a smaller parking lot, outside water and air hookups, as well as a gas pump.

Trotting behind me as I circle the entire building, Casey asks, "Are you thinking of this for your bike shop?"

Shrugging my shoulders as I round the front of the building, I say, "Maybe. I mean... depends on price."

"But don't you want to be in Raleigh... closer to Zoey?" she asks as I stand on my tiptoes and try to look inside the small, squared windows on the first garage door. Unfortunately, it's too high for me to see.

"Is that panic in your voice?" I ask her drily with a cocked eyebrow. Can't help it… for all the strides Casey's made, she still radiates a resounding skittishness over anything remotely resembling commitment. "Afraid I might be moving here to be near you?"

"No," she exclaims quickly, but I'm not buying it because of the pink tinge of embarrassment on her cheeks. "I just know that the reason you're relocating to North Carolina is to be near Zoey. She's in Raleigh, ergo, I thought you'd live in Raleigh."

"Well… I'm thinking I might move to get primary custody of Zoey," I say absently as I turn and head toward my bike. "And if I do that, doesn't really matter where I live, right?"

Casey's hand snags ahold of one of my belt loops and pulls me to a stop. I turn to look at her, and her eyes are apologetic. "I really didn't mean anything negative about you looking to live here, Tenn. Despite what you may think about me, I am trying to be open about all of this."

I immediately wrap my hand around the back of her neck and pull her in close to me. Her arms go around my waist, and I have to tilt my head way to the side to place a kiss on her neck since she's still wearing her helmet. "I know," I say with a breath of apology. "You're trying hard, and I appreciate it."

And she is.

She's let me into her home, she's let me take her

out on dates, and she's even opened herself up to me personally. She's trying hard.

But the mere fact that she has to try *hard* worries me, because that means this whole concept of having a relationship is still foreign and frightening to her. It's still very much a struggle to Casey.

♦

"MAN… YOU SCORED one smokin' hot prime piece of—" Kyle says as he punches me on the shoulder.

"Don't even fucking go there," I warn him in a low voice as we both sit at the bar and watch Casey as she plays pool with Gabby.

Andrea's party is in full swing and the bar is packed, which is testament to just how well she's fit into this community in a short time. The entire "gang," as Casey calls them, is congregated at three tables that sit along the wall right beside one of the pool tables.

They're tight knit. You can tell at first glance, the way they carry on easy conversation, give hugs to each other, and playful smiles. They look like a fucking episode of *Friends* or something, and it reminds me very much that I am an outsider even though they were all perfectly nice when Casey introduced me to them. And past that introduction, Casey made one valiant attempt to encourage me to come over and hang with them, but she hasn't tried again since I told her I was fine just sitting at the bar with Kyle. He's going to be heading back to Wyoming tomorrow, so I wanted to spend a little bit of time with him tonight.

Which irks the shit out of me. Irks me that Casey is part of a group that I'm not comfortable with but within which she is very secure, which means she really has all of the support she needs. But mainly it pisses me off to some extent because Casey isn't trying harder to include me.

Logically, I get that. This is all new for her, and she's forging unchartered territory. So she'll be cautious with every action she takes.

But it still drives me bat-shit crazy that she just can't give into it... whatever it is that we're develop-ing. I know she can feel it... the ease with which we come together in conversation and even in quiet times. The physical connection... I know she feels that too. I know she feels it harder and deeper than she's ever felt it before, because she as much told me that last night.

I fucking feel it in every fiber of my body. I've never felt it before with another human being. It's a feeling that feels so fucking good, that I'm actually considering setting up a business on this island and making it my home so I can be near her. Now, how fucking insane is that?

"Dude... you two have it bad for each other," Kyle says with a smirk on his face.

"Oh yeah?" I ask in skepticism. "What makes you

say that?"

"Because you two may be sitting on opposite sides of this room, but you can't keep your eyes off each other. You... well, you're just staring straight at her and not bothering to look anywhere else, and Casey... well, she keeps sliding covert glances at you when she doesn't think anyone's looking.

I snort with a jerk of my head because that's Casey... keeping our relationship in a dark and dirty closet, not wanting to admit to the world that she's making a change in her life.

"I gotta take a leak," I mutter and launch myself off the stool, mainly in an effort to get away from Kyle's keen perception.

The men's bathroom is empty, so I have my choice of urinals. I unzip my pants and get to business when the door opens behind me. One figure steps to my left and another to my right, just three men now pissing out our beer.

"You're awful antisocial," the guy to my left says and when I turn to look at him, I see Hunter standing beside me. When I look to my right, Brody's standing there. At least I think it's Hunter on my left and Brody to my right, but that's only because the guy on my left had his tongue down Gabby's throat about twenty minutes ago.

I grunt an acknowledgment, shake my dick, and zip it away. A quick flush to the urinal and I head over to the sink to wash my hands.

"So what's the deal with you and Casey?" Brody asks as he comes to stand beside me at the other sink. I rinse, shake my hands off, and step to the side to grab some towels while Hunter squeezes in to wash his hands.

"What do you mean 'what's the deal'?" I ask Brody as I ball up the wet towels tightly and throw them in the garbage.

"He wants to know what your intentions are with our little sister," Hunter supplies helpfully.

Oh great. I'm getting the concerned older brother speech. While I top each of them by a good two to three inches and a good thirty pounds, there are two of them and just one of me.

Which makes it pretty stupid when I say, "Not really any of your business."

"Well, yes… see it is," Brody says affably as he claps me on the shoulder and then gives me a push backward into the wall. I stumble briefly and right myself. He tries for another push, but I'm ready this time and I don't budge an inch.

"Strong fella," Hunter chuckles and Brody actually grins at me.

"Yeah… I guess I could see why Casey would be attracted to him," Brody adds on as he eyes me up and down. "He's got this whole bad-boy image going on."

"And those eyes," Hunter says and then fans himself mockingly. "To die for."

My eyes flick back and forth between Hunter and Brody while they continue to banter back and forth about my attributes. Finally, just to stop them prattling, I grit out, "What the fuck?"

Brody blinks at me innocently, and Hunter says, "Oh… sorry… were we going on a little too much?"

"You two sound like high school girls at a slumber party," I mutter.

"He's hilarious," Hunter says as he loops an arm around my shoulder and starts walking me toward the door. "And here's a secret… we like you, dude. I'm not sure exactly what brand of mojo you're packing, but you have got our little sis to actually start acting like a normal woman."

"You mean dating a normal guy rather than targeting rich men for sex?" I ask blandly, because I'm curious just how much they really know about their sister.

"Hey," Brody growls as he opens the door. "Watch your fucking mouth about Casey."

I actually cringe for a moment, not because I'm afraid of Brody or Hunter, but because of the way in which I just painted their little sister and the woman who I'm coming to fall for more each day. I can only chalk it up to all of the frustrations that Casey still presents for me.

"Look," I say as I scrub my hand through my hair. "I'm sorry… that was uncalled for. And to answer your question, my intentions with her are completely on the up and up. I like your sister, even as maddening as she can be, and I'm really trying hard to build something with her, okay?"

Brody gives me a shove through the door even as he hands me a big grin. "Dude… you are preaching to the choir when you talk about how maddening our sister can be."

Hunter walks through behind me and says, "In fact… I insist we do some serious drinking tonight and discuss her in detail. We're feeling a little compelled to help you out all we can because we like the direction Casey is going."

Shaking my head, I can't do anything but follow Brody and Hunter back to the bar where they order more beer for me and Hunter, as well as a water for Brody. Then they lead me out past the pool tables toward the back deck. I cast a quick glance at Casey, whose lovely eyebrows raise in surprise, and then narrow back down in suspicion as she sees me walking out the door with her brothers. I merely shrug my shoulders and shoot her a confident wink, and I'm totally rewarded when she blows me a kiss across the bar.

◆

"CHRIST, I'M DRUNK," I mutter as Casey releases her hold around my waist and I fall down onto her bed.

"You are so drunk," she says in agreement and

starts working on my boots.

"I might need you to do all the work tonight, baby," I slur at her with a sloppy grin as I raise my head off the mattress to look down at her. "You on top, but you can start by sucking my dick a little if you want."

She snorts at me and gives a hard pull, taking one boot off my foot as my head falls back to the bed. "You're too drunk to have sex."

"I'm never too drunk to do that," I maintain… also in a slurred voice. "In fact, I'm seeing three of you right now so that means three times as much beautiful Casey riding my cock tonight."

Casey lets out a bark of a laugh as she pulls my other boot free. "You're hilarious when you're drunk."

I smile… happy she finds me funny. Happy she likes drunk Tenn. Probably would be happier if she gave me a blow job, but happy nonetheless.

"At least you warmed up to me tonight," I mutter as she crawls up onto the bed and lays her head on my chest. My arm comes around her waist, and I squeeze her into me.

"Warmed up to you?" she asks quizzically.

"Yeah… you were all aloof when we got there. Thought you were getting cold feet on me again, but then it didn't take long and you were all over me, baby."

Casey gives me a quick pat to my chest. "Honey... you were all over me. I was just accommodating you."

"Yeah... that's what I mean. You didn't push me away. You actually embraced our 'togetherness' in front of all your friends."

"Well, you are kind of charming. You're also really hot and I was afraid if I didn't stake my claim on you, some other floozy would move in on my territory."

"So, you like me, huh?" I ask as the room starts to spin a little bit. I latch on to Casey a little tighter in an effort to stabilize.

"Just a little," she says, affectionately rubbing her cheek on my chest. I'm drunk, but I fucking feel that touch down to my toes.

And because I'm drunk, I'll probably be forgiven for anything I say right now.

And that makes me realize, I'm not so drunk that I can't rationalize the fact my inebriation will give me a free pass with Casey if I say something to spook her.

Now my brain really starts working.

Going to go ahead and lay it out there... I can blame it on the alcohol later if I wig her out.

"So you like me a little?" I ask her, trying hard to annunciate clearly.

"A little," she verifies.

"That's good," I say. "Because I like you too."

"That's sweet," she says, and I can actually hear the smile in her voice.

"I mean… really, really like you."

"Oh, well… in that case, I'll admit it… I really, really like you too."

I roll quickly onto my side, coming almost nose to nose with Casey as she lies beside me. "I'm just going to go ahead and say it while I got the drunken balls to do it… but I'm falling for you kind of hard, Goldie."

And apparently, I'm not so drunk that I miss the very brief and momentary flash of panic in Casey's eyes, but thankfully, it's immediately replaced by warmth. She gives me a slow smile, leans in, and kisses my chin. "How much of this conversation are you going to remember tomorrow?"

"Probably not a word," I answer honestly.

"Then I'll also go ahead and admit to you… I'm sort of, kind of, possibly falling hard for you too."

"You mean that, Goldie?" I ask as my eyes search hers… which thankfully, I'm only seeing two of right now.

"Yeah… for the first time in my life, I really mean it," she whispers, and my drunken heart soars.

Reaching an arm out, I slip it around her waist and pull her back into me. Her face snuggles into the crook of my neck and her arm wraps around me.

"Christ… I really hope I remember this tomorrow," I grunt before I close my eyes and pass out.

CHAPTER 15

Casey

I NEVER IMAGINED in my life that I would consider being a biker babe. Well, and really… I'm not even sure what that means, but I know I do love riding on Tenn's motorcycle. I haven't done the whole braless, Harley tank top thing yet, but I could be persuaded if Tenn thought it was hot.

Admittedly, I was nervous the first time I got on his bike but then I warmed up to it, and now I may possibly be addicted. I'm sure it has absolutely nothing to do with the powerful engine rumbling between my legs or the hot, muscled man that's sitting in front of me.

I'm surprised Tenn is even up and about today. I didn't expect him to get so drunk at Andrea's party last night, and I blame that completely on my brothers. They fed him beer after beer and proceeded to tell him every embarrassing story they could think of about me. I'm not sure what they were hoping to accomplish, but I'm pretty sure telling him I had a lazy eye when I was six years old wasn't helping.

And sometimes, alcohol can be a blessing or a curse when it comes to loosening inhibitions, and I'm still not quite sure how I feel about it loosening Tenn's tongue last night. He was drunk, but I'm sure he was being completely straight up when he said he was falling hard for me.

He's not the first man that has said words of that nature to me.

He is, however, the first man that I've kept around after saying those words, and I can only take that to mean that for some reason, my psyche simply accepts Tenn and what he's telling me. I simply have to accept the fact that I'm changing and I'm becoming open to the possibility of actually having the first real relationship of my life with a man.

Let's see... since meeting Tenn, I've gone out with a man that doesn't have a lot of money, I've invited him into my home, I've slept in bed with him all night, and hell... I've even cuddled.

Me... Casey Markham. A cuddler.

I've also shared something with him that I haven't even shared with my best friend. Or my family for that matter. Tenn Jennings is the only person on this earth that has somewhat of an understanding of why I did the things I did when it came to men. He may not know it all, but he at least knows more than anyone else, and that right there tells me something.

It tells me I was being truthful when I told him

last night that I was falling for him.

Because I am so fucking falling for him.

We cruise down the main drag on the way to my house. Tenn had picked me up after work, having spent part of the afternoon looking at the garage that was for sale after I'd put him in contact with a commercial realtor I knew. He offered to take me out for dinner, but because Zoey is coming tomorrow, I want to make sure to get the house absolutely cleaned and the guest bedroom made up. For some reason I don't even want to fathom, Zoey's mother insisted on bringing her, so that should be oodles of joy meeting Tenn's fruity ex-wife.

I look at the grocery store as we slide by, thankful that I did my grocery shopping this morning. The parking lot is absolutely packed but Saturdays on the beach are big grilling and party days. Just as I start to turn my gaze back to the road, I catch a glimpse of a familiar face walking into the store, and my blood fires up nuclear hot from a surge of anger.

Jeff Parkhurst.

Without thinking, I tap Tenn on the shoulder and yell at him above the wind. "Turn around and go to the grocery store. I forgot to pick up something."

He nods and gets us turned around, the sound of the engine barking loud at such a slow idle as we pull into the lot. "Just drop me off at the front door and I'll run in really quick," I tell him, and a spark of guilt fires up that I'm not being honest with Tenn as to why I'm here.

But fuck… I don't know why I'm here. I just saw Jeff, got swamped with fury, and now feel the unmistakable need to confront this douche.

I get off the bike when he brings it to a stop, quickly take off my helmet, and hand it to him. "You need anything?"

"I'm good," he says with a smile, but then asks, "What are you getting? You had me lug up about forty bags of groceries to your house this morning."

"Um… milk," I say and start to turn away.

"You got milk," he says, and I turn back to look at him impatiently. "Yeah… but I only got skim and I like whole milk with my coffee."

And damn… more guilt with how easily that lie came out of my mouth.

"Gotcha," he says with a nod toward the rear of the lot. "I'm going to go find a spot to park over there."

"Okay," I say, and then I spin toward the automatic glass doors. They swish open, and a blast of icy air conditioning hits me. I'm not sure if it's the chilled air or the ice in my veins, but I rub my arms a bit to warm them up.

I immediately start walking across the front of the store, looking down each aisle as I go along. Finally, I see him… halfway down the beer and wine aisle, perusing the various microbrews for sale. Taking a deep breath, I push it out hard and start walking his way. I'm going to tell him off, and I'm not going to be quiet about it.

When I get up close to him, Jeff's head turns my way, and for a brief moment, just the tiniest of blips really, I appreciate how good looking he is. But I know outer beauty doesn't mean shit on the inside.

I'm a prime example of that.

Jeff's eyes round wide with surprise, and he gives me a blinding smile. "Oh, my God. Casey Markham? Is that you?"

Suddenly, my mind goes blank and I can do nothing more than nod at him dumbly. He steps forward and wraps his arms around me, dragging me in for a hug. Weakly, my arms go around his neck as he pulls me in close and murmurs. "It's so good to see you."

When he releases me, I take a small step back. His gaze travels up and down my body, making absolutely no effort to hide the gleam of appreciation in his eyes. He even pulls his chin back and says, "Damn girl… you are still just as smokin' hot as you were in high school."

Greasy tremors race up my spine as his eyes linger on my breasts, and I have to resist the overwhelming urge to slap him across the face. So many things I want to say but again, he doesn't give me a chance.

"Listen… I'm only in town for another few nights. Any chance you'd let me take you to dinner tonight?" He says this in a low, husky voice while still staring at my breasts. "You know… for old time's sake?"

Of all the sleazy, scummy things that he could say to me, that is something I didn't expect. But then again, Jeff has no clue the bitter feelings I've harbored for him for going on eight years. I should blast him out about it now, but when I see the hunger in his eyes and the way he is mentally undressing me... already figuring it's a foregone conclusion he can take me out to dinner tonight and then talk me in to bed, I am struck with sudden brilliance.

I'm going to make him suffer far more than just a berating from me. I'm going to make him think he's good enough to have me, and then I'm going to make sure he dies of blue balls when I refuse him.

I give him a bright smile, wrap my finger around my lock of my hair to twirl it all bimbo-style, and cock a hip out sexily. Then I start calculating how to make this all go down.

First, I need information though, because I want to know exactly how far I can make him fall. "So, are you married or seeing anyone?" I ask innocently. Of course, I know the answer to this because Gabby told me he has a fiancée.

And even though I really expected no different, my stomach recoils when he shakes his head and says, "Nope. Absolutely single."

Liar! What a fucking liar and my anger starts surging again.

"What about you?" he asks as he glances down at

my left hand.

I'm sorry, Tenn, I think to myself. "Nope. Single and free."

"So… how about dinner? And then maybe after, we could um… figure out something fun to do," he says as he dips his head lower toward me. I actually have to lock my knees to stop myself from inadvertently bolting away from him.

"Dinner sounds fabulous," I purr at him even as I push past my nausea. "And I'm really looking forward to seeing what kind of 'fun' we could have after dinner."

"Eight o'clock? La Papillon," he says lecherously, and really… I'm surprised he's even offering me dinner based on the way his eyes continually rove over me. I expect at any moment he's going to throw me down on the grocery store floor and start humping my leg or something.

"Eight sounds perfect. Gives me just enough time to get home and get showered," I say, and then reach into my purse for a pen. I click it on and then take his hand in mine, turning his palm up. "Here's my address."

I take my time writing my address and even put a little heart beneath it, quelling my urge to vomit over the ludicrous act I'm putting on. I wonder what the maître'd will think seeing me in there again. I'm sure he'll remember me from the way Tenn pulled me out of there.

Jeff glances down at the writing on his palm and then back up at me with glittering eyes. I think it's the first time he's looked at my face since the hug.

Movement at the end of the aisle catches my attention and I look past Jeff's shoulder to see Tenn standing there looking at me curiously. I hold up a finger to him to wait, turning back to Jeff to whisper. "Can't wait to see you tonight."

"And I can't wait to see you… all of you tonight," he says almost on a half moan that gives me the freakin' willies. I give him a smile, hope he can't see the distaste in my eyes, and scoot past him.

When I reach the end of the aisle, I turn toward the front door as Tenn walks behind me. "What about the milk, Casey?"

"I decided to stick to skim," I say offhandedly as we make it back through the automatic doors. I don't want Jeff to see me with Tenn. I don't want anything to happen that will thwart my plan for revenge tonight.

"Who was that you were talking to?" Tenn asks casually as we walk side by side through the parking lot.

"Jeff." I answer him honestly because I have no intention of hiding this from Tenn.

Tenn's hand on my arm stops me in my tracks. "Jeff, as in THE Jeff?"

"That's the one," I say, pulling my arm free. "Now hurry… I need to get home because he's picking me up at eight for dinner at La Papillon."

Tenn puts a vice-grip hold on my elbow this time and I expect him to pull me to a stop again, but instead, he propels me forward to the back of the lot where his bike is located. His long legs eat up the distance and I have to trot to keep up with him, which is fine by me... I need to hurry so I can get ready.

When we reach the bike, Tenn spins me around and his face is thunderous. "What the fuck? Are you going out with that guy tonight?"

"Yes, but it's not what it seems because—"

"You're going out with the same guy that for whatever reasons caused you to lock yourself away from relationships?"

"Yes," I tell him impatiently. "I had this idea—"

"Jesus fucking Christ, Casey," Tenn barks at me, and his eyes are blazing with fury. He steps up to me, leaning down before gritting out, "You're fucking going out with another man?"

"To get revenge," I assure him quickly and then attempt a confident smile. "Make him suffer."

Tenn spins away, drags his hands through his hair, and then clasps both of them behind his neck. He turns back to look at me and shakes his head in disbelief. "I can't believe I'm entertaining this stupid as fuck idea, but just exactly how are you going to make him suffer by going out with him tonight?"

"I'm going to make him crazy with wanting me.

I'm going to make him think he actually has a chance with me. I'm going to make him beg like a dog, and then I'm going to tell him fuck off because he's not good enough for me."

I think it's a brilliant plan now that I just said it out loud.

Tenn just stares at me hard, a muscle popping at the corner of his jaw. Then he quietly asks, "And just how are you going to drive him crazy?"

"Well, I'm not sure—"

Stepping back into me, Tenn wraps his huge hand around the front of my throat, gripping me lightly. He pushes up, causing my face to tilt so I can't help but look at him. "Are you going to touch him?"

"That's probably—"

His hand squeezes a little. "Are you going to give him a bit of a hand job first? Just to work him up good?"

"Tenn, that's—"

His hand now tugs on me, raising me on my tiptoes until his nose is almost touching mine. With barely controlled rage, Tenn asks so softly. "Are you going to let him kiss that mouth? Especially after you used it on my cock just this morning?"

"Please, Tenn. You have to understand—"

He releases his hold on me abruptly and asks in a strangled voice that causes my heart to squeeze painfully. "Are you going to do any of those things, Casey?"

"No," I say immediately, and I know it's true. While I may not have thought this plan through all the way, Tenn has made me consider my options, and there is no way in hell I can let that sleaze touch me. My body belongs to Tenn and no one else at this point in my life.

"It's a stupid plan, Goldie," he murmurs. "I don't know what this guy did to you, but it's not worth breaking down everything you've been working to build up."

"What do you mean?" I ask cautiously.

"I mean, you become just like him if you engage in this mind fuck."

"I am nothing like him," I snarl, stepping forward. Poking him in the chest, I say, "You have no idea what he did so you can't possibly know how important this is to me."

"Then tell me," Tenn pleads as his arms come to my shoulders. "Tell me what he did and let me kick his ass for you, but don't go through with this."

Shaking my head, I turn away and walk up to Tenn's bike. I grab my helmet and with my back to him, I say, "I'm not talking about it. You'll just have to trust me when I say it was bad enough that I have to do this. That I think this is the only way I can get some type of vindication. Some type of peace."

Then I turn to look at him and with imploring eyes, I say, "I'm asking for your support on this and to trust me that I won't cross a boundary that's disrespectful to you."

Tenn's shoulders sag and he steps up to the bike, grabbing his helmet. He stares at it thoughtfully for a moment and then says with resignation, "The mere fact you would do something like this… that would cause me worry… that would tear my fucking guts up to even think of you making sexual promises to that fucker… well, I'm sorry, Casey… but that's already disrespectful to me."

"What are you saying?" I ask as I can feel my lungs starting to deflate in anxiety.

Tenn turns those beautiful blue eyes my way and says, "I'm not sure I can handle it. When I said you'd be breaking down everything you've been working to build up… I'm not just talking about you, Casey, and the way you've changed. I'm talking about what you've built up with me."

He's giving me an ultimatum. He's telling me that if I go through with this, which to my way of thinking is just going to be dinner with me getting Jeff worked up with fake promises, he's going to break up with me. Clearly, he doesn't trust me. Clearly, he doesn't understand or support the importance of this to me.

I stick my chin up and even though I know in my heart this is probably the wrong thing to do, I say, "So be it."

Tenn's eyes go distant, and he gives a sad smile. "Get on the bike. Guess I need to get you home for your date."

I go ahead and climb on, my feelings raging an absolute war inside me that causes my chest to ache and my stomach to roll with queasiness. I'm doing the right thing... I can feel it in my bones. The only way I can let my past go is by standing up for myself and making Jeff understand exactly how it feels to have someone reject you. While I know his ego won't be as fragile as mine was at the tender age of eighteen, I know it will hurt him just a bit. And at least I'll be able to expel all of my bitterness at him. That has to be psychologically beneficial, right?

The ride to my house doesn't take long. Tenn doesn't turn the bike off and the loud rumble doesn't exactly make it conducive to a fruitful discussion. But I do try one more time as I take my helmet off and hand it to him. After he stows it in the saddlebag, he turns to look at me.

"Tenn... please don't hold this against me," I ask beseechingly.

He shakes his head and gives me a wry smile. "I won't," he says simply, and my heart lightens. "I'm going to hold it against me that I even thought to get involved with someone like you. Tired of the fucking games, Casey."

Tenn doesn't spare me another glance, which means he doesn't see the tears that immediately start pricking my eyes. Instead, he puts the bike in gear and rumbles off down the road, and I watch until he fades off into the distance.

My first real relationship already over.

CHAPTER 16

Jenn

C HRIST… THAT WOMAN is maddening.
     She's stupid, ignorant, willful, and bratty.
Heartless.

That's what she is… absolutely fucking heartless.

She's a woman that's been hurt, a voice says inside of me. *It changed her into something no one should ever have to be.*

Not my problem though. Not up to me to try to change her.

"Fuck," I yell out to the wind as my bike motors down the highway. I figured I'd go to The Last Call and get fantastically drunk tonight. Maybe Hunter and Brody will be there, and I can rant to them about what a stupendous idiot their sister is.

Or, you could go and stop this shit in progress, a voice inside me says. *Drag her ass out of the restaurant. You've done it once before.*

Yeah, that is so not happening again. It's different this time because Casey knows I have feelings for her, and she's choosing to do this despite the havoc it could cause. She's ignoring my feelings in this matter.

Just like you're ignoring her feelings, that little voice says.

"Shut the fuck up," I yell out to the wind.

Just shut the fuck up, I tell myself, so I can rationally think this thing through.

Okay... Casey admitted she's falling hard for me. I fucking remembered every bit of our conversation from last night, so I wasn't as drunk as I thought. She's truly changed and she's changed because she wants to try to build something with me.

She's also a smart woman and most of all, I've come to see that she has a heart the size of the ocean. She would never do anything to intentionally hurt me.

I trust her. I really do trust her that she would never let this get physical. I expect her plan for revenge is to work him up good over dinner, maybe even spouting some of the dirty talk I've taught her over the last few weeks, and then let him down with the force of a plane plummeting out of the sky. I expect his ego will make a resounding *splat* when it hits.

Is that really so bad? If she does that?

Will it give her closure and remove any further barrier that might present itself to a potential relationship with me?

Now that is some fucking food for thought.

Letting my heart guide my bike, I go ahead and make a U-turn on the highway and head back into the town of Nags Head. I don't know what's going to happen inside that restaurant but best-case scenario, Casey walks out with her head held high and vindication in her eyes. Worst case, that fucker tries to do something to her or causes her pain in some way, and I really, really need to be there if that happens.

♦

I SIT SIDEWAYS with my ass perched on the seat of my bike, legs stretched out in front of me. Same position I was in the first time Casey and I were together when she walked out of The Last Call. Except now, I'm waiting outside of La Papillon where I fortuitously got a spot thirty feet from the front door. I know if Casey's plan goes down, when she walks out that door, she's going to need a ride.

Glancing at my watch, I note it's 8:10 PM and figure that she'll work the fucker up good over the course of dinner. Because it's a fancy French restaurant, I'm thinking dinner will last a good two hours at least. I know I'm in for a long wait but in my heart of hearts, I know Casey is worth it.

The door to the restaurant swings open, and I blink my eyes as Casey strides out. My eyes cut down to my watch. 8:11 PM.

Well, damn.

Casey looks left, then right, possibly considering the best place to get a taxi, when her eyes roll right over me. She pauses, and then her gaze snaps back my way.

"Thought you might need a ride," I call out to her.

She stares at me a moment and I can read nothing on that beautiful face. She looks gorgeous, wearing the same little black dress that she wore the other night when I pulled her out of this very restaurant and fucked her in the alley.

Casey throws her shoulders back and starts my way. My eyes focus in on those long legs, her feet encased in stilettos that give me very dirty thoughts. The thought of that little dress riding up her thighs as she sits on the back of my bike starts to get me hard.

"What are you doing here?" she asks tentatively, crossing her arms over her chest protectively.

I stand up from the bike, and her face tilts to look at me. My fingers reach out and trace the edge of her collarbone a minute, and then I drag my gaze up to her eyes. "Figured you might need a shoulder to cry on, although I was really kind of hoping I'd have the opportunity to kick this dude's ass for you."

She smiles as her eyes cut down quickly. Putting my finger under her chin, I nudge her gaze back up. "What happened in there?"

She shrugs her shoulders, and then throws her hands out to the side. "I couldn't go through with it. I knew it would hurt you, and I couldn't do it. But why are you here? I thought you made it pretty clear that this was sort of a deal breaker for you."

My hand drops from her face, and I shove my hands in my pockets. With a shrug, I casually say, "Yeah… well, I sort of worked it out in my head after I got done being pissed. I understand why you needed to do it and I also realized I trusted you not to do anything that would betray me."

"Oh," she says softly, looking back down to the pavement and then back up again to me. "So where does that leave us?"

"I think it leaves us exactly where we were the minute before you hatched this idiotic plan," I tell her simply. "Although… I am still completely willing to go in there and stomp the shit out of him for you."

Her eyes crinkle up, and she nibbles on her lower lip. "That would be kind of awesome, but I don't want you to get in trouble."

"I'd gladly take an assault charge for you," I tell her gallantly, although I'm sure my dad would blow a gasket if I got arrested. "So… what excuse did you give him why you were leaving early?"

She looks up at me coyly and says, "I didn't. Told him I had to use the restroom and then I jetted."

I throw my head back and laugh. "Oh, Goldie… you're brilliant. You're a hot mess, but you're brilliant."

Just then, I see the door to the restaurant open

over Casey's shoulder and the douche himself comes out. Just like Casey, he looks left and then right, utter confusion on his face.

"Looks like your date is looking for you," I tell her, and then give a nod in the direction of the restaurant. "Want me to handle this?"

She huffs out a gust of frustration but shakes her head. "Nope. I got it."

Turning away from me, she starts toward the restaurant at the same time his eyes land on her. I can see the confusion melt off the guy's face and sizzling lust replace it as he eyes her up and down. My fists clench and it takes every bit of willpower I have not to leap forward to strangle the fucker.

"Casey... what are you doing out here? Our drinks just arrived," he says as he takes a few steps to meet her. He loops an arm around her shoulder with the intent of steering her back inside, and I start to take a step forward. Casey shrugs his hand off though, so I halt myself and wait.

"Jeff... I'm going home," she says matter-of-factly. "The truth is... I never intended to do anything with you tonight, so I figured I'd save you a buck and just go ahead and leave."

The guy is so self-absorbed that he doesn't even notice me standing there ten feet away. He doesn't notice me and the menace that is pouring off my body in waves, otherwise, he wouldn't attempt to touch her again. His arm comes back to her shoulder and he says, "Come on, baby. Thought we were going to have fun tonight?"

Before I can make a move, Casey steps away from him. She takes a deep breath and says, "Look... I only agreed to come out with you tonight with the intention of getting you worked up until your balls were blue and then leaving your ass."

The guy is kind of thick because he says, "Work me up, huh? Now that sounds fun and I'm sure we can avoid the blue balls thing, right?"

Casey narrows her eyes at him and places her hands on her hips. "Are you dense or do you just think so much of yourself that you can't see when someone is plainly not only *not* interested in you, but is actually completely disgusted by you?"

He blinks at her... large eyes as round and blank as a fucking owl's. "I don't understand."

"Because the only person you really care about is yourself, Jeff," Casey says, and then she steps up to him and snarls, "You're a pathetic loser."

He takes a hint... takes a cautious step back. "Oh-kay," he drawls out. "Apparently, you got hit with a little case of the crazies today, so I'm just going to head back into the restaurant—"

"I'm not crazy," she says quietly. "I merely wanted to confront you for what you did to me all those years ago."

"What I did to you?" he asks in confusion. "What the hell did I do to you?"

"I heard you that night," Casey says softly. "At the beach party that I couldn't go to. I snuck out of my parents' house and went there... and I heard what you told your friends."

The guy just stares at Casey with a blank face, completely not remembering anything about that night. It makes my gut tighten in sorrow for Casey, that whatever he did to her, it apparently didn't mean anything to him because he'd forgotten it.

"I gave you my virginity after you gave me false comfort over my brother going to prison and told me you loved me. Then you turned around and told your friends I wasn't good enough for you. I didn't have the "credentials" to be a part of your circle. You said I wasn't the type you marry, but I was the type of woman you'd fuck behind your wife's back. But hey... at least you told them I was a fantastic fuck."

That motherfucking douche bag scummy fucking asshole.

My head feels like it's going to explode so great is the rage that rockets through my system now that I know exactly what went down. I don't even think twice but start walking toward the guy with a film of red haze over my eyes for what he did to Casey. For what he said about her.

For fucking hurting my woman.

I'm going to kill him, and he has no clue it's coming because he's staring at Casey.

Ten strides from him, the sheepish look on his

face morphs and his eyes glint with malice at Casey.

Eight strides from him, and he shrugs his shoulders and says, "What can I say, Casey, you were a fantastic fuck."

Four strides from him, and he says, "But yeah… you are the type you fuck behind your wife's back."

Two strides from him, and I see Casey raise her hand to smack his face and then her hand is striking at nothing but air because I have the fucker by the neck and I'm walking him backward toward the restaurant. Both of his hands come up and try to claw at my one that has him gripped tightly. His eyes bug out of his head and his face goes beet red as he tries to suck in air.

I push him back up onto the sidewalk, where he nearly stumbles but I pull him up, then I'm slamming him up against the exterior wall of La Papillon, knocking off one of the lighted wall sconces to the left of the door. His head makes a nice *thudding* sound when it smacks the brick and his eyes start to roll in the back of his head.

The door to the restaurant flies open, and the little maître'd comes out to see what the noise is all about. He takes one look at me, I growl at him, and he goes scurrying back into the restaurant.

Swiveling my head back slowly to look at this scumbag, I loosen my grip a tad, let him suck a gulp of air, and then tighten my hold again. His eyes bug once more.

I'm amazed at how calm my voice is since I'm

practically buzzing with the need to do serious violence. "Now, that's my girl there that you just insulted. And do I look like the type of guy that's going to let something like that pass?"

He shakes his head frantically at me.

"That's right," I say calmly... and yeah, with maybe a slight taunt. "So I'm going to give you one of two choices. You can either apologize to Casey or I can stomp your ribs in with my boots, and just so you know... the toes are reinforced with steel."

I loosen my grip, he wheezes in air, and then I tighten up again. Eyes bug out once more.

"Now, since you currently can't talk, I suggest you hold up a hand and indicate which option you want... one or two."

His hand immediately flies up, and he's holding up one finger while his eyes silently plead. I wait a moment and consider, then I loosen my grip slightly but still keep it tight enough that I can easily pull him away from the wall. He stumbles immediately but I haul him back up by the neck, turn him, and march him back over to Casey, who is now actually reclining back on the seat of my motorcycle, watching me with amused eyes.

"That was really hot," she says, her eyes sparkling at me mischievously.

"Thanks, Goldie," I return jovially, and then give old Jeff a little shake. "Now, I think this guy has something to say to you. Right, Jeff?"

His head frantically nods up and down. I give him

a little push toward Casey as I release him. Stumbling, he drops to one knee right at her feet. He starts to rise up, but I squat down and clamp my hand on the back of his neck to hold him in place. "Uh-uh," I admonish him. "I actually think I like you kneeling down before my girl."

Casey snorts and when I look, her eyes are admonishing. "Now, you're just being mean, baby."

"I'm sorry," Jeff blurts out, and I can feel his entire body shaking under my grasp. "I'm so fucking sorry, Casey. What I said... it was awful. Rude. You totally didn't deserve that."

She stares at him a moment, and then asks, "Do you really mean that, Jeff, or are you just afraid Tenn here is going to put you in the hospital?"

"I really mean it," he practically screams, and the smell of ammonia greets my nose. I tilt to the side and look at the dude's crotch, which now has a wet stain starting to spread.

"Uh-oh," I say with a chuckle. "Jeff here just pissed his pants."

Casey dips her head and covers her mouth with the back of her hand to hide her smile. She looks at me and shakes her head, telling me it's done.

I release my grip on the fucker's neck and stand up, walking around him to my bike and my girl. "You cool, baby?" I ask her as my fingertips stroke her cheek.

"Yeah," she whispers with gratitude in her eyes. "I'm actually really cool."

CHAPTER 17

Casey

"**W**AKE UP, TENN," I say as I shake his shoulder. He's in the classic position I've found him in almost every morning. While we go to sleep wrapped up in each other's arms, I always wake up on one side of the bed, practically clinging to the edge, while he sprawls out on the other seventy-percent of the mattress. Face down, arms wrapped around a pillow his head is resting on, gorgeous naked ass for me to look at.

I shake him again. "Come on, dude. Places to go, people to see."

Tenn groans and opens one bleary eye to look at me. "What time is it?"

"Eight," I tell him and give him a tiny shove. "Zoey will be here soon."

"She won't be here for another two hours," he says and then turns away, giving me his back. "Plus... she's not coming here. We're meeting them over at the Sand Shark. Remember?"

Yeah… we decided to meet them at the Sand Shark because it was right at the intersection where the highway ran north and south up the islands and connects to the mainland. Apparently, Zoey's mom and her boyfriend were going to make their way south and spend a few days down there, so we agreed to meet them at a convenient place.

"I know… but I want to make sure we get the bed made in here, and then see if there are any last-minute arrangements we need to do, and are you sure I got all of Zoey's favorite foods? Do we need to run to the grocery store again? It probably wouldn't—"

"Jesus, woman," Tenn growls at me as he flips over so fast I have no clue what's going on until he has me flat on my back and he's pinned me down. "Why can't you seriously just sleep in a little?"

"Because there's too much to do and I want everything to be perfect for her," I say quickly.

"Relax, Goldie," he says with a soft smile. "I swear Zoey is going to like you. Stop trying so hard to impress."

My cheeks heat up with embarrassment that he's calling me out over my insecurity. "I just… I really, really want her to like me. I mean… if she doesn't then there's no hope for you and me, because do you realize how stressful that can be on a relationship? Because your loyalties will be with Zoey, as they should, so it's really important to make sure—"

Tenn slams his mouth down on mine, shoves his

tongue halfway down my throat, and kisses me quiet. His lips move with surety over mine, his goatee tickling my skin. I can feel him start to grow hard between my legs, and a tiny whimper pops out.

He lifts his head and peers down at me. "Casey… she'll love you. Trust me, okay?"

I nod, my lips still tingling from his onslaught. Giving him a sheepish smile, I give a little push on his chest. "Fine. Sorry. You can roll back over and get some more sleep."

"Nope," he says and rolls his hips so his erection is now placed squarely in between my legs. "I'm awake now, and I think you need a diversion to help you relax."

"What did you have in mind?" I ask him with a sly look.

"Well, remember last night… when we got back from your "date" with that douche?"

With eager eyes, I nod at him quickly and suck my bottom lip in between my teeth. I hold it a minute, and then let it pop free, loving the way his eyes watch me and go darker. "You were so gallant."

"Yeah… right… gallant. Anyway, you were so grateful to me for rescuing you from that douche, that you gave me the best blow job I've ever had in my life."

"I remember," I tell him breathlessly. "It was really good, wasn't it?"

"So good," he says as he quirks those sexy lips at

me. "I was thinking of returning the favor."

"Yes please," I say as I wiggle my hips under him.

He cuts me a sinful grin and starts sliding down my stomach. When he makes it only halfway down, I bring my hands up to his head and slide my fingers into his hair on either side. I grip it and tug, stopping his progression.

Tenn tilts his face up to look at me in question, resting his chin right above my belly button.

"You've been in relationships before," I murmur. He doesn't nod or say a word, just waits for me to continue. "Is this what relationships are all about? I mean… is this what I've been missing? Is it always this good?"

His eyes soften and he dips his face to press a kiss on my stomach before peeking up at me again. He's so beautiful, with his dark hair sticking up all over the place, his broad shoulders and tattooed arms, and just behind, the swell of his rounded and tight ass. I sigh deliciously.

"No, Goldie," he says seriously. "It's not always like this. But sometimes it is."

That makes me sad. "Does it just get old?"

He shakes his head and stares at me with warm intensity. "No, it has nothing to do with the length of time you're together. It has everything to do with the person you're with."

"Oh," I say, not really understanding, then I completely understand and say in an enlightened voice, "Oh."

"Yeah, oh," he teases. "It's like this for me because it's you, and it's like this for you because it's me. Get it?"

"I get it," I tell him, and then give him a push on his head. He grins at me and starts moving back down my body again.

♦

I PULL MY Jeep into the parking lot of the Sand Shark, and Tenn points over at a white pickup with an extended cab. "Right there. That's Kip's truck."

"Oh, my God," I mutter. "I'm so nervous."

Tenn reaches out and squeezes my thigh. "It will be fine, Goldie."

My sweaty palms on the steering wheel beg to differ. I pull into the spot behind the pickup and watch as the passenger door opens and a tiny, dark-haired girl comes flying out. Tenn has his door open just as fast, and I have to blink back tears as I watch him engulf her in a huge hug.

A man gets out of the driver's side, wearing a navy baseball cap, t-shirt, and shorts, and then a woman, who I presume to be Zoey's mom, Brianna, gets out of the passenger side. She's wearing a sundress that's obscenely short—definitely something I would have worn in my sluttier days—and looks over at my Jeep with her lip curled.

She intimidates me... no doubt. Not only was she married to Tenn and has known him for like a gazillion years, but she's also a bit whackadoodle according to Tenn and seems to think she has some proprietary interest in him. I find this odd since Tenn assured me she's in a committed relationship with Kip, but I didn't pretend to understand.

I take a deep breath and pry my sweaty fingers from the steering wheel, give them a quick wipe on my shorts, and get out of my Jeep. Because I happen to be on the same side as Kip, he shoots me a friendly smile and sticks his hand out to me. "Hey, I'm Kip."

"Casey," I say and hope my hands are still dry.

He motions for me to precede him and we walk between the two vehicles to where Tenn is now standing with his arm around Zoey's shoulder. Brianna stands there with her arms crossed over her chest, looking like someone peed in her Corn Flakes.

Tenn ignores her though, so I do the same, focusing a smile on Zoey instead. I walk up to her, my heart pounding so very hard because of how desperate I am for her to like me, and I stick my hand out to her. "Hey Zoey... I'm Casey."

And to my utter surprise, she squeals and launches herself at me, wrapping me up in a hug that is surprisingly powerful for such a tiny thing. "Oh my God," she gushes through straight and even teeth that I can tell were the product of braces. "I've been dying to meet you. My dad has told me so much about you when we talk on the phone."

"Um… okay," I say as I squeeze her back, looking at Tenn smile at me over her shoulder. "We're going to have a blast while you're here."

Zoey releases me and then bounds for the truck. "I'll get my bags."

"I'll help you, squirt," Kip says, and it's clear they have a nice relationship.

I turn my attention to Brianna, who is glaring at me. I bite the bullet and stick my hand out to her. "You must be Brianna. It's really nice to meet you."

She stares at my hand for a second before turning to Tenn. "I don't like it. Staying at her house with Zoey."

"Not up for debate," Tenn says in warning. "You have no say so."

"I most certainly do," she sneers, shooting me an evil look. "I won't have you shacking up with your summer floozy with my daughter around."

"Now wait a minute—" I start to say, but then Zoey is bounding back up to us, a backpack over her shoulder with Kip right behind carrying a suitcase. My mouth snaps firmly shut.

"I'm ready," she says with a big smile, her light blue eyes exact replicas of Tenn's.

"I mean it, Tenn," Brianna snaps. "You'll have to stay somewhere else. Not with her."

Zoey's eyes get wary, and Tenn's eyebrows slash downward in anger. He looks at Kip and says, "Do me a favor... take Zoey inside and grab her a drink so I can talk to Brianna."

Kip nods, sets her suitcase down, and holds his arm out to her. "Come on, Zoey."

She rolls her eyes and mutters, "Leave it to Mom to totally mess things up."

I duck my head down and turn toward the restaurant. "I think I'll join them."

Tenn's arm shoots out and snakes around my waist, pulling me in to him. "You're not going anywhere."

Brianna snorts and says, "So caveman, Tenn. I remember when you used to do that to me."

"But not anymore," he says quietly. "Now, I'm only going to say this once... you do not open your mouth with any form of disrespect to Casey. If I see you treat her with anything less than abject politeness, I am going to rain so much misery down on you that you will not be a happy camper. And I'll start by getting sole custody of Zoey and making sure your bitter, crazy ass can't influence her anymore."

Bri's eyes widen and she opens her mouth, but Tenn cuts her off. "And if I hear you say anything disrespectful about Casey outside of my presence—say to our daughter, for example—you can expect the same misery. Are we clear?"

The woman wisely holds her tongue but refuses to give him any acknowledgment.

"You need to know that Casey is in my life. I'm

looking at permanently relocating to this area and I expect you will be seeing Casey over and over again as you and I attempt to parent our daughter. This is non-negotiable, Bri. I mean it... do not fuck with me on this."

I can actually hear the woman gritting her teeth in anger, but again, wisely, she keeps her mouth shut. She gives a jerk of her head at Tenn, and then spins on her foot to head toward the diner. "I'll say goodbye to Zoey in there."

When she walks through the door, I let out a huge, pent-up breath of relief. "Wow. She's just... um... wow."

"But Zoey's great, right?" Tenn says with a playful grin before leaning down to kiss me on the side of my neck.

"She's fantastic. She's a miniature you," I say reverently. "And you've obviously raised her right... to be open and kind to people. I'm kind of guessing that comes solely from you."

"You're nice to say that," Tenn says humbly. "My parents spent a lot of time with her as well, so I think she gets it from them too."

"How come you've never told me about your family?" I ask suddenly.

Tenn's body stiffens slightly, but he tries for a casual shrug of the shoulders. "Guess we've been busy doing other things."

I snort, because I know exactly where we've been

spending our time and most of it has only led to dirty talk and touches. Which now that I think about it, makes me a little apprehensive. What if this thing with Tenn is no different from my other flings?

"We should talk about your family," I say with desperation. "It's what people in relationships do, right? They talk about things that are... you know... non-sex related."

Tenn pulls me to the front of his body and wraps his arms around me. Leaning down, he kisses the top of my head and says, "Relax, Goldie. Those are all details we'll continue to learn about each other. Things are fine."

"But... I don't want this to just be about sex," I insist as I push away from him. I know my voice sounds desperate when I say, "Damn it... if I'm going to change my ways, I want this to be different with us."

Tenn's eyes soften in empathy and a hand comes up to stroke my hair. "It is different with us. You know that deep down, right? You feel it? And while the sex is fucking phenomenal, it's also pretty fucking phenomenal to just hold you like this."

"God, you're really good at this," I say with a dreamy sigh and rest my head on his chest.

"But you feel it?" Tenn asks again, and although he's asking me a question, it's almost a foregone conclusion in his mind.

"I know I feel something I've never felt before," I

tell him shakily. "Scaring the shit out of me half the time and making me paranoid the other half."

He gives a hearty laugh. Pulling me away from his chest, his eyes twinkle at me with humor. He kisses me... hard... swift... possessively. "Well, I think you're very brave, Goldie, to give it a shot."

"Okay, I'm ready," Zoey yells from behind us as she comes running. "Mom and Kip are going to stay in there and eat a late breakfast."

Tenn releases me, turns to Zoey, and holds his arm up so she gets the message that he wants to tuck her into his side. She slams herself against him, her arms going around his waist, and he squeezes her in close.

God, that right there. That is so freakin' sexy to me.

Tenn turns toward my Jeep, guiding Zoey along with him. He reaches his hand back, palm open toward me in a silent indication he wants my digits locked with his. I slip my hand into his grasp and we all walk back to my car, with Zoey now babbling a hundred miles an hour.

"I cannot wait to get on the beach. Oh, and I read online that they have wild horses up in Corolla. Can we go see those? And I'd like to try to surf... that looks really cool, and Dad said your brother was a professional surfer, right Casey? So maybe he can teach me. And Dad... I'm kind of hungry. Can we go somewhere for something to eat first? Then maybe the beach."

Tenn shakes his head with a smirk on his face. He looks over at me and mouths the word, "Teenagers" at me.

"I bet there are a ton of cute boys on the beach, right Casey?" Zoey asks as her dad opens up the passenger door.

"And, that's my cue to go back and get her suitcase," Tenn mutters as Zoey hops in the back. He turns and gives me a grave look, "and you better tell her there aren't any cute boys on the beach."

Leaning in to him, I give a whisper, "I think she's going to figure out on her own that there will indeed be cute boys. And trust me... she's so pretty that she's going to have them surrounding her."

Tenn looks perplexed a moment before giving a confident shake of his head. "Nah... those boys will be too busy ogling you in your bikini and too busy being intimidated by her big biker dad to come anywhere near her. She's safe."

Sweeping his hand up to the passenger seat, Tenn says, "Hop in. I'll drive."

"Alpha man," I quip as I jump into the passenger seat.

"Your man," I barely hear Tenn say before he closes the door on me and heads toward Zoey's suitcase.

"I'm so glad you're dating my dad," Zoey says from the backseat. "He really likes you."

"Oh yeah?" I twist in my seat so I can see her.

"Yup," she says with a grin as she leans forward over the center console to get closer to me. "Talked about you a lot. He wanted to make sure I was cool with him spending time with you while I was visiting, and also that we'd be staying at your house."

"Um… yeah, about that," I stumble a bit. "Your dad and I… we um… that's to say, he'll be sleeping on the couch."

I have no clue if that's true or not. Tenn and I didn't discuss it much other than to agree that we'd have to be very discreet when we had sex, and we'd also have to be a whole lot quieter than we normally were.

Zoey rolls her eyes and gives me an admonishing look. "Puh-leeze. I know you're having sex. It's what adults do when they're together. Plus, I heard my mom say that Dad was probably only interested in you for the sex."

I blink at Zoey hard, trying to figure her out. My head spins a little. Did her mom really say that about me? Does Zoey believe that?

"But I think my mom's full of horse shit," she continues rambling on just as Tenn opens the back tailgate to put her suitcase in there. Zoey leans in a little bit closer to me and whispers, "I can see the way my dad looks at you. He's never looked like that with any other women he's dated. Oh, and I'd appreciate it if you didn't mention to Dad I cussed just now."

Wow. Just wow. She's like a little supercharged dynamo.

Tenn throws the suitcase in and slams the tailgate shut, walking toward the driver's side. I quickly whisper to Zoey. "I want to hear all about the women your dad dated in the past, okay? In return, I won't tell him you cussed. Deal?"

I reach my hand back and hold my pinky out. She grins and loops her pinky with mine. "Pinky swear," she giggles as Tenn opens the driver's side door.

"What's so funny?" he asks as he pushes my seat back and climbs in. He's in uncharacteristic shorts today since he's not on the bike and his powerful legs look magnificent as he folds into my Jeep.

"Nothing," Zoey says coyly, shooting me a wink before sitting back in her seat.

I think it's going to be just fine... having Zoey here. We're off to a pretty damn good start.

CHAPTER 18

Tenn

T HE POUNDING ON Casey's bedroom door jolts me upward and out of bed. Before my eyes are even fully focused, I know… just by sensing… that Casey's not beside me. Rubbing my eyes, I turn to her side and yup… she's gone.

"Come on, Dad," Zoey yells through the closed door. "Get up. Casey and I are ready to go down to the beach."

Christ… what do the women in my life have against sleeping in?

"I'm coming," I grumble as I roll off the bed and because I'm a complete dude and Casey's not around to laugh at me, I go ahead scratch my balls as I lurch into her bathroom.

Of course, I scratch my balls through the pair of workout shorts that Casey insisted I put on last night before we went to bed, just in case Zoey came into our room unannounced. Fat chance, since I locked the door, but it made Casey feel better.

I made sweet love to her last night with my hand clamped over her mouth to keep her quiet and moving extra slowly so the bed wouldn't creak or the headboard slap against the wall. Zoey had been asleep for a few hours, having been exhausted from the afternoon we had spent out on the beach together, but I didn't want to take any chances she'd hear us. She's a smart kid. She knows what's going down between Casey and me, but I don't want her *hearing* what goes on between us in private.

After doing my business, brushing my teeth, and not bothering at all to try to tame my hair, which is sticking up all over the place, I decide against shaving and get dressed. A pair of swim trunks I had bought last week and a t-shirt are good enough for someone who promised to spend all day on the beach with his daughter.

When I get out into the kitchen, I see Zoey sitting at the kitchen table eating eggs and bacon and chattering at Casey, who is leaning back against the counter, holding a cup of coffee, and smiling down at my daughter. And I'm not sure how it's possible, but Casey actually looks more beautiful right now than I've ever seen her before. No makeup... hair piled into a messy bunch on top of her head, a ratty old t-shirt, and a pair of shorts. And yeah, Casey is such a gorgeous woman, even without paying any attention to herself, she's ten times more beautiful than most women.

But what really strikes me this morning is the way she's looking at my daughter. A mixture of genuine interest and amused delight. She really, really likes Zoey, and there's something about that right there that makes me very possessive feeling. Like I want to drag her down to the nearest tattoo parlor and have my name tattooed over her heart. And maybe her name over my heart.

Shaking my head, because fuck... I'm a putz to be thinking those things... I walk into the kitchen.

Walking up to Zoey first, I lean over and kiss her on the top of her head. "I can't believe you're waking me up so early, brat."

She smiles while she happily chews her eggs, cutting a sly grin at Casey, which means she was behind this devious plot to get me out of bed.

Turning to Casey, I walk up to her, place my hands lightly on her hips, and lean in to brush my lips over hers. I slide my mouth over her cheek, right up to her ear where I murmur, "You were in on it too. Gonna make you pay for that later."

And she fucking shivers... right there, over the promise in my voice. When she whispers back, "Lucky me," I have to abruptly let her go and turn toward the coffee pot before I start to get a boner.

"Why are we up so early?" I ask curiously.

"Because... we want to get down on the beach," Zoey says.

"And I'm needed for that because?" I prompt.

"Because we both want to spend time with you," Casey says as she slaps my shoulder, "and I have to go into work at twelve today, so my time is limited."

"Oh, yeah… right," I say with a grin as I pour my coffee. "I'm made of so much damn awesomeness that my girls can't get enough of me."

Casey snorts, and Zoey gives me an eye roll.

I lean back against the counter, my own hip bumping up against Casey's. Looking over at Zoey, I say, "You know… instead of the beach, maybe Casey could take you shopping this morning for a few new bathing suits."

Casey remains noticeably quiet but Zoey gives me another eye roll, and then pins me with a look that says, "Seriously, Dad?"

"What?" I ask defensively. "What's wrong with that? And what girl doesn't love getting new clothes?"

"I have a bathing suit," Zoey says before turning her eyes back to her eggs.

Since subtle didn't work, I go for overt. "It's too revealing," I say pointedly. "Your mom shouldn't have bought that for you."

I expect Zoey to start a full-blown argument, so I'm surprised when Casey says, "I thought it was lovely."

"See," Zoey says as she shoots Casey an adoring look. "Casey thinks it's fine."

Yeah, well Casey doesn't have a fourteen-year-old daughter who had plenty of boys on the beach looking at her yesterday. They were looking at Casey too, but that didn't bother me. If I was going to beat up some punk kid for ogling, it will be for ogling my daughter, not Casey. She can hold her own.

Now, if it's a full-grown man… maybe one with a big, fat wallet… then yeah, I wouldn't mind stomping his ass into the sand if he ogled Casey, but that, thankfully, didn't happen yesterday.

My head turns slowly to look at Casey, one eyebrow cocked. "You think it's okay? What she had on yesterday?"

Casey looks a little torn, now that I've put her on the spot. I know she wants to stand by my side, and I'm sure she understands the parenting is left up to me, but I also know she wants to give her own opinion.

"Just give it to me straight, Goldie," I say.

"Um… I think I'll just stay out of this," she says hesitantly, and I know her need to appease me is winning out over her need to bond with Zoey. She averts her eyes and turns to pour the rest of her coffee down the drain. "I'm actually going to go get my bathing suit on and I'll be ready to go."

Zoey doesn't look back up at me but continues eating. I watch Casey walk away, and I'm stuck not knowing whether to argue with Zoey or not. I'm a little out of my depth here. It's the first time I've had to worry about these things with my daughter, and I don't want to fuck up. I want to be protective, but not stifling.

Pointing at the sink, I tell Zoey, "Wash your dish when you're done."

I follow Casey back into her bedroom, where I find her tying the strings of a tiny, white bikini at her hip. For a few moments, I get sidetracked, watching her work... looking at the narrow waist, the way her hips swell out beautifully, then her long, toned legs. When she finishes, she pulls her t-shirt off, and then I really get distracted by her beautiful breasts as they swing free. She pulls her bikini top on quickly over her head, the top strings already tied.

Casey shoots me a taunting look and says, "Want to tie the back for me?"

I stride over to her as she turns her back to me. I run my eyes down the golden skin of her back, focus in on a tiny mole she has just over the back of her right hip, and then to the beautiful ass below. I reach up, pull on the strings to make sure the cups are adequately covering her breasts and tie them at her back.

Stepping in closer to her, I bring my arms around and cup her breasts with my palms. She presses back into me and lets her head fall back onto my shoulder. I pinch each nipple between my thumbs and forefingers, relishing her whimper and the way they harden under my touch.

"Did I ever tell you how sexy you are?" I ask, tilting my head to run my lips up her neck.

She nods, and I can hear heat and longing in her voice. "You tell me a lot. You show me just as much."

Releasing her breasts, I wrap my arms around her waist and squeeze her tight, resting my chin on her shoulder. "Seriously… tell me honestly what you think about Zoey's bathing suit. You copped out in the kitchen."

Casey turns in my arms and loops hers over my shoulders, letting her fingers play in the hair at the back of my head. "Honestly, Tenn… her bathing suit is fine."

"It's a two-piece," I point out.

"And a modest one at that. It adequately covers her boobs and her butt, and even has a ruffle on the back end. It's sweet. I wore suits like that at her age."

"But she's exposed," I grumble. "And boys… did you see how many boys were vying for her attention out there yesterday?"

"I hate to tell this to you," Casey says with a sympathetic smile, "but your daughter is stunning. Doesn't matter if she's wearing a two-piece or a one-piece, they are going to swarm."

Lowering my forehead to hers, I let out a sigh. "She's growing up too fast. Makes me feel old and prudish."

Casey laughs, tilts her head up, and touches her lips to mine. "You are most definitely not prudish. Have you even listened to yourself when you talk dirty to me? You'd make a porn star blush."

I grin at her, kiss her quickly, and say, "I do like me some dirty talk."

"I like it when you talk dirty too." She grins back.

"So the suit is fine?" I ask again, just to verify one more time.

"It's fine. Besides, it's not like they're going to try anything with you sitting there."

"Fine," I say before kissing her one last time, thinking to make it quick, but when she slips her tongue in my mouth... well, there's no disregarding that move. So I kiss her deep instead but ultimately pull away when I start to feel lust stirring me below the waist.

My phone starts ringing, so I release Casey and walk over to her dresser where I had left it charging last night. I see it's Nix calling.

"What's up, man?" I ask as I connect the call.

"Looks like Emily and I can come down this weekend. Would that be good?"

On the heels of my visit to see Nix in New Jersey, we've continued to brainstorm over my business idea. I told him about the garage for sale here in Nags Head, and while he's questioning the locale, he did agree to come down and see it.

"Yeah, that sounds great, man. How long can you stay?"

"We'll stay a few nights... make it a mini vacation," he says. "Emily's dad actually has a friend with a house on the island, so we have a kickass place to stay."

Nix's fiancée Emily has connections. Her dad is a U.S. Senator, and the rumor mill is he's looking at a presidential run. Her family also comes from insane money, which gives me a little pause for concern, but I don't say anything about it just yet with Casey standing in the room with me. That's not a beast I've figured out how to tackle, because I do think some of Casey's views about rich people could be a little skewed.

"Okay, man… why don't you text me the details of when you'll be in and we'll arrange a time for you to see the garage, and then I figured we could get together one night and pound some beers," I tell Nix as Casey sashays past me into the bathroom.

"Works for me," he says and then disconnects after a quick, "Later."

"Nix coming down to visit?" Casey asks from the bathroom as I watch her take her hair down and rearrange it back up into something that looks just like the tousled pile she had up there before.

I walk over to the doorway and lean my shoulder against the jamb. "Yeah… this weekend."

"Cool," she says. "Although, I wish I had room to let them bunk here."

"They were able to get a place for a few days," I say vaguely and luckily, she doesn't ask me more details. I figure in the circles that Emily Burnham travels in, the house that was probably loaned to them is a mega-mansion like her friends Gavin and Savannah live in. I haven't seen it yet, but Casey tells me it's monstrous.

I'm not sure why I'm reticent to bring up the fact that Emily comes from a powerful family and lots of money. Casey has friends that are rich… Gavin, by way of example. And Brody's fiancée Alyssa is an heiress as well. But those are her friends… she knows them in the context away from their money, so I'm assuming Casey makes exceptions. But past that, Casey is admittedly judgmental when it comes to the power money gives people and the way in which it changes them.

Based on her experience with Jeff, she intimately ties money and power with a man's character, and that totally gives me concern because I haven't been overly forthcoming with Casey about my own background.

In a cowardly maneuver, I've glossed over a lot of the details about my family when Casey's asked. It's not because I'm necessarily hiding it, but it's that I don't want to give her any room to be skittish with me. After the "Jeff" ordeal, there's no telling what will come into that head of hers and her fragile sensibilities regarding relationships.

"Okay… I'm ready," Casey announces as she turns toward me and holds her arms out to the side for inspection.

My eyes slide over her… over golden skin that

I've pretty much licked every square inch of. Looking back up to her, I give her a smirk. "I guess you pass muster."

"Pass muster?" she asks dramatically with narrowed eyes. "This is the hottest thing you'll see on the beach today. I think I more than pass muster."

I grin licentiously at her, grab her by the waist, and pull her in for a kiss. After I rob the breath from her lungs with said kiss, I smile and rub my nose against hers. "You are the hottest, sexiest thing ever. You more than pass muster. You outshine the sun."

"God… your dirty talk is good, but your sweet talk is even better," Casey mutters as she shimmies past me and out the door of her bedroom.

I watch that fine ass as it sways out the door for just a moment before I follow her.

It's a massive production to get set up on the beach but by nine AM, we are in business complete with foldout lounge chairs, a cooler with ice and water for Casey and Coke for Zoey and me, towels, and the ever-needed sunscreen. I suggested getting one of those large umbrellas you stick in the sand, but Casey actually sneered at me.

"Shade is for wusses."

I threw up my hands in quick defeat and said, "Sorry, Miss Beach Goddess. Didn't know there were rules."

She just smirked at me, and then put on a production by slathering the front of her body with sunscreen. It took some concentrated effort on my part not to get turned on by that, but I managed and mainly because of my daughter being there. It's amazing how free I am with Casey when it's just me and her… having no boundaries when it comes to expressing our mutual desire for each other. With Zoey here, it's a bit different. I have to check myself so I don't say something completely dirty to Casey or I don't get a full-blown hard-on when she does something as simple as putting on sunscreen.

Casey and I get settled in beach chairs next to each other while Zoey heads down to the water's edge. She starts walking south, stopping every once in a while to pick up shells.

"I have off tomorrow and I'd like to take Zoey up to Corolla to see the wild horses," Casey says as she tilts her face up to the sun.

"Am I invited?" I ask playfully as I tilt my face up too, closing my eyes against the glare.

"Sure," she says impishly. "Why not?"

"Gee thanks," I mutter, slightly put out.

"It's just… I know how much Zoey loves horses, so I thought that would be something cool I could do for her."

"I love horses too, Goldie," I point out.

The creaking of Casey's chair has me opening my eyes and swiveling my head to look at her. She's turned over onto her side, one hand propping up her head and the other arm resting gracefully along the length of her ribs and hip. This position really catches my attention because her breasts squeeze together and… eyes back up to her face before I get a woody.

"So what was it like working on a ranch?" she asks curiously, her one hand now fiddling with the bow tie of her bikini bottoms at her hip. I swallow hard and make my eyes slide back to focus on her face, which… fuck… that's so beautiful, that alone would give me a hard-on.

So I decide to concentrate on the conversation. "It's hard work… up at dawn, usually done about the time the sun goes down. It's physically grueling, especially during the calving and branding seasons. And sometimes boring… many days are spent on horseback just riding the perimeter of the property, checking the fence line, and protecting the cattle from wolves and coyotes by our presence out there."

"Do you love horses or your motorcycle more?" she asks, her blue eyes looking lighter in the overhead sun.

"Hmmmm…" I pause to think because that's a damn good question. Something I've never considered before, and while I don't miss working the ranch, I do miss riding every day. "I'd have to say horses. I've been riding them since I was practically a baby. The motorcycle thing has only happened in the last several years."

"Alyssa has a horse that she keeps over at The Haven now," Casey says. She had told me about The

Haven, which was Alyssa and Brody's no-kill animal shelter they ran together. "She said I could bring Zoey over there to do some riding if I wanted."

"She would love that," I tell her, completely warmed over her thoughtfulness to give something to Zoey that she loves so much.

"You could ride too if you wanted," Casey adds on. "I think you'd look really hot on a horse."

"Hotter than on a motorcycle?" I ask, turning her original comparative question back on her somewhat.

"No way," Casey says firmly. "The hottest is you lying on my bed naked, on your stomach and sleeping. The way your arms curl around the pillow make your biceps bunch, and I get to see all of your beautiful tattoos. And your ass... damn, boy... it is the hottest, sweetest ass I've ever seen. Or licked for that matter."

I groan and lean my head back against the chair, closing my eyes and wishing I could close my ears. "I need you to stop talking now, Casey. You're getting a little too good at dirty talk."

She chuckles, and I can hear the creaking of her chair as she rolls over onto her back.

CHAPTER 19

Casey

TENN ON A motorcycle? Very hot.

Tenn on a horse? No words in the English language can describe.

I took Alyssa up on her offer to let Tenn and Zoey ride her horse, Sasquatch. He's an Appaloosa gelding that she rescued a few months ago. After she rehabbed him, she'd grown way too attached and decided to keep him. This necessitated her hiring Gabby to expand the current barn outward to add another stall.

Not knowing much about horses, I kept my distance as Alyssa and Zoey got him saddled. He seems to be a relatively calm horse, but his size intimidates me a bit. Not Zoey, though. She hopped right up and took off after Alyssa pointed her to a riding trail she and Brody had cleared out last year.

While we waited for her, Alyssa put Tenn and me to work helping to bathe some of the dogs. This is, of course, one of my favorite things to do when I volunteer at The Haven. It's the perfect thing to do on a hot summer day too, and it doesn't hurt to have a gorgeous man by your side doing it.

We got a grand total of five of the dogs done when Zoey came trotting back up to the back of the kennel, easily swinging her tiny frame off the big horse.

And looking like he'd just won the lottery, Tenn's eyes shined with excitement as he took the reins and hauled himself up in the saddle. One would think a tall man wearing faded jeans, a Harley t-shirt, and black biker boots would look odd in the saddle, but my damn mouth watered as I looked up at him. He had pulled a beaten-up University of Wyoming ball cap out of his back pocket—courtesy of his brother, Woolf, who he had told me graduated there—stuck it on his head, and cantered off.

It was only when the dog that I was bathing decided to shake the wet soap off, spraying me in the face, did I turn my gaze from Tenn as he rode away on the horse.

"You really like my dad, huh?" Zoey asked as she squatted down beside me at the large, metal tub.

"Yeah," I say with another glance at his retreating form in the distance. "I really kind of do."

"He says you have commitment issues but he's working on fixing that," Zoey says innocently, now sticking her hands into the soapy water to help scrub down the Springer Spaniel who looks at us with morose eyes.

Shaking my head with a smile on my lips, I can only let Zoey's words roll over me. Over the last week she's been here, I've learned that fourteen-year-old girls don't have much of a filter over their mouths. Zoey, in particular, says whatever is on her mind, never with any ill will or malice, but with a brutal honesty. It's why I give her a pass, because true enough… I do have commitment issues.

"What do you think of my dad moving here?" she asks, and when I cut my eyes to her, I see a little bit of overprotectiveness in her gaze.

And damn… that's sweet. She's checking me out on behalf of her dad.

Taking the spaniel by the collar, I help urge him to hop out of the tub so I can rinse him down. He's only too happy to comply as this dog clearly doesn't like "bath time".

"You want my honest thoughts?"

"No sense in lying," she says with a grin. "I can smell a liar a mile away."

Laughing, I tell her, "Here… come hold his collar as he's likely to jet away when I turn the water on."

When Zoey has the pup in her control, I grab the hose and start running the stream over his back, using my hands to push out the soap as I go along.

"So… your dad is pretty amazing," I tell her candidly. "He's made me look at things a bit differently."

"He's good at that," Zoey says with a nod.

"Yeah, well, I can be pretty pigheaded about certain things, so he's like really good at it," I say with a chuckle. Continuing to rinse the dog, who intermittently tries to shake out the water of his coat, I tell her, "Without telling you the details, some guy messed up my head a long time ago. Hurt me pretty bad and then I sort of used that as an excuse to close myself off from relationships."

"Because you didn't want to get hurt again?"

"Exactly. I was protecting myself," I confirm as I step away from the dog and turn the water off. He gives a vigorous shake, spraying Zoey down nicely.

She just laughs and turns her face away until he's done, then looks back over him at me. "Good thing my dad came along and set you straight."

"I'm sort of a work in progress," I tell her truthfully. "Still scared but because your dad is so amazing, I'm really trying to push past that."

She considers that for a moment and then with a voice that borders on almost pleading, she says, "Please don't hurt him. I think you have the ability to do that."

Ouch. That hurt.

Letting the hose drop to the concrete, I step over to Zoey and squat down so I'm eye level with her. "I promise you that I will never intentionally hurt him. And I also promise I will continue to work hard at moving past my insecurities. Your dad is extremely good at pushing me nicely but also giving me room to falter. That's how people learn the best."

"Good enough," she says, and then with a completely unfiltered mouth adds on, "because it would be awesome if y'all got married."

I shake my head at her as I stand up and give her an admonishing smile. "Your dad and I have known each other going on four weeks now. I don't think marriage is something we should be talking about at this point in our relationship."

"But he loves you," Zoey says with innocent candor as she stands up, keeping her hand on the spaniel's collar.

Her words... so simple, said with somewhat of a child's view on the world, and yet they slam into me like a nuclear punch. My voice actually shakes when I ask her, "Why do you say that?"

She gives me a sly smile and leads the dog over to a hook on the wall that has a leash. Taking it, she snaps it to his collar. "He looks at you the way he looks at me. That's how I know."

An overload of emotion swarms through me, making my chest ache and feel warm at the same time. Only one man has ever said he loved me and that was a man who absolutely lied about it. Other men have come close, but I never let them get the words out of their mouths, the thought of hearing it almost sending me into a full-blown panic.

Which begs the question... does Tenn really love me and if so, how do I feel about it?

Little bursts of panic that recede just as quickly as they exploded, then a nice feeling of comfort settles over me. A secure feeling. Peace, maybe?

The thought of Tenn loving me is… actually okay, I think.

Now I just have to figure out what my feelings are for him, because as much as I've learned over the many years I've played at being a seductress, the one thing I know absolutely nothing about is what it really means to love a man.

◆

"ARE YOU SURE you're okay walking up there by yourself?" Tenn asks Zoey for the third time as he hands her over a twenty-dollar bill.

Typical Zoey, she shoots him the old teenage eye roll. "Yes, Dad. You can see the pier from here. It's not like I'm traveling to Mozambique."

I snicker and start walking up the stairs to my house. We just got back from The Haven, and I have to get ready for work. Zoey asked if she could go up to the pier because some of the friends she had made on the beach over the last week will be up there hanging out. Tenn is about ready to freak out about his daughter wandering off, and I think it's adorable.

"When will you be back?" he asks.

"Few hours?" she asks back, to make sure that's okay.

"Fine," he grumbles, and she turns to start running back toward the public beach access. But he can't help himself when he calls out to her, "You have your phone on you, right?"

She waves a dismissive hand over her head and doesn't answer. He continues to watch her until she's out of sight, and I feel compelled to walk back down the steps to him. Placing my hands on his shoulders, I lean forward and kiss the back of his neck. "Relax, Daddy. She'll be fine."

Tenn doesn't answer me for a moment, continuing to look at the walkway over the dunes where she just disappeared. When he finally does turn to face me, his eyes are filled with white-hot lust, blazing so intensely that I actually jerk backward.

"Get upstairs and get naked now," he growls at me, placing his hands on my hips and roughly turning me around. A small push on my lower back to start climbing and he says, "Really, really need to fuck you, Casey."

Heat scorches me from the inside out and my belly flutters. It's stupid to say it, but I argue, "I have to be at work soon. I can't be late."

"Fuck work," he says, pushing me faster up the stairs, and when I reach the top, he simply spins me around, bends over, and throws me over his shoulder. "Give me the keys."

I pass him my key chain and he deftly unlocks my door, pushing it open and leaving it that way as he makes his way through my house. The keys drop to the floor and then he's in my bedroom, tossing me on the bed.

Tenn starts stripping quickly, eyes focused first on his boots, then on his belt. He glances over to me, sees me just leaning on my elbows while I watch him undress, and growls again. "Naked, Casey."

Even as I reach to pull my shirt over my head, I grumble, "I'm going to be late for work."

Tenn snorts as he whips his shirt over his head, the muscles in his stomach flexing with the action and giving me a peep at the washboard that apparently resides just under the skin. "I seriously doubt your brother will fire you."

He takes his jeans off lightning fast, pushing his boxers right along with them, and then he's gloriously naked at the foot of my bed, stroking a very magnificent and beautiful erection. I take a moment just to appreciate, and then I start shimmying out of my shorts and underwear. Tenn pounces about the time they get pushed to my knees, jerking them the rest of the way off me.

I start to undo my bra, but he mutters, "Leave it" and places a large hand on my chest to push me down. Roughly jerking my legs apart, he turns my insides to jelly when he levels me with a promising stare. "Going to eat you out... fucking devour you actually, then I'm going to fuck you hard."

"God, that's sexy," I moan, spreading my legs

further to him.

His eyes glitter at me and as he strokes a finger through my wet folds, he says, "This quiet lovemaking we've been doing has been supremely nice, Goldie, but I've been dying to hear you scream. Now that Zoey's gone… well, I really am looking forward to *making* you scream."

"And, I could just come from your words alone," I say as a full-body shudder overtakes me.

Tenn levels me with a wicked grin and then dives down in between my legs. His long fingers spread me apart and his tongue works his magic, causing every muscle in my body to clench hard over the pleasure he gives me. He alternates spearing his tongue inside of me to fluttering the tip over that home-run spot, and when he adds two fingers that push deep inside of me, my hips fly off the bed as I start to come.

A long moan tears out of me and even while spasms are still playing havoc on my body, Tenn is flipping me over and pulling me up to my knees.

"Grab the headboard, Casey," he grits out with urgency. "You're going to need to brace yourself."

And wow… just wow… the threatening promise in those words causes mini orgasms to fire up and slingshot up my spine. My hands go out and grab onto the edge of the wood and the minute I grip on tight, Tenn is thrusting hard into me from behind.

He lets out a groan of such deep satisfaction and fills me so completely, more spasms shoot up my back.

And then he does indeed proceed to fuck me hard. He pulls that long length out of me, almost to the tip… almost to the point of empty desolation within me, and then he's ramming it back in so hard his balls slap against me.

Every time… he grunts, hisses, or moans from the friction he's causing.

Every time he slams into me, more tingles race up and down my back and another orgasm builds.

Every time he fills me up, I feel my heart filling up as well.

Tenn leans forward over me, bringing one hand up to lay beside mine on the headboard. The other comes to the back of my head where he fists my hair and pulls on it, twisting my head to the side so he can close his mouth over mine. He kisses me deep, his thrusts going a bit slower as he takes the time to let our tongues mate. Then he pulls his mouth away, drops his hand from my hair to my shoulder, and then uses his leverage by holding onto the headboard to fuck me harder yet.

His thrusts now are hitting me so deep, the entire bed is rocking back and forth and we have to pull our hands back a bit so our fingers don't get slammed in between the wood and the wall. Tenn merely uses that as an opportunity to lace his fingers with mine, and then push them against the front of the head-board for continued leverage.

"Tenn," I whimper as he continues to heave inside my body.

"What is it, baby?" he gasps as he pumps in and out, over and over.

"Feels so good," I tell him… my words coming out in choppy spurts because he simply steals my breath in all ways.

Tenn leans over me again, moving his hand from my shoulder to wrap his entire arm over my chest. His stomach presses into my spine, and I can feel his forehead drop to the back of my head. "I am never letting you go," he says through clenched teeth. "And I don't care if it scares the shit out of you. You're going to have to deal with it."

My heart squeezes hard.

Oh… Tenn… what are you doing to me?

"Want you to see everything you've been missing," he says softly as he continues to tunnel in and out of me. "Want you to crave me the way I crave you."

My eyes start misting with tears over the need in his voice. A ball of pleasurable tension contracts tight in my center as he continues to drive deep into me.

"You're mine, Casey," he says dangerously. "And nothing will stand in my way to keep you. Not even you."

The confident and dominating way in which he's claiming me finally causes all of my resistance to cave. My orgasm breaks free like a thunderclap at the same time I feel the walls around my heart start to crumble with the realization... a realization deep in the marrow of my bones, that Tenn would never abuse my heart.

I'd gladly give it to him and while he holds it within his big, powerful hands, I know he would only ever give it the most delicate of care.

I cry out from the force of my release as much as from the understanding that Tenn Jennings may just be my salvation. I cry his name out loud and with deep emotion, "Tenn!"

Tenn slams hard into me once more, his body freezing in that perfect moment, and he moans, "Fucking coming... coming deep inside you, baby."

Shuddering, his breath gusts out over the back of my head. He releases my hand pinned against the headboard, wraps it over his other arm across my chest, and pulls us both upright to our knees while I can feel him pulsing wetly inside of me. He squeezes me hard... to the point of cutting off my breath, but I don't care.

It feels too good to care.

As he grinds his pelvis against my ass, tiny tremors race through me, zinging all around and plucking at my nerves. My heart feels like it's about to explode from my chest.

My. Heart. Actually. Feels.

It actually feels damn good.

CHAPTER 20

Jenn

"**A**RE YOU OKAY?" Casey asks as I pull into the parking lot of The Last Call to drop her off for work. We're in her Jeep but call it a man thing, I like to have the wheel.

I drive up to the front door and shoot her a sad smile. "Miss her bad already."

"Me too," she says, leaning across the console to kiss my cheek.

Zoey's mom picked her up this morning. We met at the same spot… the Sand Shark… and it just about killed me to say goodbye. Having her with me the last two weeks reminded me of just how much I really need her more in my life. There is no doubt about me relocating to North Carolina. It gets me far from Wyoming and the ranch and puts me right by my daughter. But one thing I've come to realize over the last few weeks, I don't think I'm ready to settle with having Zoey only on weekends, summer breaks, and holidays. I want her full time, and I talked a lot with

Zoey the last few weeks. She wants the same, so I'm going to start working to make that happen.

Oddly, I think this might just have something to do with my relationship with Casey. Every day that goes by, I can feel her stepping closer and closer to me. I can feel her fear melting and her trust building. Every day that goes by, I find myself falling more and more in love with her.

And that is one tried and true fact. I fucking love Casey Markham.

I want to make a life with her. I don't know what that means to her, but to me, it eventually means marriage and children.

Fuck... we'd make some pretty ass babies, for sure.

Six weeks and I'm already in so deep with her that I'm starting to forget what life was like before her. It's almost like I didn't exist prior to her.

With the lone exception of Zoey, it's almost as if my entire world was just waiting for Casey to walk in so that my life would have meaning. So no matter what happens with Nix on this visit, I've already decided to buy that garage for sale and start working toward building up this business. I've already committed in my mind that I'm not going back to Wyoming, even if Woolf doesn't decide to step up to the plate. I'm leaving the ranch and my legacy behind so I can start a new life here on the East Coast with the woman I love and will do whatever I need to do to make her mine in all respects.

Slipping my hand behind Casey's head, I pull her in for a soft kiss. "We'll be back to pick you up at six."

"Sounds great," she says with a sweet smile as she opens the passenger door. "Can't wait to meet Nix and Emily."

"Bye, Goldie," I say as she hops out.

"Bye, hot stuff," she says with a wink before closing the door. I wait for her to walk inside and then pull out of the parking lot.

I agreed to meet Nix and Emily at the garage as he had texted me that he was in town. They went straight to the beach house where they were staying to unload their stuff, and we decided to meet over at the garage as soon as I dropped Casey off at work. Because the realtor is friends with Casey and knew I just wanted Nix to take a quick look, he was more than happy to give me the key.

It takes me no more than five minutes to get down the highway to the garage. When I pull in, I see a nondescript dark green sedan, figuring that to be Nix's rental car. They flew into New Bern and then drove the hour and a half here, which was a much easier drive than Raleigh, although the plane schedules were not as frequent.

I pull up beside them and both doors open up. Nix stepping his tall frame out with his eyes immediately roving over the building in interest. Emily hops out and walks up beside him, casually slipping her hand in his. He looks down and gives her a smile that is both loving and reverent at the same time.

Nix is one badass motherfucker. He was with MARSOC in the Marine Corps, which is our line of elite Special Forces. He could snap Emily's neck with probably just his thumb and forefinger, but the way he looks at her now... big, bad Marine has fallen hard.

I can empathize. I feel the same.

Nix looks back to me as I get out and shut the Jeep door. "Dude," he says, jerking his chin up.

I walk up to him and hold my fist out, which he promptly bumps with his. "Dude," I respond.

And just like that, the male-greeting ritual between old friends is complete. I lean down and kiss Emily on the cheek. "Emily... looking beautiful but standing next to his ugly mug, how could you not?"

She slaps my chest and wraps an arm around Nix's waist. "My man is the most beautiful creature on this earth.

Nix winces and corrects her. "Um... honey, that's not a very studly way to describe me. Maybe I'm the hottest fucking man in the universe would be more appropriate."

I snicker and turn toward the side office, wrestling the key into the lock. Nix and Emily follow me in when I open the door. "This was used as an office and it's big enough we could do that, but it's also big enough we could put a bike on display in here as well."

Nix nods as he walks around the space. Emily walks behind the built-in reception desk and says, "I'd move this into the corner to open up the space more."

"Agreed," I tell her as I follow Nix over to a side door that leads into the garage area.

When he steps through, he whistles in appreciation. "Whoever had this didn't fuck around with equipping it."

"I know," I say with a small measure of excitement. "And all of it is included in the list price. As far as the engine work, I wouldn't have to buy much to get it up and running."

He doesn't respond but continues to circle the area, running his hand over some of the shelving and tools. Emily also comes in and looks around with a keen eye.

"I'm worried about the location… if we do this," Nix says as he turns to face me, shoving his hands deep into his jeans pockets. "It's a small community. Not much visibility. Nothing around for miles. Not much commerce."

"All true," I tell him. "But this type of business isn't going to depend on walk-in traffic. The type of product we'll sell is custom and pricey. People who buy from us won't be stumbling in. They'll find us by word of mouth, website, or referral. This is just a place for me to do the work, and I've decided I want to do my work here on this island."

Nix snorts and gives me a knowing look. "I'm assuming that has something to do with a woman."

"*The* woman," I correct him with a grin.

"Nix said her name is Casey, right?" Emily asks. "So fill us in on the scoop."

I had told Nix about her briefly when I went up to New Jersey. That was so early on in our relationship, I didn't have a whole lot to tell other than the fact I'd met a woman who was both amazing and untouchable at the same time.

Nix's advice?

Keep reaching out. Keep trying to touch. Make her touchable.

It was great fucking great advice and I followed it, but I had not had a chance to update him on everything. Dudes don't call each other up to talk about our girls, love, and romance. But with Emily here asking, I get a free pass.

"Well, let's see… she's gorgeous and sexy. Looks fucking fantastic on the back of my bike. Uncommonly beautiful but completely down to earth. You both are really going to like her. And she's a bit broken… bad history, but she's been working to overcome it."

"Broken how?" Emily asks with sympathy, her eyes warm and limpid.

"Let's just say a terrible experience with a man that left her… um… a little jaded."

"And you've shown her the light?" Emily asks with a romantic sigh.

"I've shown her something," I say with a mischievous grin. "She's warming up to me, let's just say."

"Well, she has to know what a great catch you are," Emily says firmly. "Hot dude who is heir to a cattle baron. That's enough to make any girl swoon."

I internally wince and scratch my head. "Yeah... um... Casey doesn't exactly know the details about the ranch. She thinks I'm just an unemployed mechanic with a bright business idea."

Nix's jaw drops. "Dude... you can't keep shit like that from her if you're trying to build something here."

"It's like lying," Emily affirms. "And why would you care if she knows that? It's a good thing, right?"

"Casey's a little jaded when it comes to rich men," I say bluntly. "The guy that fucked her head up was rich and entitled, and she does not look kindly on men like that now. Kind of lumps them in a category."

"You're rich dude," Nix confirms with a grave nod. "But you are not entitled. Surely, she sees that."

I shrug my shoulders helplessly. "I suppose she sees that because all she's seen is Tenn Jennings... a mechanic. And to clarify... I'm not rich. My father is."

"You have a trust fund," Nix points out in reminder. "It's what you're going to use to front this business."

"I know," I grumble as I start to head back to the side door that leads back to the office. "I know I have to figure out a way to tell her this shit. It's just… we get so caught up in other things that it never seems to be the right time."

"I'm thinking you're talking about some really smokin' hot sex, right?" Nix starts to say, but then Emily backhands him in the stomach, causing him to bend over and grunt.

"Quit asking him about his sex life, you perv," she huffs, and then looks at me as I hold open the door for her to walk through. "Take it from me… a woman… we do not like secrets. You need to out yourself sooner rather than later, Tenn."

"I'll take that under advisement," I tell Emily with a nod of my head.

And I will. I just have to figure out whether or not I trust Goldie to accept this about me. Is she in deep enough with me that it won't matter? Or will this cause her to get skittish on me again? Possibly cause her to bolt? Worse… will it diminish the trust she's put in me so far?

I wish I knew the answer to those questions. The painful and obvious thing to draw from that is the reason I don't know the answers is because I guess I don't trust that Casey is feeling the same things I am. While she has admitted to falling for me, I still have no clue what that really means. For a woman that gave so very little to the men in her life, that could mean something as little as just liking the fantastic sex. Truly… it could not mean much at all in Casey's world.

Sucks to have doubts, but there you go.

I am not deterred, however.

When I told Casey the other night that I wasn't going to let her go, I meant it. I'm sticking around, and I am going to take whatever she chooses to give me. Then I'm going to keep at her, chipping away at her walls until every last fear and reservation has been obliterated. Will it take days? Weeks? Months?

Fuck… it could take a lifetime, but I'm not going anywhere.

◆

NIX, EMILY, AND I walk into The Last Call. My original thought had been to grab Casey and go somewhere for dinner, but then I thought… why not just stay here? They have great food and great beer, plus one fantastic view of the ocean from the back deck. So I texted Casey and suggested it, and she texted back that she'd have Hunter reserve us a prime table outside.

As we walk through the growing crowd, I can see Casey's already gone from behind the bar, so I head straight out to the deck with Nix and Emily following me. We had a productive afternoon. Grabbed a bite to eat at a local restaurant, introducing my friends to the East Coast treasure of fried seafood that I've become quite addicted to. Then we went back to Casey's house and sat at her kitchen table, ironing out details.

"So what do you think?" I'd asked him... but cut my gaze over to Emily, as I knew she was part of this as well.

"We're interested," he said, referencing both he and Emily. "We've been talking about it since you came up to visit, and it could be a great way to supplement my income since my work is all commission based and requests for metal art are few and far between. What would you need from us?"

"Well, we need to work up a formal business plan," I mused as I got up from the table and foraged around in one of Casey's drawers until I found a small pad of paper and a pen. "The building list price is $220,000, and we'll need to put down twenty percent at least. We'll need some start-up supplies and a budget for advertising, most of which would probably be in a website build. Some money to front shipping costs since you'll do the metal work up in New Jersey and ship the parts down to me. I'm thinking... maybe $75,000 on the low end, $100,000 on the high end. Fifty-fifty partnership."

Nix whistled through his teeth. "That's some serious cashola. I don't have fifty grand laying around."

"I do," I told him bluntly. "I'll front the entire cost and we can work out a way for me to recoup those from first sales over a period of time. Or dude… listen, if you don't want in as a business partner, I'll contract with you exclusively and pay you on commission."

Nix shook his head. "No, I want in as a partner. It's a great opportunity and if you're willing to help me front the buy in, I'll take it."

"Nix," Emily said hesitantly. "My dad will give us the money."

Before the words even finished leaving those lips, Nix was shaking his head. "No way. We're doing this on our own."

Emily merely smiled in understanding and then turned to me. "I think we should do it. The goal should be for us to iron out the framework for a business plan before we leave on Sunday."

"Awesome," I said with a bright smile, sticking my hand across the table toward Nix. "Partners."

"Partners, man," he said gruffly as he shook my hand.

So yeah… the wheels are in motion. We have so much to do, and I doubt this will get launched at least for a few months, but we have an initial game plan. And I can't wait to tell Casey about it, because today is the day that I made the one-hundred percent commitment to stay here in Nags Head.

With Casey.

And I hope she looks forward to it somewhat.

Speaking of the woman who captured my heart, I see her as soon as I push through the glass door that leads out onto the deck. She's sitting at one of the tables closest to the ocean, her back to me as she stares out at the water that is turning pink from the sun setting behind us in the west. Her long hair hangs over the back of her chair, and she has her flip-flopped feet propped up on one of the companion chairs.

I walk over to her, come up right behind her, and lean my head over until she sees me. She tilts her head way back and gives me a beautiful, upside-down smile. I, in turn, give her a fast, upside-down kiss.

"Hey beautiful," I tell her when I pull my lips free.

Casey pushes to her feet as I step back from her chair. She walks around and stands beside me so I can put my arm around her waist as Nix and Emily walk up. Leaning over to kiss her on the side of her head, I say, "Goldie… this is my buddy, Nix, and his fiancée, Emily."

Casey leans forward to shake each of their hands. "I'm so glad to meet you both."

With greetings out of the way, we go ahead and take seats around the circular table with Casey to my left and Emily to my right, putting Nix in between both women as well. A waitress comes over, takes our drink orders, and gives us some menus.

We engage in plenty of chitchat while we decide what we want to eat, and take a moment to enjoy the colored water as the sun fades behind us while we sip at frosty beers.

"It's so beautiful here," Emily murmurs as she gives Casey a smile. "You are so lucky to live in a place like this."

"Don't I know it," Casey says with such fondness in her voice, it makes my heart clench. "It's a great community, and all my friends and family are close by."

I decide now is as good a time as any to break the news to her. And much to my dismay, my body immediately braces in anticipation that Casey may not be very excited about my tidings.

"Speaking of friends and family being close by, I need you to get your realtor ass working and find me a place to live," I say nonchalantly before taking a large swig of my beer.

Casey's head snaps toward me and her jaw drops slightly. But her eyes... fuck, can't read a damn thing in them.

"So, does that mean—?" she starts to ask neutrally.

"That I'm going to be staying?" I ask for her. "Because yeah... Nix and I decided to buy that garage and set up here in Nags Head."

Those beautiful blue eyes stare at me blankly for a moment, and I start to internally cringe. But then I'm shocked as shit as Casey comes flying out of her chair and launches herself at me. She crawls onto my lap, oblivious of Nix and Emily or the other thirty people on the deck. She wraps her arms around my neck and plasters her mouth to mine in a kiss so deep and hot I have no choice but to bring my arms around her waist and press her in tighter to me.

When she finally lifts her face away from me, I'm stunned to see absolute joy and happiness radiating from her eyes. "You're really moving here?" she asks, her voice quavering with excitement.

I just nod dumbly at her, not trusting my own fucking voice.

And then she kisses me again… just as deep, just as hot, and much longer this time. But fuck it… this is awesome, so I kiss her back and it's not until Nix starts coughing that we both break apart.

"You excited, Goldie?" I ask in wonder.

She nods at me enthusiastically. "And I'm happy. Really, really happy."

God… I fucking love this woman.

CHAPTER 21

Casey

I T'S THAT TIME again.

Monday.

Breakfast date with my girlies.

And this time, it feels completely different. This time… and for the first time… I now have something in common with every other woman sitting at this table with me. Gabby, Alyssa, Savannah, and Andrea. Like dominos, they all fell for a man… and in exactly that order.

I was the last woman standing. The one, who every Monday that we met for breakfast, would regale my girls with my sexual exploits and conquests, while they would regale me with tales of love and babies and commitment. Usually, when they did that, I would only hear *blah, blah, blah, blah*. Now, I wonder, is that what they heard from me when I would tell them about the newest, rich dude I was banging to get another notch in my bedpost of vindication?

It's hilarious to me, that at right this very moment, four pairs of eyes look at me expectantly as I doctor up my coffee. Four women know me so well that they know I'm a different person as I sit here before them.

"So spill it," Gabby says with impatience while her eyes dart back and forth from my face to the sugar I'm stirring into my cup.

"I should make you suffer and wait," I say with a degree of superiority, "but I am internally and quite quietly squealing on the inside I'm so excited, so I won't make you wait."

All four women put their elbows on the table and lean in closer to me with watchful eyes and excited smiles. I look briefly to each of them, so freakin' pumped that I can truly join their little circle.

With a huge gust of air through my lips because I'm getting ready to impart something absolutely monumental to my girls, I say, "Okay, here goes... I really like Tenn."

Four sets of eyes blink at me. Four smiles slide away and four women look at me blankly.

My head roves back and forth, looking at each woman, waiting for them to start squealing for me.

More blank stares.

"For Pete's sake, Casey," Gabby says impatiently. "We know that much."

"You do?" I ask, and now I'm the one blinking at her dumbly.

"Well duh," Alyssa says with knowing eyes.

"How?" I ask, again… more dumb blinking.

"You invited him to my birthday party," Andrea supplies.

"And you were really cozy with him," Savannah, the romantic, says with a dreamy sigh.

"And I have it from Hunter, who heard from Kent, that you were all over him this past weekend at The Last Call. The intel I received said that you climbed on his lap and kissed and dry humped him in public, while looking deliriously happy doing so," Gabby says with a confirming nod.

"I did not dry hump him," I say with offense.

Not much, anyway.

"The point is," Andrea says as she reaches over and pats my hand. "It's pretty obvious you like him. So we need more details than that."

My first reaction is to clam up… keep the warm and fuzzies close to my chest because I'm not sure I still trust them fully. While I have very tender feelings for Tenn, and while I know without a doubt there will never be a man like him again in my life, I'm still leery of admitting my feelings have turned deep. It might be the last barrier between me and my former self that's left, and as weird as it is, it's comforting to me.

But then I look at these women. All of them so strong and independent, and yet not one of them lost that when they fell in love. Not one of them gave up themselves. If anything, their lives were greatly enhanced.

Every single one of these women have stood by me, Gabby more so than the others since we practically learned how to walk together. Every one of them have watched me burn through men without a judgmental look or a reprimanding word. They let me be the Casey I needed to be, and not one of them even had a clue what was driving me. That was how supportive they were of me.

"I went on a dinner date with Jeff Parkhurst," I blurt out.

"Huh?" Gabby mumbles. "I'm lost. What the hell are you talking about?"

"Jeff Parkhurst. The night after Andrea's party," I clarified.

"But you were seeing Tenn," Savannah says worriedly.

"I was," I tell her with an embarrassed smile. "And Tenn knew about it."

"I'm more than just lost," Gabby says, her brow wrinkled in confusion. "What are you trying to tell us, Casey?"

Taking a deep breath, I look at Gabby with determination. This is for all the girls, but mostly for Gabby. "I dated Jeff for four weeks in high school. He told me he loved me, and I gave him my virginity the night that Brody was taken to prison."

"I know that," Gabby says in agreement. "I thought you saw him for a shorter period of time though."

"It was a long time ago," I say sadly, perfectly aware of how much of my life was wasted on these memories. "I overheard him about a week later talking to his buddies about me. I won't get into the gory details but he basically said I was a great fuck but that was all I was good for. That I wasn't good enough for his circle. He pointed out my dad was a fisherman and my brother was a felon."

"What the fuck?" Gabby explodes and comes halfway out of her chair, causing the cups to rattle hard. "I'll kill that asshole."

"Pipe down," Alyssa says with a restraining hand on Gabby's shoulder. "Let Casey finish."

I give Gabby a thankful smile... for having my back. Then I tell her as honestly as I can, "He ruined me, Gabs. That was when I changed."

A light sparks in Gabby's eyes, and understanding filters in. She knows me well. Now that she knows my motivator, she can easily figure out why I took the course I took.

"You only went out with men like Jeff Parkhurst," she says in amazement. "Not just rich men... but men just as conceited and self-important as Jeff. You were gorgeous and fabulous and you made those men beg you for a chance, and then you walked away. You let them know they weren't good enough for you."

I nod my head in absolute shame, my eyes lowering to my cup. "Some of them didn't deserve it."

"You never led them on," Gabby says, and she knows this about me because I've always been candid with not only my conquests, but with my friends when it came to how I treated said conquests. I openly shared my boundaries of no love, no commitment, and no hassles with friends and lovers alike.

"I didn't," I agree. "But regardless of the type of men they were, I guess no one deserved for me to take my wrath out on them."

"I want to get back to the part about you going on a date with him," Alyssa says.

"It was so stupid," I say sheepishly. "I saw him at the grocery store and I had every intention of just laying into him, but then I thought... I should do to him what he did to me. So he really knows how it feels."

"So you were going to do what?" Savannah asks in confusion.

"She was going to bring him to his knees with lust, and then she was going to walk away," Gabby says confidently. "And yeah... that was a stupid idea, Casey."

"I know," I say with a grimace. "Tenn flipped out—"

"As he should have," Gabby butts in and when my eyes flash at her, she says, "Sorry... please continue."

"I never intended to cross any line with Jeff. It was only meant to be words to get him hot. And trust me, my dirty talk is really hot. I told Tenn that but of course, he was still pissed."

"As he should have been," Gabby mumbles, and I ignore her.

"But I couldn't go through with it. I left him in the restaurant," I tell her, and she smiles at me brightly. "And Tenn was right there waiting for me... ready to support me no matter what the outcome was."

"And what was the outcome?" Andrea asks.

"Tenn totally roughed Jeff up, made him get on his knees before me to apologize, and then made him pee his pants," I say with a wicked grin.

All four women break out in loud cackles, Savannah hunches over holding her stomach, Andrea slapping at the table, and Gabby with tears rolling out of her eyes. "Tell me you're making that up," she huffs. "Because that's the funniest thing I've ever heard in my life."

Shaking my head... chuckling with my peeps, I assure her, "I swear to God. He fucking peed his pants."

"Oh my God," Alyssa snorts. "I think I'm going to pee mine."

"Tenn is like the most perfect man ever," Gabby says dreamily. "Next to Hunter, of course."

"So you see," I say, bringing the conversation around full circle. "I really like him."

"Oh, baby," Alyssa says with a knowing look.

"You more than like him."

"Maybe," I admit while nibbling on my lower lip. "I don't know. I've never had these feelings before."

"What does it feel like?" Savannah asks earnestly, her lovely face tilted in curiosity.

I close my eyes briefly, and the image of Tenn's face magically appears in my mind. "When I'm with him, it's so comforting. It's like I'm continually immersed in my favorite smell of sea salt and coconuts or like I'm being wrapped in my grand-mother's old afghan. Tenn feels like that giddy first day of summer vacation, and my insides feel like a litter of wiggling puppies whenever he looks at me. It feels strange, and dangerous, and like I'm on the edge of falling into something great and mysterious with all the promise in the world." I open my eyes, immediately seeing all four of my girls staring at me with romantic eyes and lips slightly parted in surprise. I smile at them, and lower my eyes shyly. "Yeah… it feels like the lifting of dark clouds on a rainy day… that moment when the sun peeks out and a rainbow magically appears."

"Wow," Alyssa murmurs.

"Dying here," Savannah sighs.

"Speechless," Andrea says.

"Holy shit, girl," Gabby exclaims. "You are so in love with him."

My entire body startles over her proclamation, and I immediately shake my head in denial. "No way.

It's not love," I stubbornly assert.

"That is so love," Savannah says with a knowing smile. "Except I've never heard it sound so poetic."

"I don't do love," I practically whine. "I don't know how to do it. I'm just now getting comfortable with the idea that I like Tenn. I'm just now able to be happy that he's staying in the area. I'm not ready for love."

"None of us were really ready for it," Andrea says thoughtfully. "But when it comes… you just know it."

"But I don't 'just know it'," I maintain. "I'm having all kinds of doubts still. It feels awkward to me."

Gabby reaches across the table and grabs my hand. "Push through it, Casey," she says in almost a warning tone. "Don't you dare let this guy get away. He's the real deal."

"How do you know?" I ask quietly… skeptically.

"Because… he's the reason you're even sitting here with us waxing poetic about rainy days and rainbows. You're in a relationship, Casey, and while it's awkward to you, I guarantee you that it's fantastic too, right?"

I nod at her, my eyes filling with unmeasured hope. Could I do this? Could I push past my fears and really have something serious with Tenn? Could I really be in love?

"You need to grab onto it, Casey, and make it

your bitch," Gabby says with a wink and a smirk.

"Yeah," Andrea says in affirmation. "Make love your bitch."

"That should be a hashtag on Twitter," Alyssa says, and Savannah gives another dreamy and romantic sigh.

Make love my bitch?

Hmmmmm. That sounds like something Casey Markham would do.

♦

AFTER HAVING THE most fun breakfast of my entire life, I swing by my place and grab Tenn, then proceed to take him around the island and show him five different houses for sale and three that are for rent. He didn't like any of them.

The view isn't good enough.

The carpet's too old.

The front door sticks.

The bathroom isn't big enough.

As we walk through the last house on the list today, I take in the open and airy living room that overlooks the Atlantic, a well-designed kitchen, brand-new hardwood floors, and a huge master bedroom that has a bathroom so big that it has a Jacuzzi tub. It falls well within the budget Tenn told me he had, which is apparently quite healthy due to some serious savings and equity from his house he sold in Wyoming.

"I dare you to find something wrong with this place," I tell Tenn as we step out onto the back deck.

He walks up to the railing, places his hands there, and leans forward while staring at the ocean. His profile is as stunning as the full frontal, and I stare at this beautiful man while he stares at the ocean.

"I don't like it," he finally says.

"What the hell, Tenn?" I ask in exasperation. "What could possibly be wrong with this place?"

Blue eyes stay focused on the water but he speaks directly to me. "You're not living here. That's what's wrong with it."

Tenn's face turns slowly to me and his eyes are turbulent... swirling with something that I would say almost borders on agitation. He turns his entire body my way, casually resting an elbow on the railing and clasping his hands together.

"Cat got your tongue, Goldie?" he asks wickedly.

I give a small shake to my head and practically stutter out, "Are you saying you want to live together?"

One minute, he's leaning there all casual yet self-assured, and the next minute, he has me turned so my back is to the railing and he's kissing me so hard I bend backward. His kiss conveys a message to me loud and clear. He's possessive and he wants me in his bed, wherever that may be.

When he finally pulls away, I almost whimper at

the loss of his mouth against mine. I loosen my fingers, which I find had somehow unknowingly fisted hard onto his t-shirt, and blow a huff of breath out.

"At the risk of getting attacked again," I say as I smooth my hand over my hair in an effort to appear calmer, "are you saying you want to live together?"

"Yeah, Goldie," he says with a small smile, reaching a hand up to absently tug on a lock of my hair. "I want to be in your bed every night."

"But you'd probably be there anyway if we had separate places," I point out matter-of-factly.

"And I want to be in your bed in the morning and on the couch when you get home from work. I want to eat breakfast and dinner together, and lunch when we can. I want to share closet space with you and figure out our bills together. I want to fight for space on the bathroom sink, and I want you to yell at me for leaving my clothes all over the floor. I want to know that when I think of the word home, it's the place where your ass resides with me. I want the words "home" and "Casey" to mean the same thing to me."

I reach my hands back to steady myself against the rail, because the feeling seems to have gone out of my legs. My voice is shaky… foreign sounding. "That may have been the sweetest, most romantic thing I think I've ever heard in my life."

Tenn's blue eyes lighten up and start to sparkle.

He prowls forward and steps into my body, hands going to my hips. He dips his face to look at me and says softly, "So romantic we can move in together?"

My arms smooth up the hard lines of Tenn's chest, grazing softly around to the back of his neck where my fingers disappear into his black hair. "Don't you think this is awful fast?"

"No."

"No?" I ask incredulously. "Just… no?"

"What more do you want me to say, Casey?" he asks affably. "I'm crazy about you. I want to be around you as much as possible. You didn't mind me staying with you these last several weeks. We cohabitate quite nicely together, if I do say so myself. So, no… I don't think it's too fast."

I pull back from our embrace and turn to face the ocean. He comes up behind me, wraps his arms around my waist, and rests his chin on my head. We both gaze out over the beauty of the ocean, and I wonder out loud, "What will my friends say? My family?"

A small rumble of laughter from Tenn's chest vibrates up my back. "Do you really care? The woman who hasn't cared a damn bit what people think of her for the last eight years?"

That's true enough. I've never cared what anyone's thought of me… well, except maybe my parents. I mean… I didn't like when they've been disappointed in me but hell, even their most disappointed looks are filled with so much love, it really doesn't pack much of a punch.

My friends will understand. The adventurous ones like Gabby and Andrea will pat me on the back and say, "Shack up, girl."

The romantic ones like Savannah and Alyssa will just give me knowing smiles and silent approval with dreamy sighs.

Now my brothers... that might present a problem, but only in an overprotective kind of way. The good thing is that I at least know they like Tenn already, and they both moved in pretty fast with Gabby and Alyssa.

My parents... I really have no clue what they'd think.

So, there's really only one thing to do.

Turning back around to face Tenn, I tell him, "I want you to come to dinner at my parents' house so they can meet you."

His eyes light up and those sexy lips quirk. "Want them to check me out first, huh? Get their stamp of approval?"

"No," I tell him candidly and with my chin raised up. "I don't need their approval. I say we can give this a try... at my house... for a while and see how it goes. I just want you to meet my parents so they can finally see that I've got my head out of my ass when it comes to relationships."

Tenn throws his head back, and I get a flash of

white straight teeth as he starts laughing. When he looks back at me, he says, "Fuck Casey... I adore you so much."

I adore you too, I say with my inside voice, and hope that one day I can say that with my outside voice too.

CHAPTER 22

Tenn

I WASN'T NERVOUS about the prospect of dinner with Casey's parents. She, however, assumed I was and gave me a knee-buckling blow job not long before we left, I suppose in an effort to relax me. I wanted to tell the sweet minx that I didn't need it but damn... with her on her knees before me, wrapping those lips around my dick. Yeah, well, I wasn't about to tell her I didn't need it. Sure as fuck wanted it, but didn't need it.

Casey has babbled the entire way as she directs me to her parents' house in Avon, which is about an hour south of Nags Head. We decided to take her Jeep since rain was forecasted for the early evening, but as has become our ritual, I'm driving.

Over the last few weeks, I've come to learn a lot about her family. While I know we spend an inordinate amount of time having sex, we spend a good amount of time before and after talking.

Once she got past the emotional block of sharing

herself with a man on an intellectual and emotional level, she sort of blossomed. This specifically came on the heels of her ditching Jeff Parkhurst in the restaurant and seeing me waiting on my bike for her. It doesn't mean she tells me all her secrets, and I can tell she's still holding back a bit, but she's definitely more open and free with herself. Definitely not guarded the way she used to be.

She's pretty much an open book when it comes to her family, and I believe that comes from absolute and unconditional love between everyone. I've come to learn a lot about her mom, Lillian, who is a nurse, and her dad, Butch, who is a fisherman. Despite what Jeff Parkhurst thought, Casey didn't exactly grow up poor. She wasn't rich, but her parents provided a nice, middle-class upbringing for her and her brothers. They had enough money to support Hunter's fledgling surfing career as he grew up, and with it looking like Brody was on his way to medical school being the brainiac in the family, they had plenty of money set aside in savings for him. Sadly, they ended up using that for his legal fees, but nothing could derail the disaster of him getting convicted and sent to prison for the drunk-driving accident that claimed a man's life.

Casey and I had stayed up late one night, sitting out on the back deck and drinking decaf coffee. The moon was bright and lit the entire ocean up to our right as we looked at it between the roofs of the other houses. We sat in some low-slung, Adirondack chairs with our feet propped up on her railing.

I asked her to tell me what happened to Brody.

And she did… starting way back when she was in high school and what it felt like to find out your beloved older brother who had a bright future ahead of him as a doctor ended up being convicted of Felony Death by Vehicle and put behind bars for five years. She glossed over Jeff Parkhurst and how he took advantage of her emotional frailty in order to get her virginity, but I didn't need to hear that. I knew that story and besides… it pissed me off way too much to hear it again.

But she did tell me more about what Brody was like when he came home.

How emotionally unavailable he was to everyone… and how much that impacted her, especially being a woman that withheld herself emotionally from other men. It was weird, ironic, and eye opening for her. It made her feel worse about herself, seeing Brody act the way she acted. She wanted Brody to snap out of it… let the past go… be a part of regular life again. And yet, she couldn't do the same herself.

It was a fascinating dynamic, and I was even more intrigued by her continued story when she told me that Brody wasn't the one driving the vehicle during that tragic accident. It was Brody's then girlfriend and being an overprotective, if not foolhardy man, he took the fall for her. While Casey didn't say as much, I think it had to affect her more than the other family members to watch someone who proclaimed to love her brother take advantage of him in such a sinister way. I'm sure she felt the pain of that on Brody's behalf all the way down to the marrow in her bones.

When we reach Avon, which is a blip on the map, Casey has me make just two turns off the main highway and we are sitting in front of a small, classically stilted cottage that sits a few blocks from the ocean. Like Casey, her parents don't have beachfront, but I can tell by the way their house is situated and the fact that there are fewer homes, that it means they have a better view of both the ocean and the sound.

We get out of the Jeep and round the front. At the base of the stairs that lead up, I hold my hand out to her. She looks down and then back up to me, slipping her warm palm against mine. I curl my fingers tight around her, and we walk up together.

As we reach the top step, the front door swings open wide and I'm staring at either Brody or Hunter. I really can't tell without their respective women with them as they are indeed identical and even wear their hair about the same.

Leaning to the side, I whisper, "Which one?"

Casey giggles and whispers, "Brody," just before she lets my hand go and steps into a hug with her brother.

Brody gives her a tight squeeze and looks at me

over her shoulder, giving a jerk up of his chin. "What's up?"

"Not much, man," I say in response and our male greeting ritual is complete.

"What are you doing here?" Casey asks as Brody steps back into the house and we all walk in together.

"Alyssa had to head over to Manteo to pick up a dog that's set to be euthanized in the morning, so I figured I'd come and partake of Mom's cooking tonight."

"And to make me squirm as I introduce Tenn to the family," Casey guesses sagely.

"Yeah, something like that," Brody says with a sly grin.

Casey just levels him with a look that dares him to make this difficult on her, reaches back to grab my hand, and then leads me through the living room. It's small and cozy, with plush, beachy-looking furniture in blue and white striped cotton, bleached wood tables, and tile flooring covered by a shaggy, blue rug. Framed photos are everywhere. Walls, tables, corner curio. A brief glance and I see several of Casey and her brothers, and I can't wait to look at them in a bit more detail. I want to study them, knowing that I'll see something different in her eyes in those photos that are pre and post Jeff Parkhurst.

Just as I know I'd see something different now if I were to snap a picture of her.

"We're here," Casey calls out.

Brody says, "They're on the back deck. Dad's cooking up some steaks."

"Steaks?" Casey asks in surprise. "I thought Mom said she was going to make some shrimp and grits tonight. I was looking forward to that."

We head into a surprisingly large kitchen for the moderately sized house with whitewashed cabinets and cheery yellow paint on the walls, and just beyond, the sliding glass doors that lead out to the deck.

Casey releases my hand, opens the door, and steps out. I'm on her heels but momentarily forgotten as she hugs her mom first, who is leaning back against the deck rail with a glass of red wine in her hand while watching as her husband flips some steaks.

Casey and her brothers both take after their mother in coloring but you can tell they get their height from their dad, who I'm guessing is almost eye to eye with me.

Lillian Markham turns to me and with her wine in her left hand, reaches her right arm up in a clear indication that she prefers hugging as her primary method of introduction. I step forward, bend down, and she loops that arm over my shoulders. I wrap my arms around her lightly and accept her embrace.

"It's so good to meet you, Tenn," she says in an accent that is far more southern than Casey's.

"Thanks for having me," I say as she releases me, and then I look over to her father. He quickly switches his grilling tongs from right to left hand and leans past the grill. We shake hands, and he gives me a warm smile.

"Great to meet you, Mr. Markham," I say.

He shakes his head as he turns his attention back to the grill. "It's Butch and Lillian. None of that formal crap here."

I chuckle and step up to the grill to take a peek at what he's cooking. Five nice-sized rib-eyed steaks with perfectly charred hatch marks. Out of the corner of my eye, I see Casey and her mother step back into the kitchen, presumably to get other stuff ready, and then it's just me, Brody, and Butch out on the deck.

"Beer is over there in the cooler," Butch says with a nod of his head.

I see frosty bottles of Budweiser and bottles of water. I know Brody doesn't drink anymore after the accident. Even though he wasn't driving, he takes alcohol consumption so seriously that he refuses to touch a drop, so I grab two beers for Butch and me, and a bottle of water for Brody.

When I stand up and pass the bottles, I can see surprise on Brody's face that I would know he doesn't drink. I suppose that tells them something about how their daughter and sister must feel about me... to trust me with that information.

"Casey said that you're relocating to the area and are going to move in with her," Butch says quietly as he flips the steaks and shuts the grill lid.

I'd expected this but not so soon in the conversation. I thought he'd might take a bit of time to check me out first. "Yes, sir," I answer, but I don't provide any explanation or argument about the saneness of our actions.

"Ordinarily," Butch says after he takes a healthy swig of his beer, "I'd say it's too soon, but I have to be honest... Brody here says he's seen some amazing changes in Casey since you two have been together."

I cut a surprised look over at Brody, and he shrugs his shoulders at me like he really didn't say much of anything. When I look back at Butch, I say, "I'm not responsible for her changing. That's all on Casey."

The respect in Butch's eyes increases further. "Yeah... Casey's a strong girl. She can do anything she sets her mind to. But I expect you may have been the catalyst to make her want to change."

Turning to Brody, Butch says, "Will you go get me a platter or something to put these steaks on?"

With a nod, Brody turns around and heads back inside, and then I'm alone with Casey's father.

He flips off the grill burners, reaches under, and turns the gas off the tank. When he stands back up, he levels me with a stare. "There was a time that our family was a bit broken. Brody went to prison, Casey was a wild child, and Hunter was off trotting the globe. Then it started coming back together. Hunter moved back home and bought the bar. Brody came home and we found out the bitter truth that he went away for a crime he didn't commit, but after Brody revealed that to us, I really felt us start to get close again. Both my boys settled down with good women."

He pauses and takes a sip of beer before continuing. "But Casey... she was a bit lost, and we didn't know how to reach her. Her mother and I love her very much, as do her brothers, but she always held a piece of herself away from us. Had been that way since Brody got sent away."

I don't disabuse him of thinking this all had to do with Brody. It's Casey's story to tell her parents if she wants them to know what Jeff did to her and how it made her so jaded. How it formed and directed her actions... her choices... the way in which she viewed the opposite sex.

"She's different," Butch says contemplatively. "A good different and it makes me happy."

That seems to be the end of his soliloquy, and I heard the hidden message in there. He's grateful for this. He's happy for his daughter and he's telling me that whatever has caused this change in Casey, it's affected not only her, but her family as well.

"I love her," I tell Butch bluntly, my gaze holding his.

His eyes start to crinkle in a grateful smile that doesn't reach completion before I hear the small gasp behind me. Turning my head slowly, I see Casey standing there with an empty platter in her hands, her eyes pinned to mine. Wide, uncertain... possibly filled with alarm.

But then it's gone. Acting as if she didn't hear me, she smiles at me softly before walking up to her dad to hand him the platter. "Mom said everything else is ready."

My eyes follow Casey like a hawk, wondering what the hell is going on in her head at this moment. She heard my declaration… no doubt. But the variant emotions that filtered over her face in just the breadth of a nanosecond didn't reveal anything to me. If her dad wasn't standing right there, I'd grab her by the shoulders, kiss her hard first, and then demand she tell me what was going on in that sexy head of hers.

Instead, I take another casual sip of my beer and intercept the platter from Casey. My fingers graze against her hand just before she releases it into my control.

Butch opens the grill lid and starts grabbing the steaks with his tongs and layering them on the platter. Casey turns around without a word and heads back inside.

"I'm assuming you haven't told her yet," Butch says as his lips tip upward, his eyes intent on his work.

With a sigh, I look back through the sliding glass door and see Casey helping her mom set bowls of food on the table. She's laughing at something her mom says and then Brody walks into the kitchen and grabs her in a headlock, rubbing his knuckles over her head. I can hear her squeal through the closed glass door, and I can't fight the grin on my face.

Turning back to Butch, I say with frustration, "Just never seems to be the right time."

Placing the last steak on the platter, Butch closes the grill lid and looks at me with solemnity. "Son… I'd propose it never seems to be the right time until it is the right time. You'll know when it's right."

I nod at Butch, his simple words making a fuck of a lot of sense to me.

Butch grabs the platter. I grab the sliding glass door and open it, motioning for him to precede me in. He goes through. I follow and slide it closed behind me.

"Everyone, sit down," Lillian says as she flits back and forth grabbing condiments and one more bowl of food… pasta salad by the looks of it. Butch leans over and sets the steaks in the middle of the table.

Casey and Brody immediately fight for a chair, not because I believe it holds any special importance, but because the noogie he bestowed upon her earlier has seemed to waken up her inner brat. I shake my head with an amused smile and wait to see how it all shakes out. Casey manages to win by putting her butt on the seat, pushing hard to dislodge him, and then reaching up under his armpit and viciously twisting what I'm guessing was a chunk of skin and hair. Brody yelps and jumps from the seat, and Casey gloats.

My girl. The woman who shut herself away. Who

curled into herself when her brother got ripped away from the family and another man shattered her heart and her trust. Now opening her arms to me as surely as her heart, and doing so with almost a blind faith in my ability not to hurt her.

I walk around the table and take the seat next to the one she claimed. Brody walks to the opposite side and sits down. Finally, Lillian and Butch take seats opposite each other at the ends of the table.

"Eat, eat," Lillian says, motioning to the food on the table. Brody doesn't wait and pounces, grabbing a steak first and then a baked potato. Butch and Lillian start filling their plates, and Casey starts to lean forward to grab a steak of her own.

A quick glance at her and I see a warm, relaxed smile on her face. She gives Brody's hand a little slap when he tries to grab the butter from her, and her dad laughs at them. Lillian tells Casey to quit picking on her brother, and Casey gives her mom an eye roll that would rival Zoey's.

It's at this moment that I get overwhelmed with the sudden desire to tell Casey that I love her. That no matter how she feels in this moment, I just need her to know how I feel, and I don't give a fuck that her family is sitting here witnessing it.

My phone buzzes in my pocket and I pull it out to make sure it's not Zoey calling. I'm surprised to see it's my brother, Woolf, because he never calls me. I hit the side button to decline the call, start to put in back in my pocket, and it immediately starts ringing again.

"Sorry," I mutter to everyone at the table and hit the decline button again.

"You can answer it if you need to," Casey says as she slices her potato open. "We're not formal or anything at dinner."

"It's alright," I assure her, but then a *ding* alerts me to a text. I glance down and it's from Woolf.

Call me. Emergency.

Immediately, a zap of electric fear penetrates the center of my chest and my skin starts to tingle in apprehension.

I stand from the table and mumble, "Excuse me. I need to make a call."

Clumsily, I step out from my chair and manage to bump into Casey's hard. She looks up at me as my hand goes to her shoulder to steady myself a moment.

"Tenn… are you alright?"

I try to give her a reassuring smile, but I'm not sure if I'm all right or not. I'll know as soon as I call Woolf back.

CHAPTER 23

Casey

TENN PUSHES PAST my chair as his fingers tap something on his phone and he's putting it up to his ear. I immediately scoot my chair back, put my napkin on the table, and shoot my mom a quick glance. "I'll be right back."

"Take your time, honey," she says and her eyes are as worried as I know mine are.

Hot on Tenn's heels, I follow him through the living room and out through the front door as he holds the phone to his ear. As I'm walking through, I hear him say, "What happened?"

His voice is soft... filled with dread. I know something bad is going on, and my insides start to cramp with worry over Zoey. I step around Tenn and rest a hand lightly on his stomach to let him know I'm here if he needs me, which I think he does.

The muscles in his abdomen bunch in reflex, but then he relaxes as he shoots an apprehensive look at me while he listens.

I don't know who is on the other line but whatever they're saying produces an effect on Tenn. The foreboding leaves his eyes and is immediately replaced with a hot flash of shock. That quickly melts away and his skin pales, then I'm staring at full-blown grief within those blue irises. His lips draw down, a soft rush of breath blows through his lips, and then everything drains out of his eyes until they're devoid of anything.

Flat.

Dead.

Just… nothing.

My fingers curl into the soft material of his t-shirt, and I bunch it hard with anxiety.

"I'll get the quickest flight out I can," Tenn says, his voice thick and hoarse. "I'll text you the details."

He listens a minute more and then he pulls the phone away from his ear, not having bothered to say goodbye to whoever was on the other end. His gaze shifts away from me, staring blankly at the house next door.

"What's happened?" I ask, my own voice scratchy with distress.

Tenn's shoulders sag as if fifty-pound weights are on each side, and then his head slowly turns back my way. "It's my dad… he's dead."

"What?" I exclaim as my entire body receives a sizzle of shock and my fingers tighten harder into his shirt.

"He got thrown from a horse, and then um... trampled. Took a hoof right to his chest. Ruptured something in his heart apparently."

His words are flat and monotone. I launch myself at him, burying my face in his chest and bringing my arms around his back to hug him as tight as I can. His arms immediately come around me, clinging hard, and I feel his lips press against the top of my head.

"I'm so sorry, Tenn," I murmur as I turn my face to rest my cheek against him, my arms clutching at him in a desperate attempt to convey my feelings. "So, so sorry."

He hugs me back, silently accepting my sympathy. My brain tries to process everything I know about Tenn's father. He's been notoriously tight lipped about him, and I assume it's because they weren't overly close. Tenn has told me that his father has pestered him repetitively to come into the family business of ranching, and Tenn has told me that he has no intention of doing that. I know he's just been waiting for his younger brother, Woolf, to sort of step up to the plate and fill his shoes, and now I have to imagine that in addition to the grief of losing their father, the two brothers will need to come to some sort of understanding.

And shit... it hits me all at once. Maybe this is really Tenn's destiny. Maybe he has to take over the ranch now that both his parents are gone. And that means he'll be living thousands of miles away, and even as this fills me with a weird feeling of abandonment, I also feel tremendous guilt for even worrying about this because it's a selfish thought to have at this point.

"I need to get back to your house and get packed… make some plane reservations," he says absently, looking utterly lost and vulnerable.

"Of course," I say suddenly, pulling away and springing in to action. "I'm going to go grab my purse."

"Apologize to your family," he says softly.

"There's nothing to be sorry for," I say quickly, and then fly back into the house.

I give a quick explanation of what's happened, and my mom immediately jumps up wanting to assist. She offers to pack food and get online for plane reservations, making a move toward the front door to step out onto the porch and console Tenn.

With a gentle hand on her shoulder, I say, "I've got this, Mom."

She nods and smiles sadly, sitting back down at the table.

"I'll call you and let you know what's going on," I say as I turn away from my family.

"Call us if you need us, honey," my dad says to my retreating back.

"I'll cover you at The Last Call if you need to go with him," Brody also says, and I have to smile at his offer. He hates bartending, so this gesture really touches my heart.

And I'm going to take him up on that because there's no way in hell that Tenn is going without me.

He needs me but more importantly... I really need to be there for him. It's something I feel compelled to do, not out of obligation, but out of a sense of connection I have with him. His hurt has become my hurt.

I manage to get Tenn loaded into my Jeep, and I know by the fact he doesn't insist on driving that he's out of it. Probably consumed with grief and even guilt, he does nothing but stare silently out the passenger window as I make the drive back to Nags Head. I rest my hand on his thigh and he places his hand on top of mine, then clutches my fingers gently.

By the time we walk into my house, I have a game plan in effect.

"Why don't you start getting packed," I tell Tenn firmly, giving him a push on his lower back. "I'm going to jump online and start checking out flight options. Do you want to fly out quickest or go through Raleigh and pick up Zoey?"

More pain flashes through Tenn's face. "Fuck... I need to call Zoey."

He looks lost as his eyes flutter around the living room, almost as if he can't even decide how to pick up the phone to dial his daughter.

"She was really close to my dad," Tenn mutters.

I know it's a stupid offer but I go ahead and make

it anyway, knowing there is no way in hell that Tenn would ever take me up on it. He's not the type of man that would ever shirk away from his fatherly duty.

"Do you want me to call her?" I ask tentatively.

His eyes slide to mine, and I see the real Tenn underneath the grief. His lips quirk a tiny bit as he shakes his head. "Nice offer, Goldie… but you know I need to do this. Let me go ahead and do that now, and then we can figure out plane reservations."

I walk up to him, press my body in close, and stand up on tiptoes, grazing a soft, gentle kiss on the side of his neck. "Okay. I'm actually going to go get you packed up and give you some privacy. Then I'll make our reservations once you figure Zoey out."

"Our reservations?" he asks with surprise.

"I'm going with you," I tell him firmly, leveling him a look that almost dares him to fight me on it.

But he doesn't, which is good, because there's no way in hell I'm staying here. Not after I found out he loves me. Granted, he said it to my dad and not me, but I heard the words.

He knows I heard the words.

He knows I didn't run, and it should tell him something that not only am I not running, but I'm pinning myself to his side in his time of need.

So, he might not have said the words directly to me yet, and I'm not even sure if I'll be able to say them to him any time soon, but I suspect that we both know what's going on here. It's just right now… with this tragedy unfolding for Tenn, there are more important things to do than worry about mere words.

I need to show him how I feel.

Reaching out, I lay my hand in the middle of his chest and rub my thumb over his breastbone. Then I give a soft pat and turn to head back into the bedroom to get his meager supply of clothing together, and get me packed as well.

It doesn't take long for me to get organized. I can hear Tenn's soft voice in the other room as he speaks to Zoey, but I can't hear the details of that conversation. I'm thinking this is good, because I honestly don't know if I could handle listening to Tenn console a grief-stricken Zoey right now. I know what it's like to experience loss at a tender age and it's not pretty. Brody may not have died, and I may have been a few years older than Zoey, but it was a terrible loss all the same. It was as if Brody had died, and I felt my world had been turned upside down.

As soon as I'm done packing, I place a quick call to Hunter. He had already heard what happened from Brody and told me not to worry about my shifts and that they'd cover for me as long as I needed to be in Wyoming with Tenn. That was so sweet, and the perfect example of why I love my brothers, but I didn't think I'd be there long. I wanted to help Tenn get through the funeral, but then I knew I'd have to return to my life. I just wasn't sure if Tenn would be returning with me.

After I hang up with Hunter, I pull the large suitcase I have filled with mine and Tenn's clothing off the bed and roll it over to the wall so it's out of the way. I cautiously walk back into my living room, and I don't hear Tenn talking anymore. I find him at my table, with my laptop open, leaning forward to peer at the screen.

He doesn't look up to acknowledge my presence but says, "I'm looking at flights. You sure you want to go with me?"

I walk up behind him, curl my arms around his chest, lean in, and give him a tight hug. "Totally sure."

"Well, it looks like there's actually an early flight out of New Bern that heads to Detroit, and then in to Jackson. It's the fastest," he says as he continues to scroll through the choices.

"What about Zoey?" I ask tentatively.

"Brianna wants to bring her," Tenn says, his words flat but accepting. "And that's fine... I mean... she loved my dad too in her own weird way. She can get compassionate time off from her job."

"How is Zoey taking this?"

Tenn takes in a deep breath and lets it out slowly, his hand falling away from the laptop. He places his palms over my forearms that are crossed over his chest and grips tightly as he eases his head back to rest against me. "She's devastated," he says, and his voice cracks.

I squeeze on to him hard, trying to suck the pain away from him that I know he's suffering not only because his own father is dead, but also because he's a father to a child who is suffering. I know Tenn… he'll put aside his own misery to take on every bit of Zoey's.

He lets me hold him for a few moments, even sighs when I lean to the side and press my lips to his cheek. I nuzzle against his skin and feel him melt just a tiny bit as he accepts my sympathy.

But then he's pushing out of my hold and reaching into his back pocket. As he pulls his wallet out, he says, "Are you sure you can take the time to go with me?"

"Absolutely," I tell him as I turn to grab my own purse so I can get my credit card out. "Hunter told me to take all the time I need."

"That means a lot, Goldie," Tenn says quietly, and shivers race up my spine over the gratitude I hear in his voice. It feels good… knowing I'm doing something that he really needs right now.

I turn and hold out my credit card to find Tenn already filling in information on the computer screen to book the flights. "Here… to purchase my ticket."

He just shakes his head. "I got it."

"No way," I insist. "You are not paying for my plane ticket."

"Back off, Goldie," he says in a low warning. "I'm

not in the mood to argue with you."

I heed his voice, dropping my outstretched hand. He needs to be in charge now, and this is not the time to try to assert my independence with him. For the time being, I'll let Tenn do the things he needs to do, and I just need to be there to support him.

Because we didn't eat, I head into the kitchen and find a few cans of soup I can heat up. I work on getting them opened and started on a low simmer on the stove while Tenn finishes booking our flights. When he's done, he pulls out his phone and sends a text to his brother with our arrival time, waits for his response, and then texts something back.

"Woolf will pick us up at the airport," Tenn says absently as he pushes out of the chair.

I turn the stove off and open the cupboard to the right to get some bowls. "Let's get some food in you and then we'll get a good night's sleep since we—"

My words are cut off as Tenn steps up behind me, taking my wrist that is extended toward the cupboard. He pulls it away, drags it back toward my body, and then presses into my back. Wrapping both arms around me, he envelopes me in a warm hug that is full of thanks and then morphs into need. I know it's need because I can feel him start to grow hard against my lower back.

"Aren't you hungry?" I ask softly, holding my body still to see what he really wants.

"Yes," he breathes in my ear, and then drops his

hands down to my thighs where he skims his fingers over my skin, just under the hem of my sundress.

His unspoken words? *I'm hungry for you.*

Immediately turning in his arms, I press my breasts into his chest and dip my fingers into his waistband. I look up at him and my heart hurts over the pain I see there, but know that based on the need I see there too, that I can make him feel marginally better.

My hands work at his belt buckle and I quickly undo it, his button and zipper following quickly. He stares down at me with quiet interest, but when my hands start to push down at his jeans, he stills them with just one word. "Don't," he says quietly.

I press a quick kiss against his breastbone, and then tilt my head back to look at him. "But I want to take care of you."

Tenn's fingers drag upward, taking my skirt with his hands. He curls them around to the back, squeezing my ass gently, leveling me with a heated stare. He shakes his head. "I need to drive."

"Be in charge?" I ask gently, knowing damn well that's what he means.

"Yeah… I need a bit of normalcy right now," he admits as he slips his fingers under the back edge of my panties. "I honestly don't think I can handle you taking care of me tonight."

His words are rough and strained but rather than respond… to potentially cause him to break on me, I simply nod and lift my mouth to his. He takes it... gladly, and kisses me deep.

While his mouth moves against mine, causing me to start to fall into that deep abyss of pleasure, his hands grip hard on my ass and lift me up. My legs naturally wrap around his waist and our kiss never breaks. Deepens in fact.

When my core settles against him and I give a little grind, deep gratification rumbles in his chest and he turns to carry me to the bedroom. In just moments, he has me on the bed and stripped naked. He proceeds to remove his own clothing, not rushing and keeping his eyes pinned on my face while I in turn let my own eyes rove all over his body. I take in the planes and contours of his muscles, the vibrant ink on his arms and shoulders, the patch of hair just below his belly button that dives down into those pants and points me to my favorite part of his body.

My nerves hum and my blood sizzles.

It's what always happens when I know that Tenn is going to touch me.

Taste me.

Fuck me.

I wait with nervous anticipation to see what he'll do. Will it be an onslaught of lust? Or sweet touches to slowly build me up? He's a master at both, and I don't have a preference.

But he does neither.

Instead, he kneels on the bed between my legs and

proceeds to run his hands over my skin. Everywhere. All over my entire body except my breasts and the money spot between my legs. He curves his hands around my ankles, digging his thumb deliciously into my instep. Spreads his fingers wide and palms my calves, squeezing them gently before smoothing upward to my thighs. Everywhere... hips, stomach, the inside of my elbows. He strokes my collarbone and my neck, running his fingers over my jawline.

After he has his fill, he finally brings his body down on top of mine, nestling his hard cock against me and kisses me. Leisurely and deep, not in a rush to do anything but savor.

He laces his fingers with mine, pulling our hands above our heads. He kisses me so sensually that I become immersed in a deep pool of feeling. I become so captivated by what his tongue does to mine that I really don't even notice as he starts to shift his hips so his cock presses against my warm opening.

When he pushes in a fraction, I can't control the gasp that comes out of my mouth. He sucks it down and keeps kissing me, all while slowly pushing his way inside.

And when he's fully seated... when we are pelvis to pelvis and he can't go any deeper, he just rocks against me. Presses deeply.

Over and over again.

He takes me slowly and drags out every bit of pleasure between us. Our breathing matches pace with one another, our hands grasp tightly. We build all the way up and when it's time, we take the plunge together.

Pushing in deep, he starts coming at the same time I do.

It's magnificent, and I've never felt closer to him than I do at this moment.

Knowing that he needed me and based on the low moan of pleasure and relief I hear in his voice, I know that for even just a moment, I was able to give him some peace.

When he finally collapses on top of me, I hear him whisper in my ear a direct admission. "I love you, Casey."

CHAPTER 24

Jenn

A S OUR FLIGHT turns parallel to the Teton Mountain range to line up with the runway at the Jackson Airport, I feel a moderate amount of turbulence that is typical of the high crosswinds. Casey jerks awake in her seat, and I immediately take her hand.

She didn't tell me that this was only her second time on an airplane, or that she had a slight fear of flying until we were barreling down the runway in New Bern. She clutched my hand in a death grip, imprinting little half-moon divets into the back of my hand with her nails. I only managed to get her to release her hold after plying her with two Jack and Cokes so she could relax marginally. Just before our flight left Detroit after our layover, I also had her down a few drinks before we boarded, and that takeoff was much smoother. And she's been sleeping ever since.

I still can't believe she came with me.

Fuck, I can't believe my father is dead.

Grief and guilt have been a constant companion since I got the news last night. Grief that a vibrant and beloved man is dead and guilt that perhaps I was an utter disappointment to him and he died with that on my conscience. He died without me ever having the ability to just make that final decision about what I wanted to do with my life. He died with me not knowing if he even forgave me for not wanting to continue with the family's legacy.

Casey's hand clutches at mine again, and I can feel how sweaty her palms are. I squeeze her with reassurance, and she lays her head on my shoulder.

It's a beautiful feeling.

I like her dependence on me for comfort.

I really like the fact she didn't go running after I told her I loved her last night.

Granted, she didn't say it back, but I could tell by the way her arms wrapped around me and she squeezed me so gently to her, that she was touched by my words. I know she was touched, and probably intrigued, maybe still a bit scared, but honestly... she's open to it. I know this because she fell asleep wrapped in my embrace, and that's how I found her this morning. Still glued to me... and it chased a little of my sadness away.

We make it through the process of deplaning and walking through the small, rustic airport to the baggage claim. After a short wait, our bags arrive... a large one that holds both of our clothes and a smaller one that holds Casey's toiletries. I grab the big suitcase while she takes the smaller one, and lead her out the door, where I know Woolf will be waiting.

I immediately see him... leaning up against the side of a silver pickup truck with the Double J Ranch logo on the side. He's dressed exactly as I would be if I were working the ranch. Plaid western shirt, pair of worn jeans, dusty cowboy boots, and his brown-colored Stetson pulled low over his face, the ends of his dark hair curling out from the bottom against his neck. Even with the hat pulled low, his light blue eyes, the exact duplicate of mine, shine brightly.

I step off the curb to the rear of the truck and heft the large suitcase over the back and into the bed. Woolf pushes off from the truck and walks up to me, his eyes sad with grief and the same guilt that I know is reflected in mine.

My arms open up naturally to him, and we give each other a short hug with hard slaps on the back. When I release him, he nudges the front of his hat back on his head so I can see his face more clearly. "Can't fucking believe it, bro," he mutters. "Fucking talking to him one minute, the next he's on the ground and Lucky is giving him CPR."

I wince over that grim description, hating that Woolf even had to witness our dad's death. I'd seen a lot of death when I served in Afghanistan, but I suppose it's quite different when you watch a family member die before your eyes.

"Sorry you had to see that, man. Wish I'd been here with you," I say quietly… absolutely lying through my teeth. No one would want to see that.

"Fucking liar," Woolf says with a pained grin on his face, and I can't help give him a return smile that's more sheepish than anything.

Turning to Casey, I reach my arm out and beckon her forward. She comes to me with sure steps, looking at Woolf with a sympathetic smile.

I introduce her simply, so there's no question as to her status in my life. "This is my girlfriend, Casey."

Slipping an arm around her waist to pull her in toward me, I tell her, "Goldie… this is my brother, Woolf."

Casey sticks her hand out and Woolf shakes it, surprise on his face. I didn't tell him I was bringing anyone because I didn't feel like making explanations. I also didn't feel like listening to Woolf try to talk me out of bringing someone, so it's another reason why I kept my lips zipped about her.

"Well, this is a surprise," Woolf says guardedly as he shakes her hand. "But welcome, Casey."

"I'm so sorry about your father," she says, her eyes warm and soft as she regards my little brother.

Woolf gives her an accommodating smile, continuing to look at her with a slight degree of suspicion, but at least his tone is friendly when he says, "Well… let's get you two out to the ranch."

After I put Casey's carry-on into the back of the truck, I lead her to the passenger door where I climb into the back of the extended cab and offer her the front seat so she can get a better view of my old world. I may not want a place in my family's ranching history but there is absolutely no denying… this area of Wyoming is the most beautiful place in the world. Casey's world is gorgeous with soft, pale sand and blue-green waters that sparkle with the sun, but it just can't compare to this area with the majestic Teton mountain range with snowcapped peaks even in the summer, wide valleys filled with fragrant sagebrush, and sparkling rivers that wind through filled with cutthroat trout. While I certainly believe I can come to love living on the coast of North Carolina, there is nothing that will ever replace my love of this part of the country.

The ranch is a good forty-five minute drive from the airport. Wyoming is land rich and people poor. You can drive over half an hour before seeing your closest neighbor, so if you are an overly social person, this isn't necessarily the place for you.

Casey stares with her face practically pressed against the passenger window, making small noises of wonder in the back of her throat as she watches the miles melt away and yet the Teton Mountains never seem to end. She asks a few questions but for the most part, the ride is silent, filled with an awkward tension since Woolf wasn't expecting company on this ride and no one wants to talk about how my father died.

When we get to the main entrance to the Double J, my shoulders start to stiffen. I haven't told Casey any more details about my family and the ranch. She has no clue what she's walking in to, and while I'd like to say that I simply didn't have the time to bring her up to speed, the fact of the matter is I just didn't feel up to it. I have no clue how she's going to react, but I figure it will be one of two ways. She'll either be pissed or she won't, and I figured that was going to happen whether I filled her in before or filled her in now.

The road that turns off the main highway is non-descript, paved with black asphalt for at least the first half mile. But it soon turns into a well-maintained dirt and gravel road that is fairly wide and lined on both sides by wildflowers. Another quarter mile down the road and the actual entrance to the ranch is revealed with a huge, red-stained sign that hangs over the road with carved and burned lettering that says "Double J Ranch" in large, chunky letters and below that "Teton Division".

Woolf drives under the arched entrance and casually asks Casey, "Have you ever been to Wyoming before?"

"No," she says, her voice almost reverent as she continues to look out at the amazing scenery. "But you can damn well rest assured I'll be coming back. This may be the most beautiful place I've ever seen."

Woolf chuckles, and I know that scored major points with him. He loves his home with a passion.

As we get closer to the main house, my insides start clenching with apprehension. In just a few minutes, Casey is going to understand that my family's ranch is a bit more than just a small-time operation.

The curving road finally straightens, crosses over a small bridge that traverses the Gros Ventre River, and then breaks free of a copse of cottonwood trees to reveal my family home sitting atop a butte.

Casey gasps audibly and I wince, lowering my gaze to my hands clenched on my lap.

"That's your house?" Casey asks Woolf in disbelief as she looks at the low, sprawling home that seems to cover the entire top of the hill.

"It is," he says matter-of-factly, and he cuts his eyes in the rearview mirror to me. I can see his question clearly, "Doesn't she know anything at all about you?"

The Jennings homestead is a little ostentatious, and Casey can't even see the entire house from this vantage point. While my great-grandfather, Jared Jennings, started out in a modest three-bedroom log cabin when he started the ranch, my grandfather, Louis Jennings, decided that it didn't necessarily convey the right message to the other cattle ranchers. He wanted to be the largest, most powerful cattleman, not only in the state of Wyoming, but also in the entire United States. Fueled on—no pun intended—by rich oil wells on our vast property, he built a home that rivaled that of the Vanderbilts.

Over fifteen thousand square feet of pine logs, slate stone, and three-story walls of glass make up the monstrosity that I grew up in with my parents and only sibling, Woolf. Fuck... the house is so large that Woolf and I had our own separate wings and would sometimes go days without seeing each other. From where we approach, Casey can only really see the top floor, which looks like it lays across the top of the butte in a lazy-like fashion. What she doesn't know is that it actually spills down the back of the hill, cut partially into the earth and dribbling down three stories.

"That may be the biggest house I've ever seen in my life," Casey practically chokes out.

Woolf chuckles while I wince again. He has no clue what's running through Casey's mind right now, although I have a pretty damned good idea. He thinks she's just really impressed, but I know different.

"Yeah... the house is pretty monstrous," Woolf says with a grin toward Casey as she leans forward to peer out the front windshield. "But it's a blip really when you consider the size of the property."

"And just how big would that be?" Casey asks quietly.

"Close to two-hundred thousand acres here in Wyoming, which encompasses both the cattle land

and the oil wells," Woolf says with a good deal of pride in his voice. "But we have another hundred thousand or so acres in Montana and Idaho."

I'm sitting directly behind Casey, so I can't really see the front of her face. Just the outline of her jaw, which seems to be popping back and forth. I don't miss the fact that she becomes noticeably quiet after that.

Woolf doesn't seem to notice either but follows the drive, which now turns into flagstone pavers that leads into a giant semi-circle in front of the house. Casey's head turns slightly to the right as she takes in the detached eight-car garage constructed in the same pine logs and slate stone. It's climate controlled and holds my dad's toys... a loaded Silverado pickup truck that he used for ranch work, a vintage Hummer, a Mercedes G550, and a Corvette. The fifth spot is taken up by Woolf's Land Rover, the sixth by my mother's Jaguar that my dad refused to get rid of even though she passed away almost two years ago, and the remainder of the space is filled with Gators and ATVs that my dad would use to drive the property. What Casey can't see is the long cookhouse and three bunkhouses that hold the resident ranch hands, which sit about five hundred yards past the garage.

The truck comes to a stop in front of the house, and we all exit. When I step down behind Casey, I resist the urge to reach out and try to massage the stiffness from her shoulders. I know her well enough to know she's angry and confused right now, and she won't accept any measure of physical touch from me.

But I also can't let this fester further so I bluntly tell her, "Double J is the largest cattle ranch in United States."

Her head turns to look at me, and the flash of heat and condemnation in her eyes smacks into me. "That's kind of a surprise," she says just as bluntly.

I scratch at the back of my head, trying to figure some way to diffuse her, but I'm distracted as Woolf pulls our suitcases out of the back of the truck and casually says, "After you get settled in, we need to talk about the funeral arrangements. We have some decisions to make and we need to choose a date. Governor Hayes will be attending, so we're going to have to get that information to him so his security detail can get set up."

I wince again and can feel the burn of Casey's eyes on me. Yeah... my dad was very close friends with the governor. As a land, cattle, and oil baron, my dad had a lot of political friends.

Taking our suitcases in hand, I trudge up the front steps to the long porch that sprawls a hundred feet in each direction. "Give me a few minutes and I'll meet you in dad's office," I say over my shoulder to Woolf. And then with a curt, "Come on, Goldie," I decide to get her up to my room where I can confront the beast.

Casey is absolutely silent as I lead her inside. I

imagine she's at a loss for words as she takes in the immediate fact that there's far more to the house than you can see from the front. Inside the foyer, there's a balcony of polished timber logs that overlooks the interior of the house that falls away down the butte. Below us is the great room, which is furnished in dark leather, mahogany, and rustic art, with two massive fireplaces, one on each end. The east end of the room is a floor-to-ceiling glass wall that overlooks the valley where some of the horses are grazing and the Teton mountain range in the back, along with the lazy curl of the Snake River that borders it. I cringe when I hear Casey's gasp. Ordinarily, I'd be proud of the fact she finds beauty in what she sees, but I'm afraid it only means she's going to be more pissed at me that I was hiding all of this.

I lead her down a staircase into the great room but take an immediate left down a hall that leads into the wing that holds my old room. Mom had it redecorated when I left for the Marine Corps, removing the twin bunk beds and rodeo posters I'd tacked all over the walls, trading it in for rustic pine furnishings, dark burgundy walls, and masculine plaid fabrics. I think I've stayed in this room maybe twice since I got out of the Marines.

Casey follows me into the room, immediately walking to the windows that overlook the Tetons. I drop the suitcases, close the door behind me, and wait patiently for her to say something.

She doesn't make me wait, turning slowly from the windows to face me. Her face is filled with confusion and distaste. "Why did you lie to me?"

I shrug my shoulders and offer, "I guess I was trying to avoid that look on your face right there."

It's not a good answer, I know that. It's evasive and slightly condescending, but fuck... I'm a little off my game here what with just finding out my father died.

"And what look would that be?" she grits out.

"Judgment," I say bluntly, completely on edge and poised defensively. "Don't try to deny you're not right now categorizing my family and me as entitled elite."

"How could you possibly know what I'm thinking?" she counters heatedly.

"Because I know you, Goldie," I say as I stalk up to her. "I know how you view men with money. I know what you think money does to people."

"So you were just going to always keep this hidden from me?"

"No," I say with a heavy gust of frustration. "I was going to tell you. I just wanted time first... to have you get to know me... away from all of this."

"Because you didn't trust me to accept you once I found out," she supplies, and a bit of shame rushes through me that she's struck so close to the real truth of what was driving me.

I turn away from her and stare out the window to

the land that I love. God knows my lack of desire to be a part of this dynasty has absolutely nothing to do with all the beauty this ranch beholds. It always infuses me with peace and pride in equal measures.

She's right. I guess, deep down… there was a part of me that didn't trust her to accept.

"You know," she says quietly. "I'm not quite sure how you can tell me you love me at the same time that you don't trust me. And I thought I was the one that was clueless about love."

That really robs the air from my lungs… the simple truth of that statement. It shames me and makes me defensive. Add on to the fact that I'm still reeling from my father's death, not only because of the loss of a man I loved, but the way that this is going to change my course in life, I can't help but lash out at her.

"Save the lectures on love, Casey," I snap at her, directing my self-loathing her way. "You're the last person I'd look to for a valid explanation as to what all this means."

She gasps and her body jerks as if I slapped her. I might as well have because it was a completely shitty thing to say.

But I hold on to my anger, let my grief over the loss of my father, the loss of my independence, and possibly the loss of my love, overwhelm me.

Turning on my heel, I stomp out of the room and slam the door behind me.

CHAPTER 25

Casey

I WISH I could be really mad at Tenn, but I can't.

I get why he held back on me and I do think, given the right time, he would have told me all about his family. Unfortunately, death has a way of moving the timetables and Tenn got caught in a situation of nothing more than bad timing.

So, I'm only mildly annoyed at him and even that's waning because my sympathy for him and what he's going through is starting to take precedence.

Do I forgive him for his omission?

Absolutely.

Do I question the validity of what he feels for me now?

Absolutely.

It's a very confusing time for me, but when it boils down to it, there are things that are far more important than my feelings at the moment. I still have a man that I care about deeply who is hurting and needs my support. I mean to give it to him, and we'll figure the rest out later. This is an adequate, short-term solution for me, because let's face it... I'm probably just as confused as he is.

Without another thought, I hurry to the door and throw it open, intent on trying to catch up to Tenn, as I'm sure I won't be able to find my way back to the front door without a GPS locator. It's disorienting at first when I slam into the brick wall of his chest as he stands just on the other side of the door with both of his arms raised and stretched out to hold onto the casing. I bounce backward slightly, which is good, because it gives me room to look upward to gaze at him.

Even though his lips are flattened out, I see a small flame of amusement in his eyes. I decide to take advantage of it. "What are you doing lurking outside my room?" I say indignantly.

"It's my room, Goldie."

"Since you left, I decided to claim it," I counter with my chin lifted.

"That so?" his voice rumbles and his lips journey upward.

"Yeah, well... now that I know you're all rich and powerful, I figured I should take advantage of it, you know?"

"Not funny," Tenn grits out, his lips flattening once more.

I give a coy smile and step in toward him, laying my hands just below his breastbone. "Okay, that was bad humor, I admit. But I am trying to find the humor in this."

Tenn's gaze bores into me, his eyes hard and unyielding. I think maybe he's really pissed over my attempt to lighten the mood, so I'm not overly surprised when he takes my hand and starts dragging me down the hall without another word.

I don't think to pull away or be leery, because even though he's moving at a quick pace, his hand is, as always, gentle on me. He navigates me back through the monstrosity of a house, that I have to admit is the most spectacular thing I've ever seen. When he gets to the great room, which is extremely great by the way, Woolf comes walking through.

He gives me a quick smile and then looks to Tenn, who quickly shakes his head. "Not now," he growls. "I'll be back in a little bit."

"But we need to discuss—" Woolf protests.

"Later," Tenn says, and then we're pushing through the front door. Tenn's long legs eat up the porch steps, causing me to trot down them. He takes a left and heads over to the massive garage I had noticed when we pulled up, which is constructed of the same timber as the house. Tenn pulls me through a side door, hits a button on a panel that houses multiple buttons, and one of the garage doors lifts slowly.

"Get on," he says as he mounts a dark green four-wheeler.

I scramble on after him, scoot close, and wrap my arms around his lean waist. Then we are off and roaring out of the garage.

Tenn operates the ATV with the same surety as he does his motorcycle and the horse I've seen him ride. Always in control. Always confident.

He drives us past the house, down another dirt lane, and through a heavily wooded area of a variety of trees I don't recognize except for pine. Then he bursts out into an open field where I can see a large river up in the distance. He heads that way and in moments, we are its banks with water so crystal clear, I can see all the way to the large rocks scattered across the bottom.

Tenn gets off the ATV and easily lifts me from my seat. He sets me down on the rocky shore and takes my hand, walking me to the water's edge. The Teton Mountains sit back several miles opposite of us with a flat valley in between. I turn my back to look at the way we came, and sure enough, I see the butte in the distance with the Jennings house sitting on top, except this time, I can appreciate how massive it is. It's three stories that run down the side of the massive hill, and I can easily distinguish the center of the structure which I know holds the great room, as well as two distinct wings that branch off to each side.

Shaking my head with bemusement, I turn back to Tenn to find him watching me with deflated eyes. "I'm sorry, Casey. I should have been up front with you. I was always waiting for the 'right time' but truth be told, it was the right time *every time* I thought about it."

"What's the real reason you didn't tell me?" I ask him with my head tilted to the side.

He ignores my question and instead sweeps his arm out to indicate the panoramic scene before me. "This was my favorite place in the world. I come out here every time I visit my parents. Spent a good part of my time growing up here fishing this river for cutthroat trout or hunting elk on the other side of the valley. It's the most beautiful place I've ever seen, and I didn't think it could ever be topped."

Sliding a hand around the side of my neck, he grips me gently. He lowers his face just a tad, his eyes boring into me. "I didn't think it could ever be topped until I met you, and then *you* became the most beautiful place in the world to me. Whether I'm looking in your eyes, or you're holding me in your arms, that is now my favorite place in the world to be. So why didn't I tell you the truth? Because I was afraid you might not be able to look past my family's wealth and remember the real me that you came to know. I got sidetracked by the beauty of you, both inside and out, but I didn't give your fortitude and common sense enough credit to do right by me."

I get a little dizzy, and I'm not sure if it's the power of his words or the fact I've been holding my breath, but I let it out in a rush. "Now that may be the most honest thing you've ever said to me."

"I do love you, Casey," he says earnestly. "Don't ever doubt that, regardless of some of the idiotic things I may do."

My heart thumps in pleasure over his words... over the intensity and the honesty... the utter conviction. And despite the fact he withheld from me, I understand that fear can be a powerful deterrent. I understand it better than most, and just as Tenn was patient with me... allowing me the time and space to move past my fears, I'm going to extend the same courtesy to him.

Bringing my arms up to wrap around his neck, I step up and lift myself up on tiptoes to give him a kiss. He has to bend to oblige me, but he does so with no hesitation. Just a brief meeting of our lips, enough of a touch to convey to him that I understand everything.

"We're good, Tenn," I tell him softly.

It's then that I notice that the anxiety hasn't been alleviated. I can see the strain around his eyes and feel the tension in his shoulders. I release my hold and step back from him, angling my head in patient curiosity.

Releasing a tiny breath of unease, Tenn lets go his hold on my neck and takes my hand. He leads me several paces away from the ATV over to a large rock that rests on the bank and protrudes outward into the swift-moving river where the water froths around the edge. He motions me forward and I take a seat on the edge, balancing myself with my legs stretched out and feet planted on the pebbled bank.

Tenn's eyes are worried when he says, "I'm not sure we are good, Casey."

My heart lurches, not from the words themselves, but with the despondency with which he uttered them. "What do you mean?"

Shoving his hands in his pockets, Tenn cuts a quick gaze out toward the mountain range, seemingly trying to draw some peace from the lovely scenery. "I need to tell you everything about my family."

Absolute dread starts welling inside of me, causing my chest to constrict and my lungs to deflate. The tone of his voice... the ominous vibe I'm getting... it's starting to scare the shit out of me.

"I'm sure you have some idea about the Jennings' wealth based on what you've seen so far," he says... his words coming out a bit choppy and unsure. "But what you may not see... the amount of land we own, cattle and oil, the political connections... the way I hid this from you... we're a bit more than just rich."

"What does that mean?" I ask hesitantly.

"It means my dad sat next to Zuckerberg on the Forbes list this past year. It means our business holdings are so vast they impact the economy. It means we not only have political connections but political obligations."

"It sounds overwhelming."

"It is," Tenn says with a sigh, taking a seat next to me on the rock. He reaches out and takes my hand in his, resting it on his thigh. Lifting his gaze toward his family home, he says, "It means that it's now my obligation. Even though it's the last thing in the world that I want, it's a responsibility that I just can't turn my back on."

My head snaps toward him, and my eyes widen with immediate understanding. "It means you're not relocating to the Outer Banks."

His eyes are tired, his voice fatigued. "Maybe. It depends on what Woolf wants to do, but I never wanted this life. I'm the first Jennings who has wanted to break free of the dynasty."

"And why is that?"

"I have a trust fund," he says offhandedly, but I've realized that sometimes Tenn needs to get to the answer to my question in a more roundabout way. "Got control of it when I was twenty-five. Every Jennings progeny has one and the money in it is insane. It's enough that I would never have to work another day in my life and could probably support a third-world country at the same time."

"Oh," I breathe out, finally starting to get a true understanding of what's going on. Tenn probably has more money than all the men I've ever dated combined.

"I've only touched the money twice," he says, and it's such a shock to hear him say that, I literally gasp.

"Once when I got out of the Marine Corps… I pulled some cash out to buy a house for Bri, Zoey, and me. The second time was to take out money to put as a down payment on the garage in Nags Head. Both times, I struggled and fought with myself whether or not to use the money."

"Why?" I blurt out. "It's yours… why would it bother you?"

"I didn't really need it. I made good money as a mechanic and was able to pay my bills… support Zoey. I lived simply… modestly. But mostly I didn't use it because I don't want to manage this empire," he says with quiet determination. "While I love this ranch, and I very much loved working it, I don't want to be responsible for it. It's not my dream. And because it's not my dream… because I'm not willing to commit the effort to take my place at the head of the table, I shouldn't really be entitled to any of it. I don't feel I earned it."

"What was your dream then?" I ask with interest. Because it seems odd to me that someone wouldn't want to aspire to this type of life.

Tenn shrugs his shoulder. "I didn't have a clear-cut idea at first. I just knew that I wanted to make my own way. I wanted to do something I loved, and I wanted a comfortable life. That was the general idea. After meeting you… it's become a little more specific."

My head spins, trying to fathom the implications

of everything I'm learning. Most glaringly is that despite the immeasurable amount of money available to Tenn, he doesn't really want or need it. It's also obvious to me that Tenn may be the most incorruptible person that I've ever met. I also have a sneaking suspicion that despite all that, he's not going to shirk his responsibility.

"What are you going to do?" I ask while attempting to keep my voice light and curious, when I really want to vomit over the fact that a future with Tenn may not be possible.

"I need to talk to Woolf. Both of us will equally inherit the estate and while, as the oldest son, it would traditionally fall to me to take over, I've always been clear with my dad that I didn't want it. I've pushed at Woolf to step into that role while my dad was still alive, so he could learn everything and be ready to take the helm, but up until now, Woolf has been happy just playing at being a ranch hand and partying his way through life. I'm not sure he has the maturity to do this."

"So it will probably need your attention," I add on. "At least until you can be sure Woolf could handle this."

"Even if he were ready to grow up and take it all on, I'm not sure he could do it alone. Actually, I'm not sure of anything at this point."

I'm silent for a moment, digesting his words. Taking in the sadness associated with his revelations and the immense pressure that he seems to be under at this point, not to mention dealing with the grief over losing his father. It's more than one man's shoulders should have to bear, and I hope that Woolf can help share these burdens with his brother. The selfish part of me... the one that realizes that Tenn may have to lead his life in Wyoming, wants Woolf to more than step up. That woman wants Woolf to free his brother from the obligation and release him to the life he wants to lead.

So that he can be with me.

I actually want to voice this to Tenn... to let him know my feelings on the matter. Not to pressure him, but so he can be assured that I want to build a life with him. So he knows that he has something waiting on the other side if he's able to walk away. I don't want him to have doubts about me, because he has enough weighing on him already.

I should just tell him I love him. I should do it so it makes him feel better. So that I reciprocate what he's so willingly given me, so that he feels the same warm flood of comfort that comes with such a simple little phrase.

But I can't.

If I did it right in this moment, it would seem contrived. It would seem convenient.

It would not seem genuine.

And I want to be genuine with Tenn. I want him to know that I am the person that will always greet him with total transparency with my feelings.

I want him to know that I will be his constant...
his anchor.

But before I can give that to him, I have to make
sure that I'm strong enough and committed enough
to offer that up. And that is something I'm still not
quite sure of at this point.

CHAPTER 26

Tenn

I LEAD WHISKEY out of the barn and look up to the bright Wyoming sky. For the funeral yesterday, it was overcast and dreary. Perfect weather by which to shed tears as we lowered my father into the ground next to my mom. Casey stood silently by my side, her arm wrapped around my waist and gently rubbing me in comfort, while Zoey stood next to me with my own arm wrapped tight around her. I didn't bother trying to stay composed because I've never been one to quiet my emotions. Whether I'm angry or happy, sad or pensive, I'm the type that wears my emotions on my sleeve. Didn't bother me in the least to have to wipe the grief away from my face as I said my final goodbyes. Touched me deeply that Casey was wiping away tears of grief too, not for my father, because she didn't know him at all.

They were all for me.

Because I was suffering.

And yet today, the sky is a bright blue a little

deeper than aquamarine and makes me think of Casey's eyes. Thick, fluffy clouds hang in place but in no way block the sun so that the snow on top of the Tetons sparkles like gemstones have been scattered all around. It's in the mid-seventies, and the smell of horse and hay smells damn good in my nose. It's why I want to get a quick ride in before Casey wakes up.

The last few days have been difficult for sure. Zoey arrived with Brianna the day after Casey and I got here. My little girl is devastated and when she wasn't clinging to me, she was actually clinging to Casey. I know Brianna isn't close to her daughter the way I am, and that's pretty much due to the fact that Brianna loves herself far more than she could ever love anyone else. But I also know that she does love Zoey in her capacity as a mother, and so I also know it was difficult for her to see Zoey gravitating toward my woman. This threatened Bri on two points... because she feels proprietary toward her daughter as well as me, and Casey had both of our attention.

And it was only a matter of time before Brianna's claws came out and she started a verbal attack on Casey. Woolf and I had been in Dad's office a few hours before the funeral was to start, looking through some of his ledgers, and we came out to hear Brianna's shrill voice say, "You don't belong here. This is a family gathering."

We both grimaced at each other and headed toward the great room to stop Hurricane Brianna before she could really get going.

There is no doubt in my mind that Casey could have wiped the floor with Brianna. There's no doubt in my mind that Casey has a sharper tongue than Brianna could ever imagine. And there was also no doubt in my mind that Casey would do nothing to escalate the situation, so as we walked into the room, Woolf and I watched as she just turned and walked away, heading toward the hall that would lead to my room.

It was then I noticed Kip sitting on one of the leather couches, looking completely dismayed and frustrated with Brianna. Why the guy puts up with that shit is beyond me, but hell… I can't judge. I put up with it for years.

Brianna turned toward Kip and sneered. "I can't believe that woman is trying to ingratiate herself into our family. She's probably after Tenn's money."

Yeah… fury rose and my hands fisted. But before I could even open my mouth to say anything, Woolf stormed past me and stalked right up to Brianna. To my utter shock, he got up in her face, causing her to take two surprised steps back where her legs caught the edge of the couch and she fell down into a sitting position on the cushions.

Woolf's face was red and his eyes were glowing, yet his words were calm. He stared at Brianna but addressed Kip with his words. "Get your woman and get her out of this house. And don't ever let her come back here."

Kip jumped up with a grateful look on his face, but Brianna wasn't having any of it. "You can't kick me out of this home. It's Tenn's too, and we share a daughter together."

Woolf merely sneered at Brianna and with a harsh laugh, he said, "This is Tenn and Zoey's home, but it is not yours. You lost that right when my brother divorced your vicious ass. And just so we're clear... this is my home too. Casey is my guest as well as Tenn's and because you can't keep your mouth shut, you just lost any further right to be a guest in this house."

Brianna started to lay into Woolf but luckily, Kip grabbed her by the arm and dragged her out quickly. Fortuitously, Zoey had not been around to witness that. Even luckier, Brianna was amazingly subdued at the funeral and kept her lips zipped.

Once Bri and Kip were gone from the house, I turned and looked at Woolf in amazement. It was the first time I caught a glimpse of the man he had actually become and for the first time since Dad died, I started to believe that Woolf might actually have something inside of him that could be strong enough to be a leader.

Woolf merely shrugged his shoulders and gave me a wry smile. "What can I say? I see the way you look at your woman. She's already part of this family."

I suppressed the insane urge that overcame me to

hug my brother, instead giving him a grateful nod and headed off to find Casey to make sure she was all right.

And, of course, she was. She had amazing compassion, even for Brianna, and merely said she understood it was a difficult time for everyone.

It takes me no time at all to get Whiskey saddled. He's a calm, five-year-old gelding quarter horse that's a gorgeous, pale buckskin with black stockings, tail, and mane.

"Hey stud," I hear softly, turning to see Casey walking up toward me.

And what a fucking vision she is. I had brought her into Jackson day before yesterday and couldn't resist buying her a pair of cowboy boots and a feminine, cream-colored Stetson. She's wearing them both paired with a beautiful summer dress with little blue flowers all over it that flares wide and comes down to just above her knees. The cowgirl look is complete with two, long golden braids draped over her breasts.

"You're up early," I comment as my eyes drag down her again.

She shrugs her shoulders as she steps up to me, taking a hand and running it down my ribs, where her fingers tuck into the edge of my belt. "Going for a ride?"

"Yeah," I tell her as I tighten the cinch. "Want to come with me?"

I can tell the idea interests her, but her eyes look at the horse warily. "I'm not so good around beasts that big. Present company excluded, of course."

I snort, and she shoots me a wicked smile.

"You can ride with me," I tell her. "You'll be completely safe."

She accepts that as truth and tentatively reaches out to stroke Whiskey on the neck. "Do I need to go get changed?"

"Nah," I tell her, more for my benefit than hers. I'm very much looking forward to that skirt hiked up a bit and miles of glorious, bare leg draped over the horse. "I'll put a blanket under you though. I don't want anything rubbing the insides of your thighs raw but the beard on my face."

"Dirty man," she says with a low, sexy laugh.

It's not easy mounting two people into a western saddle. Ordinarily, I'd plunk her on the back behind the saddle, but I know she won't feel as secure and I don't want her scared. So I use a mounting block to haul her up onto my lap, positioning an extra saddle blanket underneath her legs. As expected, her dress does indeed ride up but it's so loose that it only comes to mid-thigh, which is fortuitous because there are tons of other ranch hands milling about and I don't want them ogling my woman.

With an arm around her waist and the other holding the reins loosely, I let Whiskey walk slowly away from the barn and direct him over to one of the riding trails. With thousands and thousands of acres available, we have dozens of places we can go, but I decide to head toward a small lake we have on the property about two miles away. It's private and secluded and this is the first time I've had a chance to be alone with Casey other than when we have fallen asleep at night in each other's arms.

We ride in silence as Casey's head roves back and forth to take in the scenery. She starts out sitting stiff but eventually the gentle rocking of Whiskey's slow gait gets her to relax and she starts melting back into me. Her ass on my lap isn't exactly helping me to relax though as she rubs against my half-hard cock.

"Are you nervous about the meeting tomorrow?" Casey asks out of the blue.

"Little bit," I tell her honestly.

And I am, because tomorrow we meet with Dad's attorneys and financial advisors to begin discussions on what will be needed from Woolf and I to help manage the Jennings' estate. The formal reading of the will won't be for another few weeks but we all know he's left everything to his sons. Dad was always transparent about that because he wanted to impress upon us our duty to our heritage. And already, the attorneys have been making it clear that Woolf and I have a shit ton of stuff that needs handled immediately. Very important decisions need to be made, most importantly, my dad's position as CEO needs filled. The attorneys look at me directly every time they mention this, and it makes my stomach cramp with dread. Every minute that passes, I can feel the proverbial noose start to tighten.

"You know," Casey says hesitantly. "It might not be so bad... you staying here. I mean... this place is so beautiful. You have such history and Tenn... honestly... you on a horse riding the open range in tight jeans is way hotter than you on a motorcycle I'm sorry to say."

I chuckle and squeeze my hold around her waist. "Nice thought, Goldie, but if I stay, I wouldn't be riding the range. I'd be in a business suit attending meetings, entertaining political big wigs, and schmoozing business associates. I'd probably have to shave my fucking goatee so I'd look presentable."

"Oh," she says softly and after a moment of reflection, she says, "But still... maybe this is what you're supposed to do with your life."

Her words slice into me, because while I don't have a fucking clue as to what I'm really supposed to do, I had always sort of thought Casey would be my voice of reason. She'd be the one that would keep reminding me to follow my real dreams, which of course, include her.

I'm not sure what to say to her because I can see she's speaking to me from a place deep within her heart that is trying to help me figure out what is best. She's forcing me to look at all angles.

"Tenn?" she whispers, one of her hands releasing

the death grip she has on the pommel to come up and drape over my arm that's around her waist.

"Yeah, baby?"

"I love you," she says.

She says it firmly, without a shred of doubt in her voice. She says it as if it's a truth she's known all along.

She fucking owns those words.

My entire body freezes, and I pull on the reins to bring Whiskey to a halt. I lean to the side and then forward a bit to get a look at her face. She turns so her eyes can meet mine, and I'm thunderstruck over the intensity of feeling she's emanating in her gaze.

"I love you, Tenn," she says again with a clear voice, her eyes pinning me hard. "And if you love me, and you want me to, I'll stay here with you if this is where you're meant to be."

I can't explain the feeling that starts to overwhelm me because it's something I've never experienced before, and I don't know that mere words could ever do it justice. But in just the space of a sharp inhale of air into my lungs, my entire world becomes complete. In just that moment, I know, without a doubt, that my life will never be more perfect than it is in this moment.

For the first time ever, I have the love of a woman that is more precious to me than the oxygen that sustains me. More important than my dreams to open a custom motorcycle shop. More essential to my way of living than anything else.

At this moment, Casey takes up one half of my heart while Zoey takes up the other, and because it's so fucking full, nothing else really matters.

And with such an epiphany glowing within me, I realize in this moment that I want Casey more than I have ever wanted anything in my life. I draw her into me, pressing my face forward to capture her lips. Our hats bump against each other and immediately fall backward off our heads, tumbling to the ground, but that only makes the sun feel that much better upon me.

Casey turns in the saddle slightly, causing the leather to creak. Whiskey, being the good gelding that he is, just stands placidly as Casey's hands release the pommel completely and clutch at my shirt.

While my mouth claims hers, the arm around her waist loosens, and my hand drops automatically between her legs, the need to touch her as intimately as possibly completely overwhelming me. My fingers snake under the hem of her dress and pull it up high. I pull back from her lips briefly and angle my head down, looking at the tiny scrap of white lace between her legs with my fingers hovering just over it.

I glance back up at her briefly, rocked by the love and desire in her eyes, and my fingers dive under the elastic edge of her panties. Shifting my leg, which spreads her open a little further, I slide a finger deep inside her pussy. She groans and her head falls back against my shoulder.

So wet and warm.

My finger works her lazily, and her breath starts to hitch. Her hips gyrate, grinding against my cock, which is now painfully hard.

"Ever fucked on a horse?" I murmur just before I nip at her ear.

She shakes her head frantically, and then bucks against me when I start to circle her clit.

"Me either," I tell her. "But I'm about to."

"Tenn," she says shakily as her hands grab onto my wrist, attempting to halt my ministrations. "I don't want to fall off."

"Shhh," I gentle her. "Whiskey's a good horse. And I'm not about to let you fall."

"Okay," she says with a moan as I continue to pluck at her with my fingers.

I've never done this before but in my mind, I know exactly how it needs to work. I've been riding horses since I was three years old and feel as comfortable in the saddle as I do lying on a mattress. After looping the reins around the pommel and scooting back to the edge of the saddle, I easily pick Casey up and turn her around to face me, and because she's so lithe, she easily is able to make the adjustment by cocking her leg up high and squeezing it between us until we are adjusted face to face.

Whiskey takes a few slow, side steps as we adjust in the saddle, but that's more about him accommodating the new change in weight distribution and I don't give it another thought.

My only thought is my hands going under Casey's ass and using the strength in my arms alone to lift her up several inches. "Open my jeans," I tell her urgently.

Her hands drop quickly and with sure movements and some rocking of my own hips, she gets my belt and fly opened and the material pushed down enough to free my cock. And fuck... she looks down at it where I can feel it's already leaking with need and actually licks her lips like she wants to swallow me whole.

Christ... I can't wait. I haul her closer to me while she grips the base of my dick with one hand and the other slips into the crotch of her panties to jerk them to the side, baring her gorgeously slick pussy to me.

"Fuck," I say as I lower her... my face slanted downward so I don't miss a second of my cock as it slides up into her.

We both groan in ecstasy once I become fully lodged inside, her legs naturally wrapping around my waist with her boots resting on Whiskey's backside.

"Hold on to my shoulders, baby," I tell her as my hands go to the reins. "And hang on tight, okay?"

Her eyes are glazed but I know she understands me because she does exactly as I tell her to, and then goes one step further by wrapping her arms all the way around my neck and placing her cheek against mine.

With a soft cluck of my tongue and a tiny tap of my heels into Whiskey's flanks, I urge him forward with only enough rein so that he maintains a slow walk. I use the opportunity to let Casey get the feel of the motion and within moments, she rocking counter to Whiskey's gait. My cock isn't getting much friction at this pace, other than a gentle massage of her walls against mine as she grinds against me. This is fine though, because this is so fucking hot right now, I'm afraid I might bust a quick nut if I don't get some control first.

Casey's little gasps and moans though turn me on like nothing I've ever experienced with her before and with sharper kick of my boots, I urge Whiskey into a soft canter, causing both of us to gasp and moan.

With the first loping stride, Casey slides up my cock and then back down in a fluid motion and my eyes practically roll into the back of my head because nothing should ever feel this good. Casey moans loudly as Whiskey provides us with all the motion we need by which we can fuck each other.

The sound of hooves punching into the ground and the slap of our flesh against each other rings hard in my ears and then starts to fade as I begin to get overwhelmed by Casey sliding up and down on me. Tiny whimpers fall from her lips but what I really need is to hear her scream out to the Wyoming skyline.

I tighten the lead on the reins just a fraction and Whiskey immediately responds, slowing into a trot that almost has me coming immediately as Casey's body starts slamming hard on my dick. My balls ache because every crash down on me also crushes my poor nuts against the saddle, but the feeling of her bouncing up and down on my cock feels way better than the pain of it.

Casey and I have absolutely no control over our bodies. This is all Whiskey's choppy pace that has Casey fucking me harder than I've ever been ridden before, and when she starts grunting with every downward thrust, I feel my bruised balls start to tighten.

Pressing her face into my neck, I feel wetness there as Casey mutters against me, "So good. So good," and then her fingers grab my hair and she jerks my head hard as she screams my name while she starts coming all around me.

My own explosion bursts forth, and I pull hard on the reins so Whiskey comes to an immediate halt. Casey sags as I straighten my legs in the stirrups and thrust up into her one more time while I start to unload, grunting out my pleasure like a fucking caveman. My entire body shudders, and I look up to the sky to see it looks impossibly bluer. The clouds miraculously fluffier.

My heart definitely feels infinitely fuller.

I grasp onto the back of Casey's neck and pull her away from me. She looks at me with muddled eyes and cheeks flushed a lovely pink.

"You okay?" I pant hard, stroking my thumb up the side of her throat.

Her lips curl and then part, rewarding me with a beautiful smile. She nods and murmurs in a shaky voice, "I insist we have sex like that more often. It's a damn good reason for me to move here to be with you."

I laugh, pull her into me, and squeeze her tight, then just as quickly tug on her so I can see her face again. My lips find hers and I take her mouth sweetly, pouring every bit of my heart into it. She sighs in contentment and murmurs my name against my tongue.

Casey pulls back marginally and smiles... as bright as the Wyoming sky. "I love you, Tenn."

My heart squeezes in pleasure and equal parts sadness. It's because I love her and know now that she loves me that I need to do something that she might not quite understand.

"Casey... baby," I say quietly, holding her neck firmly so she looks at me. "I love you too. But you can't stay here with me."

CHAPTER 27

Casey

"**A**RE YOU STILL pissed at Tenn?" Brody asks as he dries the pot I just washed. Alyssa is wiping down the dining room table while Mom and Dad sit out on the back deck and sip at their glasses of wine.

I've been back from Wyoming for almost two weeks now and things aren't going well. And even though my preference in times such as these are to hide away with my thumb stuck firmly in my sucking mouth, I've decided to come out of hiding and join the real world again. My first order of business was accepting Mom's dinner invitation tonight because honestly… there wasn't anything that my mom's cooking usually couldn't cure, and my bad mood was in need of some fixing.

Shrugging my shoulders, I say, "I'm definitely fucking cranky with him."

Brody laughs and nudges me with his shoulder. "Have you heard from him lately?"

"No," I say sullenly and viciously scrub at the

spatula. "It's been three days."

Three long miserable days without any word from Tenn. Three days that I have thought the worst… that he's moved on with his new life in Wyoming and what I thought was true love was apparently nothing more than just some overworked hormones when we were together.

Now that we're apart, he's drifted away, and I'm so thoroughly confused and depressed, I'm doubting every single emotion the man had once made me feel.

Two weeks ago, he packed me onto a plane and told me that he needed time to figure out what to do with the mess that had been dealt to him. He told me that I couldn't stay there with him because I would only be a distraction, but then he did say something unbearably sweet and which provided me with a small measure of hope.

"I need you back in North Carolina, Goldie, so I have something to work for. I need you there to make me bust my ass to get back to you."

So, I accepted that and with my heart sad over leaving him but hopeful that we would be together again, I left.

And at first, it was fine. I missed him terribly both body and soul, but I was sustained with nightly phone calls. Random texts during the day fueled me on.

I love you.

I miss you.

Can't wait to be balls deep inside of you again.

He was romantic and utterly filthy in turns, and that first week wasn't so bad.

Tenn kept me updated as to what was going on. Both he and Woolf had meetings upon meetings with the estate attorneys, the corporate attorneys, financial advisors, the various ranch and oil well foremen, as well as some other family members that were involved in some of the ventures.

At first, I was buoyed by the fact that Woolf seemed to have finally stepped up to the plate. He assured Tenn that he was ready to take over the family businesses and give up his partying lifestyle. I remember Tenn had called me in the middle of the day, and he sounded so excited about it that I had the biggest smile on my face for hours afterward. I dreamed of the day he would come back and open up his custom bike shop and we would start our life together. Tenn assured me this was still his goal, and even told me that Nix was still on board and was content to wait until he got his shit sorted out.

But then the calls started slacking and logically, I knew this was because Tenn was extremely busy. He was putting in eighteen-hour days right alongside Woolf, and it worried me because I thought… if both of them were that busy with trying to keep things running, how could Woolf ever manage it on his own?

If Woolf couldn't manage it on his own, then would Tenn ever be able to come back to me?

And then the thing that weighed heaviest upon me was the fact that if Tenn ended up being stuck in Wyoming, would he ever want me to come back? Would he want to continue to try to build something together, or would the Jennings dynasty suck every bit of him up and leave nothing behind for me?

Four days ago, he called me really late at night and told me that he and Woolf were flying to Chicago to meet with some investment bankers at the urging of the attorneys. It was felt that perhaps the easiest thing would be to take the company public, which would alleviate some of the management responsibilities on the two brothers. I took this to mean that perhaps the attorneys weren't confident in either Woolf or Tenn's abilities to step into their father's shoes, and it felt like a backhanded slap to me.

But Tenn sounded so resigned when I talked to him, so eager for some type of game plan that could set his course in life whatever it may be, and he told me quietly, "It's a good idea, I think. Hell, I don't know. Maybe."

He was suffering under the same confusion and muddled thinking that I was, and frankly… it just plain fucking sucked.

I got a text the following morning that he had landed in Chicago… and that was the last time I'd heard from him.

And because I'm not one to sit around and wonder what the hell was going on, I called Tenn twice for an update. I left him two voice mails and asked him to tell me what was going on.

I was met by utter silence and every day that has passed since, my anger started building until I reached the point that no matter what he said when he called, I knew he'd be on the receiving end of my ire first.

"He's got a lot going on," Brody says guardedly. "He'll call when he gets a moment."

I snort and level him with a sarcastic glare. "I'm sure he has time to take a piss… probably get a bite to eat. Even a few hours' sleep. He sure as hell could spare a few of those minutes to give me a fucking call."

"Ouch," Alyssa quips as she walks back into the kitchen. "I'm thinking Tenn is going to get a major ass chewing when he finally calls."

Almost as if on cue, my phone actually dings in my pocket and despite how mad I am at him and my bratty side demanding that I ignore him so he sees how it feels, I frantically reach into my pocket for my phone.

It's indeed a text from Tenn, and my heart feels like it's going to leap from my chest.

Back in WY. Have been slammed with meetings. Sorry haven't called. Will call soon.

I stare at the text and my anger rages even hotter.

I can't believe he texts me a lame-ass apology with a vague promise to talk to me at some vague point in the future.

Don't bother, I hastily text back as Brody stares at my phone over my shoulder.

Shaking his head, Brody gives me a reprimand. "Seriously, Casey? Kind of juvenile."

"No more juvenile than when I tell you to 'bite me'," I sneer back at him, and my eyes stay glued to my screen.

The first contact in three days and it's a brief text to me? I'm apparently not important enough to warrant a quick phone call?

Asshole.

Another ding has me tensed and prepared for battle as I read Tenn's reply. *You really don't want me to call you?*

Well, shit. Of course I want him to call me. I want him to grovel in apology for making me worry and hurting my feelings, but something that I call a little bit of the Markham stubborn pride rears its very ugly head.

While I'm not willing to cut off my nose to spite my face, I take a middle of the road approach when I write back. *I haven't heard from you in three days. It's really kind of moot if I hear from you soon or not.*

I study the message carefully. It's cryptic enough he'll scratch his head, but it's by no means cutting ties with him. It's merely my way of voicing my feminine displeasure.

I hit send.

"You are such a brat," Brody mutters as he continues to read our interplay over my shoulder. I turn away from him to shield my phone and patiently wait for Tenn's reply. I expect it will actually be a phone call so he can give me a piece of his mind, so it's no surprise my stomach drops just a bit when a text comes back quickly.

It's only one word.

Brat.

Same fucking word Brody just used.

"Aaaghhh," I scream out and throw my phone across the kitchen, watching as it shatters against the wall.

Brody stares at me as if I've gone crazy, and Alyssa's mouth drops open in astonishment. Both my parents come running inside, looking around with wild eyes over the disturbance.

I look around at each of them, their gazes all soaked with sympathy that Casey Markham is hurting and quite possibly going insane.

Brody is the one that acts though. He merely opens his arms up to me, and I burst into tears as I step into my brother's embrace.

♦

"FEELING BETTER?" GABBY asks as she burrows under my covers beside me in bed. We're watching our favorite movie, *Talladega Nights,* and although Gabby snorts and wheezes in laughter every ten minutes or so, I'm staring blankly at the screen.

I look down into my empty wine glass, the fourth of the evening since Brody and Alyssa brought me home. "I'm feeling drunk, not better," I mutter.

After my meltdown at my parents' house, Operation Casey went into full effect. Brody comforted me with his strong arms while my mom stroked my hair and cooed words of encouragement to me. My dad made a big production of cursing Tenn as a means of showing visible support of my position, even though I know he didn't mean it. He really, really likes Tenn. Alyssa jumped on the hotline and called Gabby, who was waiting at my house with three bottles of wine.

I climbed out of Brody and Alyssa's truck, feeling like a wet noodle after I cried for half an hour straight. I immediately felt terrible for being—well, a brat. Tenn didn't deserve it, but I was operating on pure emotion and BHS... Battered Heart Syndrome.

My immediate regret turned into despair when I realized that my phone was broken beyond repair and I couldn't amend my words to Tenn. I couldn't do this even when Brody offered his phone to me, because I had no clue what Tenn's number was. It was programmed into my phone so I never had the need to memorize it.

My immediate thought was to go home and hover over my landline phone, hoping and praying Tenn would call, but then I remembered I disconnected that line over two months prior in an effort to cut down on expenses.

Now all I could do was drink wine, get drunk, and let Gabby and Will Ferrell try to make me feel better.

So far, it wasn't working.

Logically, I knew Tenn loved me and that he would not let our last interchange rule the future of our relationship. He'd find a way to get up with me despite my broken phone. However, as a panicked and irrational woman feeling like she had just lost the love of her life, I was convinced I'd never talk to Tenn again. Oh, he would assuredly text me back, and hell, he'd probably try to call. But the texts and voice mails would all go unanswered because I BROKE MY FUCKING PHONE.

Letting my head fall back, it thumps against the headboard and I give what may have been the longest, most pitiful sigh of the evening yet.

"I'm so undeserving of him," I moan to Casey.

"Oh, shut the fuck up," she growls at me, never taking her eyes off the television. "You'll get a new phone, and you'll call and apologize to him."

"I can't afford a new phone," I whine.

"I'll buy you one," she says before finishing the dregs of wine in her glass.

"It won't matter," I say despondently. "By the time I get one, he'll have already found someone else. He's too good of a man, you know? He won't stay single for long."

Gabby gives me a tremendously vicious eye roll but when her eyes come to rest, they aren't on the movie but rather on me. "Casey… baby… I love you like I love Will Ferrell. But you are really starting to irritate the crap out of me. Where in the hell is the self-assured, take-no-prisoners woman that I grew up with?"

"She got whipped by love," I tell her with a drunken smile. "My poor heart has been battered by love and I'm not sure it will ever recover. In fact, I'm pretty sure even my ovaries shriveled up and died tonight. I'm a loser."

She mutters something… I think confirming my loser status, but then reaches over to the nightstand to open up another bottle of wine. Silently, she unscrews the cap—because that's the way Gabby rolls—and fills her glass up again. She then tops mine off and puts the bottle back.

Reaching out, she clinks the lip of her glass against mine and then takes a sip. I, in turn, take a huge gulp and after I swallow, I lay my head on Gabby's shoulder.

I'm drunk, I'm sad, and that's a recipe for tears. They pool in my eyes and with the first blink, start sliding down my face. "I just want the same chance,"

I say quietly and maybe a bit slurred.

"Same chance at what?" Gabby asks as she grabs the remote control and pauses the movie. She can tell I'm in a mood for some serious talk.

"Love," I tell her tremulously. "I want what you and Hunter have. I want what Brody and Alyssa have. Gavin and Savannah, Wyatt and Andrea. I want what you all have, and I want it now. I want it with Tenn and no one else, and Gabby… I swear to God… if I lose him, I'll never smile again."

She pats my hand briefly then wraps her fingers around mine, giving them a reassuring squeeze. "Casey… trust me on this, please. You are going to have what all of us have. And I'm just optimistic enough for the both of us to know you're going to have it with Tenn. Right now… you both are going through some tough times, but I know one thing… that man is crazy about you. He is not going to give you up, no matter what the fuck is going on back in Wyoming. No matter how big of a brat you were to him. I guarantee you that he is doing everything humanly possible to make his way back to you, and you know what? If he isn't able to get out from underneath those obligations, he's going to bring you to Wyoming. I don't want to lose you, but I'll gladly pack you up and send you off to him, because I know that this is what you are destined for. You and Tenn are meant for each other. You're going to get married, have the most beautiful babies in the world, and you are going to become a full-fledged member in our Club of Love."

"Club of Love?" I ask with a true smile on my face for the first time since I broke my phone. "Is that what it's called?"

"Well, we haven't officially voted on the charter name yet, but I think it sounds great," she says with another squeeze to my hand. And then in a voice that sounds so confident, I actually feel a tiny kernel of hope start to take root, she says, "I swear to you Casey. You are going to get your happily ever after with Tenn. You deserve it more than anyone else I know."

I push up off her shoulder and turn my despairing eyes her way. "You really believe that? That I deserve something that good?"

"You more than deserve it," she says confidently and then levels a stern gaze my way. "Now drink your wine, get a bit more hammered, and start watching this movie with me. It's our favorite."

I grin at her as I swipe the back of my hand across my cheeks to dry them. "You're my favorite, Gabby."

"Aww," she says with her eyes going soft and round. "You're my favorite too."

CHAPTER 28

Tenn

I CAN'T DECIDE if I'm going to spank Casey first when I see her, or fuck her first. Maybe spank her while I fuck her and kill two birds with one stone.

But truth be told, I feel so terrible that she's clearly hurting and confused, I'm probably just going to hug the shit out of her until she forgives me for being so distant the past few days. I was a dumbass for even thinking a text would suffice after we hadn't talked in three days.

My shame turned into panic when Casey wouldn't respond to my "brat" statement. Then I called her and got her voice mail. Four calls and four messages later without a peep from her, and I went apeshit.

Despite Woolf pitching a fit, I booked the next flight out of Jackson.

"We got shit to iron out," Woolf yelled at me as I packed a small bag.

"I'll be back in two days," I assured him. "Our

shit won't be any more wrinkled in that time frame."

Jackson to Detroit, Detroit to Raleigh, and the longest fucking three-hour drive of my life from Raleigh to Nags Head.

I stopped at The Last Call, because I came upon it first. Although I didn't see Casey's Jeep, I still went inside and thank fuck... Hunter was there. It only took one look at my face and about twenty seconds, and he had me filled in on what was now called the infamous Casey Shattered Phone incident.

He assured me that she was at her house, having gotten gloriously drunk with Gabby last night, and was refusing to come in to work today because and he quoted, "I don't fucking feel like working with a broken heart."

I couldn't help the grin I leveled at Hunter before I sprinted out of the bar and jumped back in my rental to make the short drive to Casey's house.

It's fully dark by the time I get there and I'm on the brink of absolute exhaustion, but something about the warm lights winking from her living room windows invigorates me.

Because this is truly my home.

Because Casey is inside.

I leave my bag in the car, almost too tired to carry it, but grab the envelope that I stuffed down into the outer pocket before I left. I put it my back jeans pocket, eager to show it to Casey.

Despite my fatigue, I end up trotting the staircase

and bang firmly on her door as soon as I hit the top. Her soft footsteps pad closer and then the door opens.

And my heart leaps in absolute recognition of its other half.

Her eyes go wide when she sees me but that's all I see because then I have her in my arms, pulling her against me tightly. "I'm going to spank you, then fuck you, but I'm going to kiss you hello first," I say to her just before slamming my mouth on hers.

I expect a fight.

I expect angry and jilted Casey.

Instead, she throws her arms around my neck, and she's the one that proceeds to kiss the fuck out of me. She kisses me so damn good my knees almost buckle, so I lock them hard and, just for good measure, drop my hands to grip hard onto her ass.

She gives me a tiny taste of tongue, but then it's gone all too fast as she pulls back. "I'm so sorry," she blurts out, and then she starts to ramble. "I was pissed. But then I threw my phone, and your number... I didn't know what it was, so it turned into a night of wine and Will Ferrell, and I felt even shittier today, and..."

She stops... seems to be at a loss of words. Her gaze drifts away from me, and she nibbles on her lower lip.

"Casey?" I say softly to get those beautiful eyes back on me.

They slide back and they look a bit clearer...

more confident. She smiles and says, "I'm just really glad you're here."

"Me too, Goldie," I assure her. "And I'm sorry I was such a lousy communicator. I should have never ignored you for three days. I don't have any excuse other than to tell you things started happening really fast and my head was just fucking spinning with it all."

Her hand comes up, and she places soft fingers over my lips to hush me. "Don't," she says gently.

"I have so much to tell you," I say as her fingers fall away.

"Later," she says as she takes my hand and starts leading me toward the bedroom. "First… you promised a spanking and a fucking. Then we can talk."

Christ above, I silently pray as I follow her back. *Thank you for bringing this woman into my life.*

◆

UNFORTUNATELY, EXHAUSTION GOT the better of me and after I heated Casey's ass up, I fucked myself into a coma, promptly falling asleep after I had the mother lode of all orgasms.

When I awoke, Casey was gone from the bed and the sun was streaming through the windows. I rolled off the mattress, pulled my jeans on, and promptly found a message written in lipstick on her bathroom mirror that said, "Down on the beach." Not even bothering with a shirt or shoes, I make my way over to the public beach access and find her sitting in the sand with a cup of coffee.

Her face tilts up to me when I reach her side, and her soft smile fills my heart as I plop down beside her. She leans over and grazes my jaw with her lips. "Sleep good?"

"Yeah," I say as I run my fingers through my hair. "Guess I was more tired than I thought."

She turns her face back to the ocean, but I continue to stare at her a moment.

So fucking beautiful. So fucking mine.

I reach out, take her coffee, and help myself to a sip. I can't help but grimace over the creamy sweetness that hits my tongue, so I push the cup back into her hands.

"So what's going on, Tenn?" she asks with an impish smile. "You don't write... you don't call. What's a girl to think?"

My hand goes to the back of her head, threading my fingers through her hair and turning her face to me. I stick my nose right alongside hers and kiss the corner of her mouth. "The girl... she knows, without a doubt, that I love her."

She presses her forehead against mine and says, "I do know that and I love you too. But if you ever go three days again without talking to me—"

"I don't intend to go three more minutes without

you by my side," I tell her earnestly as I give her another kiss and release my hold on her.

"So what's been going on?" she asks quietly.

I take a deep breath and wrap my arms around my knees. "It's been a mess... trying to figure things out. The corporate attorneys really started pushing Woolf and me hard to take the company public. That was the reason for going to Chicago."

"But," she prompts me along.

"But we're not going to," I tell her. "We thought about it hard and honestly... we were really close to doing it, but then something happened."

She turns to look at me with curious eyes. I merely reach into my back pocket and take the envelope out. Unfolding it, I hand it to her.

"Just before we were getting ready to walk into the meeting with the board of the investment bank, my dad's personal attorney, Bob Stoops, handed this to Woolf and me. He said it was a letter my dad had written to us, and he had specifically asked this attorney not to give it to us until at least one month after his death. However, Bob, who was also very good personal friends with my dad, felt like it was more important we read it before going into that meeting, so he sort of made a command decision to deliver it a little early."

Casey looks down at the envelope and then back to me with uncertainty. I give a nod toward her hands and say, "Read it."

She opens the envelope and pulls out two sheets of paper that bore my father's last words to his sons in his neat but rustic penmanship. I read along over her shoulder.

Dear Tenn and Woolf:

It is my hope that as you read this, I can offer you both some words of wisdom and encouragement that perhaps I didn't have the fortitude to tell you when I was alive. I know I put a lot of pressure on you both to follow in my footsteps, but truly, I don't ever want that to have been the biggest disservice I may have done to my sons.

I've asked Bob to give this to you after I die, but it's my hope that you can figure things out on your own so I've asked him to wait at least a month to deliver it. If for some reason you are faltering or unsure of what to do, please take these words for what they are… merely a way for me to be a father first and foremost and not a businessman.

Tenn… my oldest son… you will never really know the pride you have brought to me. You may not be the exact chip off the old block I had envisioned, but you have surpassed what I could have ever hoped for in a son. You served our country in such a way as to humble me, and you gave me a beautiful granddaughter who I hope is more like you than me any day of the week. I know my dreams aren't your dreams, and so the one thing I want you to know... no matter what... you follow your heart.

Woolf... my youngest son... you are a chip off the old block, and it is in you that I pin all of my hopes and dreams for the future of our family. I know that may seem like a lot of pressure, but I have absolute faith and trust in your abilities. I know you may feel lost and afraid over everything that is facing you, but this is when you lean on your brother for support, and you surround yourself with good people to help you along the way.

Whatever you both decide to do, know that your mother and I will be looking down on both of you with love, pride, and complete satisfaction that we raised our children right.

Love,
Dad

My eyes mist up again as I read the letter. I've only read it about twenty times since I opened it a few days ago, and each time, the impact of his words momentarily stuns me. I guess I never gave my dad enough credit for being just a dad.

His words had such an impact on Woolf and me as we read them that we walked into the meeting with the investment bank, politely listened to what they had to say, and then just as politely declined their help. Neither one of us had a fucking clue what to do, but fueled by our father's words, we knew we'd figure it out.

Casey gives a little sniffle, and I watch as she blinks back tears. She folds the letter up, puts it back in the envelope, and lays it down on the sand between her feet. Leaning forward, she turns her face and lays her cheek on her knees to look at me.

"What does that all mean?" she asks.

"It's still complicated, and I'm still going to have to be involved somewhat in the family business, but it also means that I'm going to still pursue my dreams."

"Would those dreams include me?" she asks hesitantly, and I can't let her go another moment with any doubts.

Reaching out, I pull her over to me, lowering my legs to the sand and situating her on my lap so she straddles me. My hands go to her perfect face and kiss those perfect fucking lips.

"My dad said something really important in that letter," I tell her. "He told Woolf to surround himself with good people."

She nods, not really understanding.

"The main reason the corporate attorneys wanted us to consider going public was to alleviate management duties on us. It was just shifting the burden, so to speak."

"Because they didn't trust you and Woolf?" she asks.

I shrug my shoulders. "Maybe, but we understood that. We don't have much business experience. But then we started thinking... let's take Dad's advice and bring in good people to help us rather than do it all ourselves. I mean, my dad did everything, sure, but that didn't mean we had to."

"So you're going to hire people?"

"In a nutshell," I tell her as my hands go to her lower back where I rub at her gently. "For each enterprise, we're going to put a business manager and CFO in place, and they'll report to Woolf and me. And we've talked Bob into coming on board with us full time to act as our personal attorney and advisor. He knows more about my dad's business holdings and the way they operate than anyone does. Woolf is going to run the ranch himself though. That's where his passion is and he's got a good grasp on it."

"What about you? What's your role?" she asks, and I don't miss a slight tone of fear in her voice.

"I'm going to help Woolf oversee things, but if you'll still have me, I'm going to do it remotely from here. When I get things settled down, I'm going to open the bike shop. But I think... for the first year or so, I'm going to have to travel back and forth quite a bit. Live there part of the time."

Casey starts worrying at her lower lip, lowering her eyes shyly. When she finally raises them, I see a hint of determination though. "And what about us? Will this be a long-distance type thing?"

I smile at her, leaning forward to give her a quick kiss. "Did you not hear the part where I said I'm not going another three minutes without you by my side?"

She nods, her eyes hopeful yet still guarded. "Spell it out for me."

"It means I want you by my side, whether it's here in Nags Head or in Wyoming. I'm not going to be separated from you, and if you don't want to live in Wyoming, then I'll just tell Woolf he's going to have to go it alone from the start. I mean it, Casey… you are far more important to me than the Jennings fortune. I'm not giving you up."

"I'll go," she says quickly and throws her arms around my neck, hugging me tight. "Wherever you go, I'm there."

"It's only temporary," I assure her as I squeeze her to me. "Our real home will be here."

"Doesn't matter," she says softly with her lips near my ear. "As long as I'm with you."

"God, I love you so much," I tell her and don't give her a chance to reciprocate because I kiss her hard and deep, sealing her promise to stay by my side.

She pushes back on me, causing my lips to falter. When I stare into her earnest eyes, she says, "I love you, Tenn. And I am so thankful for you because I would have never known this feeling if it weren't for you. You've taught me so much… shown me so much. My eyes have never been as wide open as they are right now, and my heart has never felt this damn good in my entire life. You are my everything, and I would follow you to the ends of the earth."

My throat turns dry and something pricks at my eyes, but I manage to croak out. "Baby… going to make you so fucking happy."

She gives me that bright, Casey Markham smile, and leans in to press her lips against my neck.

"Going to marry you too," I tell her boldly, expecting that might shock the shit out of her. Instead, I can feel her smile against my skin.

"And I wouldn't be averse to knocking you up quickly with a kid or two," I press forward, and she actually moans against my neck.

Fucking moans over me telling her I want to impregnate her.

"We'd make some pretty babies," I murmur as my hand comes up to cup the back of her head and hold her against me tighter.

"I've been told that recently," she whispers as her tongue comes out to taste me right at my jaw line. "But we have to be married first."

"Say the word and I'm there. We can hop a plane to Vegas right now and throw your birth control pills away."

Casey giggles and leans back to look at me. She gives a serious shake of her head. "The ranch. I want to get married on the bank of Snake River… your favorite place in the world."

"Second favorite," I remind her. "You're my favorite place."

"And I only want our family and close friends there," she continues. "And we have to work on getting custody of Zoey. She has to be with us permanently, okay?"

I tilt my head, overwhelmed by the capacity of her heart. "Sure, baby. We'll get started on that real soon."

"And Tenn?" she says with sparkling eyes and joy practically pouring off her.

"Yeah, baby?"

"It's going to be physically impossible for you to make me any happier than I am right at this moment," she says assuredly, linking her fingers through mine. "You've given this girl more than she could have ever hoped for."

"Oh, Goldie," I tell her in a low warning voice. "I'm just going to have to prove you wrong about that."

"Bring it on, baby," she says before leaning in to kiss me. "Bring it on."

EPILOGUE

Tenn

MENTION MARRIAGE AND babies to Casey Markham just once, and it's all over.

Four weeks to the day since I mentioned wanting to marry her while we sat out on the beach facing the Atlantic Ocean, and I'm now about half an hour from making it a reality.

While I had to get on a plane the very next day and get back to Wyoming, Casey stayed behind and put her mother and Gabby to work planning the wedding with her. Since she already had the venue picked out—and that would be on the shores of a river in Wyoming—she was able to do pretty much everything else on the internet.

A few days later, she had no hesitation picking the date and sent it to me in a simple text. *July 30th. Our wedding. Be there.*

Later, she told me that it had to be done then because Zoey would have to be back in North Carolina a few weeks after to start school, and Casey had decided she wanted Zoey to go on our honey-moon with us. That came in the next text.

Zoey and I want to go to New York City for our honeymoon. Cool?

Of course, I texted back that it was cool. Whatever the hell she wanted, as long as she remained gung ho to tie herself to me. And even though I'm swamped with shit that needs to get done with my father's estate, I told Woolf to plan on me being gone for at least a week in August.

Casey and I decided that it would be best to move for custody of Zoey once I established permanent residency in North Carolina, so for the time being, she was going to stay with Brianna until I could get the ranch under control. I didn't have it in me to take on that fight while trying to pour all of my energy into getting myself out from under the Jennings family business. But once I was free from it, there was no doubt that Zoey was going to be with Casey and me.

I finish buttoning up the white western shirt with black stitching and put on a bolo tie with a pewter buckle that Casey gave me. It has the Double J logo stamped into the metal. I have no clue what Casey is wearing to the wedding and she told me that she didn't care what I wore, so I chose a western theme since she gave me the bolo, went with a white shirt because it's a wedding, and then chose a pair of dark denim jeans, a black belt, and boots.

Grabbing my black Stetson off the dresser, I leave my room and head over to Woolf's side of the house to get him. He's my best man, of course, and I have strict instructions from Casey that we are to be riverside at least ten minutes before the ceremony is to start. Which means I don't have much time to get our asses on our ATVs and head that way.

Woolf's bedroom door is ajar so I push it open. "Come on, dude… got a woman to marry."

"Just a second," he groans, and then my eyes take in Woolf standing there with his head thrown back and his hands gripping onto a woman's head while she deep throats him from a kneeling position.

"Fuck," I mutter, quickly turning on my heel and exiting the room, slamming the door shut behind me.

And just my luck, the closed door isn't enough to diminish Woolf's roar of release as she finishes him off. I lean back against the wall and jam my hands down into my pockets, waiting for my brother to zip up and get his ass out here so we can meet my bride down by the river.

Fucker. I can't believe he's in there getting a blow job on the second most important day of my life, the first being the day Zoey was born. And yeah… maybe that's a little bit of jealousy on my part since my girl gives the best head ever and I had to sleep apart from her last night. Casey insisted on staying at a hotel in Jackson with her crew because she wanted to preserve some wedding traditions.

The door suddenly flies open and Carlie Payton stumbles out, giggling at something Woolf says with her lips all puffy and red. I hadn't recognized the waitress from over at The Shady Pine bar when she was blowing my brother, but I nod a greeting at her.

"Hey Tenn," she says breathlessly, and then turns to accept a deep kiss from Woolf, who practically bends her in half.

"That was amazing, baby," he says just before releasing her. Giving her a quick pat on her ass, he turns her around and pushes her toward the hallway.

"We still on for some tag-teaming at Scandalous tomorrow?" she asks as she walks backward away from him.

"Yup," he says with a charming grin, his eyes raking up and down her body. "Looking forward to it."

She blows him a kiss followed by a husky laugh and spins away.

"What the fuck is tag-teaming? And what the hell is Scandalous?" I ask him as I push away from the door and follow him down the hallway while he refastens his belt. He's wearing a mint-green western shirt along with his ratty, old, brown Stetson, but at least he's washed and pressed. He loves that fucking hat more than life itself so I don't say anything.

"It's just a private club over in Driggs," he says vaguely and then completely changes the subject on me. "You have the rings?"

My heart lurches for a second, and then I remember I had put them in my back pocket. I reach back and pull out a simple, platinum wedding band that I bought last week along with another platinum ring flashing with diamonds. Three to be exact.

The center one is a cushion cut and weighs in at just over two carats. There are two trillion diamonds, one on each side of the center diamond, and total carat weight came in at just under four carats total.

This is Casey's engagement ring that she insisted she didn't want or need, but I couldn't fucking help myself. She should have something nearly as perfect as she is on her hand and for the third time in my life, I dipped into my trust fund.

So fucking worth it and I can't wait to see her face when I put it on her finger. Granted, it will go on maybe a second before the wedding band goes on, making it the shortest engagement in history, but Casey is the one that hurried this whole wedding along so it's all good.

As I hand the rings to Woolf, we make our way out of the house and over to the garage, deciding to drive the Gator down to the river.

In just under fifteen minutes, I'm going to make Casey Markham mine forever.

♦

Casey

I FIGURED I'D have butterflies in my stomach or my hands would be sweating, but I actually feel a sense of immeasurable peace within me as the wagon rocks back and forth as we head down to the river.

Tenn has no idea how I'm arriving to the wedding. He hasn't asked for any details but even if he did, I wouldn't tell him. I'm going to enjoy seeing the look on his face. I can imagine what it must look like now as he stands down at the river with only Woolf, Kyle, Bob Stoops, and the minister. I can't help the small giggle that escapes imagining the look of confusion on his face that no one else is there.

But when I decided I wanted to get married in Tenn's second favorite place in the world—the first being me—I knew it would be important to have my family and friends with me. And when I mean with me, I mean *with me*.

So I arranged to have this wagon pulled by two of the ranch horses take my crew down to the wedding site. For me, it symbolizes that they are all giving me away to Tenn.

Probably very gladly.

I'm so lucky that they were all just able to drop everything in their lives to travel out here to watch me get married. My mom and dad, of course, being the most important part of the equation. While they were a little shocked over the speed with which I decided to move, they've been fully supportive. Truth be told, I think they had given up hope for me so they are actually quite excited I want to get married.

My brothers, as well, would never have missed this. Apparently, I must have inspired Gabby and Hunter with the rashness of my actions because just last week, they decided to elope down to South Carolina to get married. They went by themselves, and even stopped at the ever fun but completely cheesy South of the Border, which sits on the North Carolina/South Carolina state line and ate tacos and drank a beer for their "honeymoon." It was completely outrageous, yet I wouldn't have expected anything different from them.

The wagon is filled with those people most important to me. My parents, Hunter and Gabby, Brody and Alyssa, Gavin and Savannah, and Wyatt and Andrea, who have finally decided their wedding will be next summer in the Outer Banks. And clearly... something is in the air because apparently Gavin must have finally gotten inspired to make Savannah an honest woman. Last night, he got down on bended knee at the Million Dollar Cowboy bar and proposed to her in front of about five hundred strangers. And shit... her engagement ring was so big I was afraid she'd topple over. It's so shiny that her daughter Clare is right this very moment plucking at it with her little pudgy hands while she sits on

Savannah's lap.

Oh, man… I can't wait to have one of those. Two actually… a boy and a girl, and I hope they both look like Tenn, although he tells me he hopes they look like me.

Sweet man.

As our wagon exits the dense forest and hits the field laced with wildflowers and sagebrush, I finally get my first look at Tenn standing on the river's edge along with Woolf to one side and Kyle and Bob to the other, the minister just a few feet back. The smile on his face is bright as he takes in the huge wagon filled with the North Carolina crew, and he just shakes his head in amusement.

There's no wedding march, only the sound of the rolling river and the wind softly rustling through the treetops. It's absolutely perfect.

The driver stops the wagon as instructed about twenty feet from the groom's party and everyone unloads. The men jump down first and are handed the babies, then they help their women down in gallant fashion. I left it up to everyone what they wanted to wear, and in trying to keep with the western setting, I'm happy to say everyone doesn't look even slightly out of place in their cowboy hats and boots.

When everyone has gotten down, that leaves two women in the wagon.

Zoey and me.

I hold my hand out to her, and she places hers in mine. She smiles at me and says, "Ready to do this?"

"I was born ready," I tell her.

"Do I have to call you mom?" she asks with a mischievous grin.

"I'll smack you around if you do," I tell her seriously, and then we both stand up and walk to the edge of the wagon. Brody helps me down while Hunter helps Zoey.

And then we all arrange ourselves exactly as I had envisioned it. Zoey and I holding hands tightly with our other hands holding matching bouquets of miniature white roses and fragrant clippings of wild sagebrush. The rest of my crew forms a large semicircle around me and after I take a deep breath, I take the first step toward Tenn.

As a pair, Zoey and I walk together.

As a group, my family and friends surround me, each of them sharing in my joy.

Every person around me taking part in the ritual of giving me away to the man I love.

We all walk together down a makeshift wildflower aisle of black-eyed Susans, cow grass, and fairy slippers, with the peppery-sweet scent of sagebrush teasing our noses. The Teton Mountains tower behind Tenn majestically and the dancing river sings to me.

This may possibly be the most perfect moment in the history of moments.

And wow... Tenn looks so impossibly handsome, my heart swells with pride that this is my man. Even with his Stetson on, I can see the clear blue of his sparkling eyes as they are pinned on me. He's wearing the bolo tie I had made for him with the Double J ranch logo, and while I definitely love him in his Harley t-shirts and shit-kicker boots, he makes a fucking fine ass cowboy as well.

Tenn's eyes roam over me slowly as I get closer. He's taking in the cream-colored sundress with spaghetti straps I had bought to match my cream-colored Stetson, and because hey... it's my wedding... I bought a pair of cream-colored boots to match. The only hint of color on me is in the lilac-colored ribbon that's tied to the ends of the braids I put in my hair, along with little sprigs of baby's breath.

Before I can reach my groom, he steps away from his group to meet me. As if planned, my group halts their progress and within a few steps, it's just Tenn and me standing in front of each other.

"Hey," I whisper.

"Hey, Goldie," he says huskily as his eyes roam down and then up my body. "You look gorgeous in your wedding white."

I give a soft laugh and lean in a bit closer to him. "This is actually cream. I couldn't go with pure white because... hello... I'm marrying *you* and there's not a virginal bone you've left untapped in my body."

Tenn's bright, white teeth explode from behind his lips as he laughs. "Consider me educated on wedding colors then."

We stare at each other, completely oblivious to the other souls around us. Completely uncaring that there's a wedding waiting on us.

"So, what did you do last night?" I ask him curiously.

"Couldn't sleep because I was missing you too much." And, there goes the butterflies in my stomach. "What did you do?"

"I got a little tipsy and tattooed your name on my ass," I tell him sincerely.

His eyebrows disappear under the brow of his hat and his mouth hangs open slightly. "You're kidding?"

"Yup, kidding," I tell him. "It's actually here on my wrist."

His hand jets out and turns my hand palm up, taking in the delicate cursive writing of his name on my skin. I remember he told me once that he intended to ink my name somewhere prominent on his body because it didn't get any more permanent than that. I figured I should do the same, although I didn't have it in me to get anything big because... well, that shit hurts and I wanted it over as soon as possible.

Tenn lifts my arm and brings my wrist to his mouth, where he places a light kiss on it. "I love it, baby," he says softly.

My cheeks turn a little pink over the adoration in his voice. We stare at each other some more, both of us getting lost in each other. Oh… his eyes. The most beautiful thing ever invented. Perhaps my favorite place in the world.

A coughing sound from behind Tenn has me blinking slightly, and I lean to the left to peek around his shoulder. The minister smiles at me kindly and says, "Are you two ready to get going?"

I give him a smile, nodding my head and then pulling back to look up at Tenn. "You ready?"

Tenn takes my hand and turns his body to face the minister. He tucks my arm in his and starts walking me across the pebbled shore of the river. "I've been ready for you my whole life, Goldie. Let's go do this."

Other Books By Sawyer Bennett

The Cold Fury Hockey Series
(Random House/ Loveswept)

Alex

Garrett

Zack (Releasing 6/9/15)

Ryker (Releasing 9/8/15)

The Off Series

Off Sides

Off Limits

Off The Record

Off Course

Off Chance

Off Season

Off Duty

The Last Call Series

On The Rocks

Make It A Double

Sugar On The Edge

With A Twist

Shaken Not Stirred

The Legal Affairs Series

Objection

Stipulation

Violation

Mitigation

Reparation

Affirmation

Confessions of a Litigation God

The Forever Land Chronicles

Forever Young

Stand Alone Titles

If I Return

Uncivilized

About the Author

New York Times and USA Today Bestselling Author, Sawyer Bennett is a snarky southern woman and reformed trial lawyer who decided to finally start putting on paper all of the stories that were floating in her head. Her husband works for a Fortune 100 company which lets him fly all over the world while she stays at home with their daughter and three big, furry dogs who hog the bed. Sawyer would like to report she doesn't have many weaknesses but can be bribed with a nominal amount of milk chocolate.

Connect with Sawyer online:

Website: www.sawyerbennett.com
Twitter: www.twitter.com/bennettbooks
Facebook: www.facebook.com/bennettbooks

Made in the USA
Middletown, DE
11 February 2017